MW00830891

ACROSS TIME

PARALLEL SERIES BOOK 3

ELLE O'ROARK

Copyright © 2019 by Elle O'Roark

Developmental Edit: Tbird London

Edit: Stacy Frenes, Grammar Boss

Copy Edit: Janis Ferguson

Cover Design: Emily Wittig

ISBN: 978-1-956800-02-9

All rights reserved.

No part of this book may be reproduced in any form or by any electronic or mechanical means, including information storage and retrieval systems, without written permission from the author, except for the use of brief quotations in a book review.

PROLOGUE

1918

The woman walks with brisk steps, her dress sweeping her ankles. She'd forgotten what a bother it was, having skirts so long. She's tripped over them three times already, but hastens toward the square anyway, eager to have this behind her. The sun has begun to set, and there's a prickle of tension along her spine. She tells herself it's merely that she's longing for home, for 1935. Her daughter will be waiting there. Marie-Therese is seventeen but remains a child in some ways. *A child who still needs her mother*, the woman thinks, her heart drumming in her chest.

The square, sitting in the shadow of Sacré-Coeur, is unnervingly quiet. She can't escape the feeling that today is an ending of sorts, and thinks again of her children—Marie at home and Henri, away in England now. They're too young to be orphans.

"Chin up," she says, forcing her feet forward. Her children are the reason, after all, that she is here in the first place. They both will play a role in the prophecy, with the help of the woman who is coming. She can at least do this much to set them on their way.

A gust of wind whistles through her wool coat, whipping leaves around her skirts. The sound almost masks the crunch of gravel behind her...but not quite. She hears it and she knows, before she's even turned her head, that this was a trap.

A needle plunges into her neck. As she falls, her thoughts are of her children. She prays this is a beginning for them, rather than an end.

And that the woman who will save them doesn't take too long.

1

1987

Saint Antoine is one of those crumbling, quaint cities you see on travel shows about France. The streets are cobblestone, every restaurant has al fresco dining, and the shops sell things you would never buy at home and wouldn't buy if you lived here either: champagne bottles full of candy, bags that say *J'aime Saint Antoine*, boxes of macarons. The passing tourists are excited, gleeful, hitting me with their bags and elbows as they unfurl maps. I wish I were one of them.

Sleep deprivation begins to weaken my resolve. *Am I really going to do this?* I've upended my life to get to this point, but for the briefest moment I fantasize about backing out. I'm only twenty-one. Shouldn't I be allowed to wander the streets like a normal college girl, buying things I don't need and stuffing myself full of brioche? *Someday*, I swear to myself, *I will be that normal girl.*

But I won't be her today.

I find a pay phone and dial my mother's number with a churning stomach. The coins I've stacked in front of me are optimistic. Odds are she won't answer, but even if she does our conversation won't last long. She didn't care for me before Kit died. It became exponentially worse afterward.

"Hi Mom," I say when she picks up. "It's me." The words come out too eager, too needy—something she hates. I wince at the mistake.

"Oh," she says, a blunt, disappointed sound. "Why aren't you calling from your own number?"

I swallow hard. I guess I know why she answered.

"School ended last week," I tell her, taking a deep breath—this where the lies begin, and she always knows when I'm lying, though perhaps it's just that she always assumes I'm doing something wrong. "I'm in France. For my internship. It was supposed to be in New York but something better came up."

She sighs. The sound is disgusted but also weary, as if I've failed her and it is nothing more than she expected from me. "What about Mark? I thought he was proposing or something."

My stomach churns anew. This was the one week Mark and I would have had together in months. I bought him off with some promises I wasn't quite ready to make, but he still didn't understand. There's so much he doesn't know, and telling him the truth—*my dead sister is haunting my dreams, demanding I help a stranger in France*—wouldn't exactly have cleared things up. Especially since he doesn't even know I had a sister.

My relationship with him is the only thing about me my mother has ever approved of, so my answer will only disappoint her. "He's in Nepal most of the summer," I reply. "I guess it'll happen when I get back."

"You do realize," she says, "that if he ever finds out what you are, it's over."

What you are. She makes it sound like I'm some kind of demon or vampire. In her eyes, I suppose, I am. "I'm changing," I whisper. "Really."

"I'll believe that when I see it," she says, her voice hard. "Well, I should go. Steven and Natalie are coming over for dinner."

"Okay, take care of—" I begin, before hearing the dial tone. "Yourself," I conclude quietly, hanging up the phone. For a single moment I allow my forehead to rest against the wall. I was stupid to have hoped the call would go any other way. My ability feels more like an addiction than a gift most of the time, especially when I hear myself swearing I'm going to change. Until I stop, there's no chance of earning my mother's forgiveness.

But until I've used it one last time, there is no chance of earning Kit's.

I CLIMB into a cab for the final leg of my journey, staring at a picture of me and Mark as if it can offer me a way out. It's from the summer we met, when I was interning at a gallery in New York City and he was getting ready to leave for grad school. It's all kind of a blur now, but I remember how happy I was then—perhaps for the first time.

I made him happy too, and I want to keep doing so. I want to be the woman he believes I am, and that's not possible right now. The nightmares have gotten so bad that I'm barely getting through the day anymore, jumping at every unexpected thump, terrified of falling asleep. The night before last I woke in my bathtub with the shower on, screaming at the top of my lungs, and it wasn't the first time. I can't let Mark see that version of me, have him hear me crying for the sister he doesn't even know I had.

Which leaves me stuck, once more, with this ridiculously vague plan, based on nothing more than a terrifying dream. *Find them*, Kit begs me every night. *Save them, help Marie.* No mention of what they need saving from or how I'm supposed to help.

What I know about Marie-Therese Durand, thanks to my

sister's hints and a long day at the library, is almost nothing: she was born in 1918, and lived on the outskirts of Saint Antoine until 1940. There is no record of her beyond that, and I don't know if this means she died during World War II or if she simply left home—given it's the year France fell to Germany, either possibility seems likely.

The cab comes to a stop in front of some massive industrial farm. There are thousands like it back home in Pennsylvania, but I'd expected a quaint farmhouse, not huge silos and aluminum siding. I suppose my mistake was expecting anything in the first place, since I'm going into this blind.

This, right now, is my last chance to back out. I pay the cab driver and climb from the car. *One last jump*, I swear to myself, *and I'll never, ever do it again.*

The sound of the door closing feels unsettlingly *final*. And with what lies ahead of me, it's entirely possible it is.

2

When I pictured pre-war France, I envisioned sun-dappled fields of lavender that would capture me like a fragrant cloud. But that is Provence, not Saint Antoine, and I've landed indoors despite my best efforts. I hit a hay bale so hard I flip over it—I'm pretty sure I'll never master a graceful landing—and I know before I even open my eyes that I will find hay wedged into my hair, my mouth and...other parts. This hay has now hit more bases than Mark ever has.

On the bright side, the barn I've landed in is not the modern one I saw only moments before. It's old enough that the wood has warped to let sunlight into open spaces. I see no trucks, hear no machinery.

As I force myself to stand, I feel the deadening fatigue setting in, my head fogged as if I have one of those colds that puts you to sleep for days. My limbs are growing heavier by the moment, weakness setting ever faster into my bones. A cow not four feet from me bellows a warning, and I can't even summon the energy to jump in surprise.

And I'm hungry. My God I'm hungry. *If I could just eat*, I tell myself, *I'd have the energy for this*. I spot an apple sitting on a stool five feet to my left—small and dull, barely fit for livestock, but right now it might as well be a large pizza with a side of cheese fries

I grip the stall door and take one small step on trembling foal legs, but catch movement outside before I can take another and dive back down to the hay, trying not to cough as I inhale the dust around me.

It's a man who's entered. I can tell by the heaviness of his tread, the certainty of it. He moves through the barn and a bucket clangs against the metal hinge of the stall next to mine. There is a moment of silence, during which I hear no movement, no breath. "*Ici*," he says—to the cow I assume—and then mutters something else in French that I don't quite make out as he sets the bucket down.

The steps recede, and after a moment of silence I rise, forcing myself, one foot in front of the other, toward that apple. I've never wanted anything more in my entire life. Just as my hand closes around it, the man steps back inside the open barn door, this time pointing a gun straight at my head.

He is about Mark's age and handsome—a lock of dark hair falling over his forehead like some old Hollywood film star. Though I freeze in surprise, it's hard to picture him as a killer. I'm more bothered by my nudity than I am his gun.

"*Pourquoi etes-vous ici?*" he demands. He wants to know why I'm here.

Good question, I think. *I wish I knew.* I'm too exhausted and unsettled to form a reply in French. "Can I... Give me your shirt."

His eyes flicker downward. I guess he didn't notice I was naked until I pointed it out. My hair covers my breasts and my hands cover the rest, but he looks unsettled anyway. "I think not," he replies in perfect, British-accented English. "In order to give you my shirt I'd have to put down my gun."

It's illogical, but his British accent sounds sort of posh and James Bond-ish and puts me at ease. Granted, lots of villains in

James Bond movies have British accents too, but they generally don't look like this guy.

"I'm looking for Marie? Marie-Therese Durand?" I explain. "Do you know her?"

I wait for a sign of recognition. Instead his eyes narrow and he raises the gun higher, pulling back the hammer. "There is no one here by that name," he snarls. "You need to go back where you came from."

I sway on my feet again and grab the stool to hold myself steady. "Please lower the gun," I whisper.

A hint of softness passes over his face before he blinks it away. He grabs a horse blanket hanging off the wall and throws it at me. "Are you ill?" he demands.

I somehow manage to catch the blanket and wrap it around me, but the effort of standing up on my own is getting to be too much. With each moment that passes I feel a bit further away from him, as if I'm sinking fast in a deep, dark lake.

"No. Please just let me talk to Marie-Therese and then I swear I'll go." I meant to sound stronger, more forceful, but it feels as if I'm speaking to him from under water.

"Again, there is no Marie here," he says. "So you can go right now. Don't think for a moment I'm reluctant to use this gun."

I don't entirely believe him, but even if I did, I wouldn't have the energy to obey. I'm barely remaining on my feet.

"Please," I beg. "I can't...I'm too—" I reach for the wall and use it to stay upright. If I allow myself to fall asleep right now, I'm not certain I will ever wake up.

Footsteps approach and from around a corner comes a shockingly lovely girl about my age. I recognize her from the photo I found, the one that led me here, and my hunch is confirmed: she is a time traveler. Our looks are what set us apart, and though I'm blonde and fair, while she's brunette and olive-skinned, there's a similarity between us as well, in the symmetry of our features and in our eyes, which are backlit, as if a fire shines just beyond the pupil.

"Mon Dieu," she whispers, staring at me as if I'm a ghost. She hisses at her brother in rapid-fire French and he lowers the gun.

My mouth opens to tell her why I'm here. But I pitch face first to the ground instead.

3

When my eyes open, I'm lying on a grossly uncomfortable bed in a sunlit room. It takes a moment of staring at the exposed wood ceiling, listening to squawking chickens in the distance, before I remember I'm not in my own time.

My arrival here is a bit of a blur, sort of like when you rise in the middle of the night to deal with something you're only half-awake for. I remember the man with the gun, and an exhaustion like I've never felt before.

Most importantly, I remember that I found Marie. Now I just need to figure out what it is she needs from me.

I rise slowly. Every muscle in my body hurts and the fatigue weighs so heavily on me that I am sorely tempted to lie back down. But the sooner I get downstairs, the sooner I can return home.

I'm still naked, but a dress lies on the chair across from me, white and dotted with small pink flowers. It's already too hot for a dress. I think longingly of home, of tank tops and shorts and air conditioning, before I slowly pull it over my head.

I limp down the stairs like an old woman, gripping the

handrail for support, and find myself in a room that is plain by the standards of home: stiff velvet chairs, a small coffee table covered with a lace tablecloth, a few vases. But the house itself is well-constructed and elegant, with high ceilings, arched windows, and French doors that lead to a small stone porch off the side of the room. If you have to pass out in a strange place, this wasn't a bad one to choose.

"Ah, awake at last," says a musical voice. I turn to find Marie-Therese there, smiling at me as if I'm long-lost family. "Three days you've slept! I thought you'd never get up!"

Three days, and I'm still so drained I can barely put one foot in front of the other. Any hope of getting this all over with quickly and catching Mark before he leaves for Nepal begins to dwindle. I blow out a breath. It was silly to hope for it in the first place, and I probably ought to focus on my present difficulties anyway.

"You're much friendlier than the guy was," I suggest, wondering for the first time if he *still* plans to hold me gunpoint and make me leave.

She glances over her shoulder before she gives me a small nod. "I'm sorry. My brother Henri—he didn't like that you knew who I was and *what* I was, but he's being ridiculous. You already know what I am on sight, just as I know what you are. Come. You must be famished."

She turns and I follow her into a kitchen that is slightly less ancient than I was expecting, but still pretty rustic. Cracked farm-house sink, old cabinets that appear hand-made, copper pans hanging from the ceiling and a big white and black Aga stove.

"Please sit," she says. "You must be famished. Is it always like that with you when you time travel? It must be highly inconvenient." She speaks of the gift so openly, so plainly, as if it's the color of the sky or the day of the week. I was raised to do the opposite.

I take a seat at the rough-hewn trestle table where she's placed a loaf of bread and a small pot of jam. I long to shove the bread into my mouth like a savage, like it might be ripped away from me. I'm so hungry it feels as if I could never get full. It's only by force that I take reasonably sized bites.

"I'm not sure. I've never gone this far back before." I flush. How is it possible that I'm ashamed of what I'm able to do, and *also* ashamed of the fact that I'm not good at it? "What year is it? I'm...not great at landing where I plan to."

"It's 1938," she replies.

Three years closer to the Nazi occupation than I intended. I should have been more careful. "Then I've traveled...about fifty years."

"*Mon Dieu,*" she says on a gasp. "Fifty *years?*"

For better or worse, the future remains a mystery to her, just as my future remains one to me. While the past is neatly blocked off, what lies ahead for my kind is hazy. It would be like jumping off a ledge on a foggy day, clueless to whether you were five feet in the air or five hundred.

I open my mouth to say more, but am cut off by a preemptory knock as the door swings open. A woman steps over the threshold, basket hanging off her arm. Her mouth is pinched, her eyes narrowed. "*Marie, tes poules sont—,*" she begins, her words dying off as she notices me. "*Qu'est-ce que c'est? As-tu un invité?*" She sounds positively indignant to find me here.

Marie-Therese's mouth has opened to reply just as Henri bursts through the door, looking at the two of us with panicked eyes. I remember thinking he was handsome when I first saw him, but in truth the word barely does him justice. He has features that would be called exquisite were they on a woman— high cheekbones, full mouth—but with a strong jaw and broad shoulders that render him not feminine by any stretch of the imagination.

"*Oui,*" says Marie, shooting an alarmed glance at Henri. "*Notre cousine...um...Amelie. Amelie Durand.*"

"Our cousin Amelie," Henri translates, looking me hard in the eye, as if I'm a child in need of scolding. "Amelie, this is our neighbor, Madame Beauvoir. *Amelie est Americaine. Elle ne parle pas le Francaise.*"

I'm tempted to argue that I do indeed speak French, but the guy *did* just hold me at gunpoint. It might prove useful to overhear what he believes he's saying in private. Between my exhaustion and how fast they talk I struggle to follow the conversation anyway. I catch a few sentences here and there: *she's had a long trip, the daughter of our uncle, we were not expecting her.* Mostly what I get from the conversation is Henri's eagerness that I be gone. For every time his sister expresses pleasure at my arrival and suggests I might stay a while, her brother says precisely the opposite.

Eventually I tune them out and let my gaze drift toward the window, realizing for the first time that their home is in the middle of a vineyard, lush and peaceful in the late May sun. *I wish Mark could see this*, I think, though in truth it wouldn't be his cup of tea. He'd want a luxurious vineyard experience, the kind that offers 600-thread-count sheets and a butler. Probably the sort where they actually *want* guests, too.

At last Madame Beauvoir rises to leave. She looks me over from head to toe like a dress she might consider purchasing, though she doesn't especially like it. "*Elle est très belle, n'est-ce pas?*" Madame Beauvoir thinks I'm beautiful. Maybe she's not as awful as I thought.

Henri shrugs, looking me over once from head to foot. *I don't see it,* he replies, *but not all men have options.*

My teeth grind in response.

He walks her to the door and watches her drive off before turning back inside and latching the door behind him. "*Dieu,*" he says, glancing at me. "Trust the old witch to barge in just as the new witch finally wakes."

Witch harkens a little too closely to the type of words my mother used all my life, because she views time travel as something akin to drug dealing or human trafficking. And I might put up with them from her, but I'm definitely not putting up with them from him. "I'd watch who you start calling names."

He raises a brow. "Is that right? Because I'm fairly certain you can't jump right now, and I'm the one with the gun." He turns to Marie-Therese. "And why exactly would our *American* cousin have a French name?"

Marie-Therese heaves a sigh. "I panicked. The only American females I could think of were Amelia Earhart and Eleanor Roosevelt. And she's too pretty to be named after Eleanor Roosevelt."

He comes forward with heavy steps, reluctantly taking the seat across from mine. "And did you get her actual name," he asks Marie-Therese, "or were you too busy giving her yours?"

My mouth opens but Marie-Therese holds out a hand to stop me. "No, don't. For your own safety, it's best you give us as little information as possible about who you are or where you're from. So for now, you are Amelie Durand. I am Marie-Therese, as you know, and the sullen one here is my brother Henri."

A muscle ticks in his jaw. "Well don't get attached. We have no idea who she is or what she's capable of."

"What she's *capable* of?" Marie-Therese asks with a laugh, setting a round of cheese in front of me, along with more bread. "She was comatose for days after she traveled here. You can't think she's capable of much."

She's right, but it's not the most flattering defense I've ever heard.

"Maybe it was all an act," he counters.

I turn toward Henri with an exasperated exhale. "What on earth do you think I'm planning to do? I'm a college student, not a criminal mastermind."

He rolls his eyes. "Believe me, I know you're no criminal mastermind. You couldn't even manage to steal an apple from my barn without being caught. Now tell us why you're here."

I'm deeply tired again, and my temper has begun to fray. "I'm here to help you, though you're making me wish I hadn't bothered."

Henri leans back in his chair, arms folded across his chest. "*Help?*" he scoffs, his pretty lip curling up at the corner. "Is this a joke?"

"Henri," snaps Marie-Therese. " *Tu es impoli.*"

"You've forgotten," Henri says to his sister, "that our future *savior* doesn't speak a word of French."

I'm officially sick of his shit. "You don't have to be rude about it."

He sighs. "And you don't have to be idiotic about it. Who arrives naked in a country where she can't speak the language and can't even stay awake?"

Marie swats his arm and turns to me. "Ignore him. Our mother insisted we both become fluent in several languages. Henri seems to forget not everyone has been so fortunate. Please continue."

"By all means," says Henri, turning back to me, "you were in the process of telling us how you—who showed up here naked and defenseless and proceeded to sleep for over two days—could offer assistance?"

His attitude leaves me longing to lash out rather than respond, except...he has a point. I'm young and terrible at time jumping. Aside from giving them some vague warnings about the future, I have nothing to offer.

I sigh, trying to think back to the weeks and weeks of nightmares before they finally got a little too realistic. They were always about Marie-Therese—other things came up too but since they made no sense to me, I mostly ignored them.

"My sister told me to find Marie-Therese, and I was hoping she'd understand. All I know is it's got something to do with saving people and a circle of light."

Marie-Therese's jaw drops and the legs of Henri's chair land heavily on the floor. They exchange a quiet, stunned look that worries me. It obviously means way more to them than it does to me. "*C'est elle*," Marie-Therese breathes, so stunned she's reverted to French. *It's her.* "*Ma mere*—my mother, she told me you would come."

Ummm...what? "I don't know your mother. This is the furthest I've ever gone back."

But Marie's eyes are bright, her head nodding eagerly. "She told us someone would come and would be important to us," she argues. "That you would help us. It must be you."

I shake my head. "I seriously doubt I'm the person your mother was expecting, but maybe if you told me what you need help *with* I could do something."

She and Henri exchange another look. It's clear that whatever it is she wants, Henri wants the opposite.

"Marie," he growls. "*Non.*"

We need to know, she hisses back at him before she turns to me. "My mother left three years ago without explanation and never returned. If I travel back to see her, she won't tell me anything. She'll realize she's not going to return, and she won't say a word. But *you* could go."

The conversation and Marie-Therese's expectations have begun to drag on me like a weight. It's the fatigue coming back, I'm sure, but the fact that I'm going to disappoint her in a minute doesn't help. "You really have no idea where she went?" I ask.

Marie-Therese stares at the table. "Her car was found in Paris, along with her clothes, but we don't know what year she was visiting."

A chill goes down my spine. I have a disappearance in my family as well—my aunt, who left for Paris long ago and never returned. Though it happened before we were born, the mystery of our missing aunt always fascinated Kit. More than once she suggested I should travel back in time to help her. But if two people disappeared going after the same thing, I'm certain I don't want to be the third.

"What's the circle of light thing about?"

Marie-Therese's eyes widen. "Did your mother never tell you the prophecy?"

Henri's eyes narrow. "Marie, if she doesn't know, it's not your place to tell her."

Marie shrugs. "She's a time traveler. She's supposed to know," she says before returning to me. "The prophecy says that there will be a child born after a great war—it calls her the *hidden* child —who will produce this circle of light, which is somehow supposed to keep our pasts safe."

My shoulders sag. I don't especially believe in prophecies, particularly ones passed down by word of mouth. Honestly, it's a little shocking that both my aunt and their mother might have believed in it enough to actually go seek it out.

"What's it supposed to keep you safe *from*?"

Henri frowns. "From you," he says. At my startled look he begrudgingly completes the thought. "Not you, specifically. But from future time travelers. My sister, any children she might have...even those of us who don't have the power, we are all at risk. Any one of you can come from the future and destroy every-thing, can't you? Even this impromptu visit right now...what if you've changed something? What if the simple act of your arrival has led to some trickle that will become an avalanche?"

I close my eyes and take a small breath. Even in 1938, I can't escape people who think I'm evil. Not that I disagree with them.

Marie-Therese frowns at him. "You've done nothing wrong," she assures me. "My mother believed the circle could keep us from having our futures stripped away."

I could point out that their futures could be stripped from them anyway. I did a fair amount of research about what's coming for this part of France when I was preparing to jump to the 1930s. Saint Antoine, given its position between Germany and Paris, will be Nazi-occupied throughout the war, but I hold onto that information for now. I'm not here to change the past any more than is necessary to get back home.

"I don't really see how I can help you with any of this," I tell her. "I'm sorry I got your hopes up."

"Please," Marie-Therese begs. "If you could get her to tell you her plans, we might still be able to save her."

Henri's face is drawn and sad in a way that makes him, momentarily, hard to hate. "Marie," he says quietly, "she's not trapped. She's dead, and that's something even you can't fix. No matter what year she went to, she'd have found her way back to us by now if she were alive."

"You don't know that," Marie breathes. She turns to me. "Please consider it. I have to find her."

I think of the nightmare that led me here. Kit, sitting up in her coffin, her skin a mottled blue and white like a sickly robin's egg —the way it looked when they pulled her out of the lake.

You have to find them, she told me again and again. For one horrible moment I wonder if it wasn't Marie I was supposed to save, but her mother and my aunt. I dismiss the thought immediately. Wherever they went, it was obviously very dangerous, and no time traveler alive is more ill-equipped to make that journey than I am. Even Marie shouldn't attempt it, and I'm not sure I want to help her try.

"I'm sorry," I reply. "My aunt also went missing in Paris, which tells me that what you're talking about might be a little harder than it sounds. And I'm just doing this one thing for my sister. Once I return to my own time, I'm never jumping again."

Marie-Therese laughs as if I'm joking, or a child making insane promises I can't keep. "Of course you'll continue to jump. We can't stop ourselves."

Her laughter irritates me, perhaps because my greatest fear is that she's right. I've done nothing *but* try to stop since I started jumping a decade ago, and yet here I am, time traveling again when it feels like my whole future depends on giving it up.

"*I can*," I reply

Marie-Therese's hands press to the table. "Your aunt is missing, my mother is missing. How many others must there be? Don't you at least want to see if you can help?"

"I'm mostly interested in not dying," I reply. "Maybe we should all just take their failure as a lesson and stay the hell away from wherever they went."

Marie-Therese's shoulders drop. I barely know her and I already hate that I've disappointed her. "But your sister said you were supposed to help me."

My stomach swims uneasily. The nightmares have been unrelenting for weeks and escalated dramatically before I got here. If I don't provide *some* kind of help they'll start back up. I'm sure of it. "Maybe I can help in other ways. I can tell you what's coming."

"We don't want to know what's coming," Henri says firmly.

I'm officially too tired for this. I press my head in my hands, resting my eyes. "Fine, whatever. I'm sorry I'm disappointing you. If you could give me one day here to rest, I'll be out of your hair."

"You're not going anywhere," says Henri. "You've identified my sister, a secret we've guarded our entire lives. I can't just let you go back and tell others."

Panic begins to rise in my chest. I think about my arrival, his hand on the hammer of the gun. He was really prepared to shoot me for being here. I wonder if he still might be.

My head swivels, looking for the exits and his eyes follow mine. "There's one exit to this home, and I stand between you and it. Don't even think about trying to get by me."

First he's demanding I leave, and now he's basically holding me hostage. One extreme to the next, and both extremes suck. Henri is proving to be far less delightful than those pouty lips of his might lead a female to believe.

"And how do you propose to keep me here once my powers

have returned?" I demand. "You're going to kill me? That's your plan?"

A muscle ticks in his jaw. "No. It's not my plan. I just haven't come up with a better one yet."

I was being sarcastic. I'm not sure he is.

"Look," I say with a heavy exhale. "I don't know what you think is going on here, but I'm not evil. I'm just a stupid college student who thought she might be able to help you, and you live more than five decades before my time anyway. What possible use is your sister's location to me?"

Marie-Therese looks at her brother as if it's a valid point, but I see something in his eyes before he averts them. Fear, knowledge. What does he know about this situation that his sister does not?

"You may remain until we figure it out," says Henri.

He rises and I watch as he returns to the vineyard. My sense of self-preservation tells me I should run at the first opportunity. Except I've barely got the energy to walk, so running is out of the question.

Marie places a hand on my shoulder. "Don't worry. I know my brother. He talks big but he doesn't have it in him to kill a pretty young girl."

I raise my worried face to hers. "I'd feel better if you'd just said he doesn't have it in him to kill anyone."

Her smile falters. "I wish I could tell you that too."

4

I return to bed for most of the day, so ill I'm beginning to wonder if perhaps I just truly have the flu, because the exhaustion feels exactly the same. Even when I try to wake up I find myself drifting back to sleep, my dreams feverish and illogical, blending the morning's incidents with memories from home in various ways I'm certain never happened.

When I finally get downstairs again, Marie-Therese pushes me to sit and I'm too tired not to obey, but I also feel guilty just lounging here while she appears to be doing five things at once.

"Let me help with something," I say.

"You could knead the dough?" She slides it to me on a floured wooden board and goes back to check on whatever's bubbling on the stove.

When she turns back a minute later she laughs. "What are you doing?" she asks. "You have to form a ball and punch it down, with your ummm..." She holds up her closed hand. "Fist? Is that not how you do it in your time?"

I raise a shoulder. "I don't know. I've never done it before."

Her jaw drops. "Never? Mon Dieu. How? You must be quite wealthy."

My family is anything but wealthy, which is sort of ridiculous given how many ways my ancestors and I could get money. "It's just not a thing people do in my time," I explain. "We're too busy. We just buy it at the store."

She frowns. "What is it that keeps you all so busy?"

I bite my lip. I'm not entirely sure, to be honest. "Well, most women work or they're in school. They aren't home to make bread." But it's not as if Marie-Therese has a life of leisure here, and when I'm not in class I have plenty of down time. "I guess maybe we're not all that busy. We'd just rather, you know, read. Or watch TV."

"TV?" she asks.

It slipped, but is there any harm in explaining it? "Television. It's like a box in your house that plays movies and shows. I guess it hasn't been invented yet."

Her eyes go wide. TV has never struck me as a wondrous invention, but I see in her face that it really must have been something when it first came out. Like a rollercoaster that comes to your home when you want to ride it. "I've heard of something like this—it was at the world's fair, I think. I just never imagined it would become common."

"What about you?" I ask. "What do you do for fun?"

Her smile grows a little sad. "I help with the language classes at the church or sometimes see my friends. Things changed... after my mother left."

I feel my first flicker of guilt and dismiss it. I've done what I agreed to. I found Marie. If she and her brother don't want to know about the future, there's not much more I can do, and doing any more would be breaking a promise I made to myself, and also to Mark, even if he doesn't know I made it. I don't care what Marie-Therese or her brother say. The second I'm recovered I'm going back home.

≈

HENRI COMES in just before dinner. Even after a day outside, with sweat on his brow and bits of hay falling from his trousers, he's the picture of a handsome 1940's soldier or movie star. All chiseled perfection, a lock of hair falling forward.

He walks into the room and sets apples on the table in front of me. His hands are large, tan from days spent outdoors. "So you won't need to steal them," he says.

I glance up. I've got just enough energy to slap that smirk off his face, I'd bet. "Are you always so pleasant to your female guests? I'm beginning to see why you're still single."

His mouth slips up on one side. "You think I'm single for lack of options?"

Marie-Therese smiles fondly at him. "Our Henri can't throw a stick without hitting a lovesick girl," she says. "It's almost irritating going into town with him, the way they all stop us and try to talk to him."

I don't doubt for a moment this is true, but I still long for a way to take him down a peg. "I assume it must be entirely women who don't know you well," I murmur.

Henri arches a brow. "Do you always bait men who hold your life in their hands?" he asks.

I'm more annoyed by the remark than I am threatened, because I'm still hard-pressed to imagine him as a killer. "Sorry. I'm not entirely clear on the rules," I reply. "No one's ever threatened to kill me before."

He turns toward the room just past the kitchen, which I assume is his. "With the mouth on you," he says, "I find that very surprising."

~

AFTER HENRI EMERGES, freshly bathed and irritatingly handsome, we sit down to eat a dinner that is relatively simple, yet smells better than anything I've ever smelled. I'm still so ravenously hungry it feels like I might never get full.

"What happened to the bread?" Henri asks. I sigh. I should have known he'd comment.

"It was my first time."

He narrows one eye. "How exactly is it that a girl of your age has not learned to make bread?"

It's no different than the question Marie-Therese asked earlier, except that he seems to regard even the most minute things about me as indicative of some greater evil, and it's getting old.

I set down my fork. "Is there ever going to come a point where you don't act like I'm the antichrist?"

"Perhaps if I got to know you well enough," he says, cutting into his ham, "but I don't plan to. So why do you not possess such a basic skill?"

My lip curls. I think the inherent chauvinism of this era would kill me long before Nazis or my ineptitude at household chores. "Because where I'm from, we don't need to make our own bread. Once life *improves* a few decades from now, the ability to cook and produce children will not be considered a woman's foremost accomplishments."

"But you still need to eat," argues Marie-Therese. "Who cooks if women aren't?"

"People eat out a lot in my time. And cooking is easier too. Faster."

She sits forward, suddenly fascinated. "Faster how?"

"Are you sure I'm supposed to be telling you this?" I ask.

"No," Henri intones. "You shouldn't. You shouldn't even be here."

Marie-Therese shrugs. "Tell us anyway. I want to know. I want to know everything that's different. Just not anything bad."

I frown. The bad is probably what she most needs to know. I've spent less than a day with her, but already every bone in my body wants to urge her to flee—to move to the United States or some distant island that won't be touched by the war. Except it's not a choice I should make for her. As her asshole brother pointed out, I shouldn't even be here in the first place.

Ignoring Henri's thoughts on the matter, I tell them about microwaves and VCRs and MTV and drive-thrus. I tell them about air conditioning, something they could sorely use right now: even with the windows open my dress has been stuck to me all day. I explain that few people farm, and that—at least where I'm from—most people go to college and wind up working indoors.

Marie-Therese is enthralled by the life I describe, gushing over the idea of having weekends free to go to parties or movies or galleries. But Henri just listens, seeming to carefully weigh every word that comes out of my mouth with his arms folded across his chest.

When Marie-Therese runs upstairs to get her needlepoint, he leans back in his chair. "I think you'll find our small life here rather unpleasant," he says.

"There's only been one unpleasant part so far," I reply, narrowing my eyes at him. I rise to my feet, too tired to sit here being baited by him and he rises too, looming over me. Between his height and the width of his shoulders, I feel a little more vulnerable than I did when we were seated.

"You've charmed my sister, *kelpie*," he says, his eyes brushing over my face, "but I promise I won't be quite so easy."

I don't know how to translate *kelpie* and decide not to ask. I'm almost certain it isn't anything good.

5

When I wake the next day the sun is beating down on me through the open window, and the air in the room is so thick and oppressive it would make me feel groggy no matter how much sleep I'd gotten. I should be in New York City right now with Mark. There was a new gallery in SoHo he wanted to take me to, and as much as I love discovering new artists, it's the appeal of a darkened room and air-conditioning that speaks to me most at the moment.

I put on yesterday's dress and limp downstairs, a trickle of sweat rolling down my chest and landing somewhere inside the God-awful, too-small bra. Marie-Therese is bustling around, sprightly and all smiles. "Oh goodness," she says, coming to a halt. "You look worse."

I twist my hair off my neck, trying to cool off. "It's just hot," I say weakly. I take in the small basket she's packing. "Are you going out?" My heart beats unsteadily at the prospect of being left here with Henri. I still don't think he's a killer, necessarily, but I like having her here as a buffer regardless.

She nods. "I teach German on Friday mornings, but if you'd like I could take you to town when I'm done."

Despite my fatigue, the idea appeals to me. Here on the farm, life does not feel drastically different from home. But in a town, with the shops and all the people, it might truly feel as if I'm in France, just before the occupation. Sort of like a Renaissance festival or 50's day in high school, albeit it one where the participants don't realize they've got nearly a decade of suffering ahead.

"I didn't have time to milk the cows so there's only water to drink, but I left you bread and cheese," she says, grabbing the basket. "I'll be back after lunch, but in the meantime, take a bath. It might help you cool off."

I see her off reluctantly and then go to the bathroom. For a moment I simply stare at the tub, arms folded across my chest, wondering how I can avoid this. It's been a decade since I last had a bath instead of a shower, but I assume it's my only option here.

I strip and force myself into the tub, sitting in two inches of water and emptying a pitcher over my head to wash my hair. I find shampoo but no conditioner. It's depressing to exert so much effort just to have my hair feel like straw when I'm done.

Showers, conditioner, shorts and cool air. This is what I miss most, so far. That and the absence of Henri.

I get back into my clothes. By the time I'm done dressing I'm hot again, and exhausted, but I grab the pail Marie uses for milking and head outside. Though ours ceased to be a working farm once my father left, I still remember a thing or two, and Marie has enough work to do without me adding to it.

I get as far as the pump when I sense something behind me and glance over my shoulder. Henri is in the field there, a vine in one hand and shears in the other, but he's gone completely still, watching me. When our eyes meet he throws the shears to the ground and begins to march my way.

Right. Because I'm a criminal here to steal his shitty little apples or something. "You don't need to get the gun just yet," I say testily as he approaches. "I'm just milking the cows."

His tongue darts out to the corner of his mouth. He almost

looks amused. "Do you even know *how* to milk a cow? Don't you have a magical device in your time that milks the cow and churns the butter and carries it all to your tongue?"

Well, for the most part, yes. I lift a shoulder. "I assume it can't be that hard if you can do it."

His hands link behind his neck, observing me. "Hopefully you've taken on this chore in lieu of making the bread."

"Marie-Therese and I are going to town today," I reply, rolling my eyes, "so your bread is safe."

His jaw drops. "*To town?*" he asks, and then he laughs unhappily. "*Non.* My impulsive sister is so thrilled to have someone around that she's not using her head. You will stay on the farm and go nowhere else. You've caused enough trouble as it is."

I'm growing tired, standing in the sun, and though I do sort of enjoy sparring with him, my will to do so is dwindling by the second. "I must be growing on you if you're so desperate to keep me close."

"Hardly," he replies. "But Marie-Therese attracts enough attention and two of you together, in the same household? It could raise suspicion."

I throw out my hands. His paranoia is getting really, really old. "What does it matter?" I exclaim. "Is Marie-Therese a fugitive? A celebrity in hiding? Why would anyone care where she is? I don't care that she knows where *I* am."

His eyes shift away. Hiding something again. "It's never safe for any of you to know each other, and the fact that you're pretending not to know this isn't helping your case."

"How would I know that? Marie's the first time traveler I've ever even met!"

His eyes narrow. "Not your mother? Your grandmother? A sister?"

My family history is like an overstuffed closet. Pull one thing loose and you'll find yourself buried in the rest. I go with the simplest explanation instead. "It skipped my mother, and my grandmother died before I was born. I've traveled back to see her, but asking her to explain things would..."

"...let her know she'll die before her time," he concludes. He understands because it's the same reason Marie won't at least try to go back and visit her mother. I see a flicker of something in his eyes. I'd suspect it was sympathy if he were anyone else.

"Yes." I feel unsteady now, between the heat and the exhaustion. I need to end this conversation before I pass out.

He reaches back to rub a hand along the nape of his neck, flinching. "You had no business jumping back like this when you know so little. What were you thinking?"

"I was thinking your sister needed help, because the information came from a pretty reliable source." Though I'm not sure a message from beyond the grave would necessarily be considered *reliable*.

I sway suddenly and he grabs my waist to hold me upright. I can feel the pressure of his hands through my dress, and this sudden awareness of him—of his size and his strength—unnerves me. "You need to lie down," he says.

"I'm fine," I reply, but it's a lie. I can't think straight right now, between the exhaustion and his hands on me. My eyes close for a moment and he scoops me up like a child and heads for the house. I'd like to argue but I feel like I'm about to pass out. And dazed though I am, I can't help but notice that—for all his belligerence—he's gentle with me now. Gentler than I'd have thought him capable of.

"You think you're being brave," he says softly. "But bravery like that will get you killed one day, kelpie."

That word again. "That's the second time you've called me that," I murmur. "If you're going to insult me, have the balls to do it in English."

He raises a brow. "A lady would not use that expression. And not only do you not know French, you don't know your own language as well. Kelpie is a Scottish word I think. A myth."

"So enlighten me," I say, as he sets me on the couch. "What is a kelpie?"

He hesitates, his eyes on my face for a long moment before he turns away. "A monster in human form."

BY THE TIME MARIE-THERESE RETURNS, I've already taken a nap but don't feel much better for it. She prepares a broth over the stove, her mouth pursed with irritation over Henri's edict about me remaining on the farm, though in truth I'm probably too tired to make the walk anyway.

I cut carrots for her while she peels potatoes and asks me question after question about university. She wants to know everything: the classes I've taken, my plans for the degree, what it's like to live on my own. Each question sounds more wistful than the one before it.

"Did you ever think about going?" I ask.

She grabs the carrots I've chopped in two certain handfuls and drops them into the pot on the stove. "I couldn't leave Henri all alone," she says. "Perhaps when he marries."

"That poor woman," I sigh. "She has no idea what she's in for with *him*."

She laughs. "Oh no. Did you see him today? Is he still being a beast?"

"Yes, and he called me a kelpie for the second time, which is apparently a monster in human form."

A small smile graces her lips. "If it's any consolation, it's actually a monster who takes the form of a beautiful woman."

I grimace. "It's not really much of a consolation."

"Poor Henri. We finally get a beautiful girl around here and she hates him. Like I said, you've seen him at his worst. He was so different before he came back from England."

"England?"

She nods, blowing on a steaming spoonful of the broth to taste before bringing it to her lips. "He was there for university."

For some reason the news surprises me, though it shouldn't. His posh British accent was one of the first things I noticed about him, after all. "I didn't realize he'd gone."

"It wasn't for him so he left," she says with a shrug. "But please just ignore him if he's being rude. I know you can't see it yet, but there's not a sweeter, more caring man alive than my brother. Your presence here worries him, and I suppose he's lashing out a bit because of it."

"If he's threatened by me, I'm guessing he's threatened by almost anything," I say with a sigh. "As you've both pointed out, I'm terrible at time jumping and not even good at stealing."

Her shoulders fall as she turns back to the stove. "We've already lost both our parents, and I think he blames himself a bit...for not being able to help our mother."

For reasons I doubt I'll ever understand, only women can time travel. It hadn't occurred to me until now how painful it must be for Henri that his sister could choose to charge back and save their mother, but he cannot.

"He's made it his sworn duty to keep me safe and yet the Germans are getting bolder—it's said they've now crossed the river into Allemagne—and with Madame Beauvoir popping in unannounced and now you...these things happen and it makes him feel like he's failing."

I don't want to feel sorry for Henri, I really don't. But in both of them I'm seeing a life of promise that's been waylaid somehow. If I planned to stay, and I don't, I might think *this* is what Kit wanted me to fix. That perhaps she wanted me to save Marie-Therese and Henri from themselves, from this sad, isolated little life they've created, though I wouldn't have the first idea how. And it doesn't matter anyway, because I'm definitely not staying.

OVER DINNER MARIE-THERESE is all smiles and laughter, while Henri continues to regard me like some kind of vampire who might lunge forward at any moment to sink my fangs into his neck. The more his sister seems to like me, the more his aversion grows.

"Henri," Marie chides, "you must smile at least once tonight so Amelie realizes you're capable of it."

"She's the guest," he says, eyes on his stew. "I believe she's the one who should be charming."

I pat my lips with my napkin and give him a saccharine smile. "I'm not generally charming to men who've held me at gunpoint. It's a personal thing."

"And I'm not in the habit of smiling at vipers who land naked on my property and refuse to leave."

"*Refuse* to leave?" I demand. "You're holding me hostage, remember?"

His eyes meet mine across the table. "Fine. You are free to go," he replies. He glances away then. "The sooner the better," he adds, almost to himself.

I should be relieved but feel oddly hurt instead. It's an old kind of hurt, as if he's pressed upon a large bruise I've had so long I can't remember where I got it. The experience of not being wanted is something you never entirely get used to.

Marie-Therese rises, snatching things from the table. "Henri, you're being rude," she says. "Amelie will not be well enough to travel for days or even weeks, and more importantly, I don't want her to go. It's been years since I've had another female around the house."

He leans back, folding his arms across his chest. "Yes, I'm aware. And it's making you a little too comfortable. Taking her to town, Marie? You really think people won't talk about our American 'cousin' once they've seen her?"

"You worry too much," Marie-Therese says with a dismissive wave of a hand. "Humans can rationalize almost anything, and it's not as if it's a secret by now. You know what a gossip Madame Beauvoir is."

He exhales heavily. "And you don't worry enough. I've asked you multiple times to jump back and change the way that visit went. There's no reason anyone needs to know she's here."

She glances at him, and then me. "No," she says, finally. "There's no point. I think Amelie might stay with us a while, so I'm not going to exhaust myself trying to hide her."

I open my mouth to assure her I do *not* plan to stay for a while, but Henri, lovely man that he is, is way ahead of me. "*Stay a while?*" he demands. "Are you insane? She remains here until she's recovered and not an hour longer, do you understand?"

Listening to the two of them fight has made me tired, and depressed. I close my eyes for a moment and lapse into a fantasy that's carried me for years now, even before I met Mark, though it's his face I see when I picture it of late: the two of us married, living in some luxurious apartment with enough of everything that I no longer need to jump—enough money, enough support, enough care. I will be normal at last. I won't need to feel conflicted about the things I haven't told him because they'll no longer matter. If you go long enough without time traveling, you generally lose the *ability* to time travel. I picture my mother visiting us, proud of me at last.

I just need to stop jumping, and in order to do that I need to get home. As Henri himself said, the sooner, the better.

6

On my third conscious day in 1938—my sixth total—I finally rise feeling slightly closer to normal. My level of fatigue is more akin now to a serious hangover, or the day after an illness, as opposed to the worst flu of my life. My limbs are still heavy, though, and I feel an emptiness inside that warns me I probably couldn't jump up a flight of stairs, much less jump to the next decade or beyond.

Which means I definitely won't get back in time to see Mark before he leaves for Nepal. I hate that he's leaving with this strain between us, hate that we had our first argument in two years just before I left, and over something that seems stupid in retrospect. He'd asked me to move to New York City with him, which would mean dropping out of college with one year left. *My goals matter too*, I said to him. "Just transfer to a school in the city," he said—as if it was all so easy, as if leaving an Ivy League university and losing a year while I applied for the transfer was meaningless—and I reacted poorly.

My days here have reminded me, though, what a novelty it is to be wanted at all. He pushed me hard because he loves me, because he enjoys my presence. I still don't want to transfer, but I wish I'd handled it better. I wish I'd been grateful rather than indignant.

I wish, most of all, that I hadn't come here in the first place.

I SPEND the morning with Marie-Therese, "helping" her make scones and pie, though my help is nothing a six-year old couldn't provide. I cut and peel apples while she does pretty much every-thing else.

"What's with all the baking?" I ask. It's just pure laziness on my end, but if I were her I wouldn't be filling up every available moment with unnecessary work. And to me baking seems like unnecessary work.

She shrugs. "I thought we'd have tea today."

"Tea?" I ask. "Isn't that a British thing?"

She laughs. "We do tea here as well, though to be honest I thought it was also an American thing. I was trying to keep you from being homesick."

She probably doesn't realize I've never once in my entire life been homesick. Even now, what appeals to me most about my own time is not the people, but the idea of showers and air condi-tioning. "That's really thoughtful of you. It sounds like fun."

Marie-Therese smiles. "I enjoy baking anyway. My mother and I cooked together every day of my life, from the moment I was old enough to climb on a chair and stand at the stove beside her." Sadness flickers over her face. "She'd have liked you, my mother. Though she'd have convinced you to cut your hair. Is that really the style, in your time? To wear it so long?"

I shrug. "There are lots of styles. I keep mine this length so it covers things up in case I land somewhere naked. Unlike you, I don't seem to have much choice about where and when I land."

"I've been thinking about that," she says. "I wonder if you struggle so much because you have some other ability. Perhaps the energy I devote to landing in the right time and place is for you...diverted elsewhere. To some other gift."

I laugh aloud. "Trust me, I have no other gifts. And it doesn't matter anyway, because I will never jump again, after this." My eyes catch on Henri outside, walking past the window on his way to the pump. He's down to a t-shirt today, and I'd be lying if I didn't admit that he has the most amazing biceps I've ever seen in my life. Mark spends hours at the gym each week lifting weights, but apparently working on a farm provides a little added *oomph* no gym can provide.

"Of course you will jump again," she counters, combing through the pantry. "You haven't visited my mother yet."

Henri pulls the t-shirt over his head and I stare, fascinated, at smooth olive skin and muscles I didn't even realize were possible until now.

"I'm not going to visit your mother," I say faintly. "I told you that."

Henri cups his hands and drinks, then cups them again to dump water over the top of his head, shaking it out of his eyes as it falls. I flush, suddenly aware that I'm gawking and my hands have fallen still.

"I know what you said," she replies with a small smile. "But I feel increasingly certain you're wrong. We're out of sugar. I'll be right back."

Before I can ask where she's going, her dress has fallen to the floor and she is gone. When I choose to jump, I'm a lot like someone trying to justify breaking her diet: *here's why I should make an exception and I've been super good and it's a once-in-a-lifetime opportunity.* But Marie-Therese treats time travel as if it's spinach or kale—something without a single negative repercussion, the kind of thing you can binge on without guilt.

I've barely blinked before there's a clatter upstairs, and then she's walking back down in a new dress, calmly grabbing a full tin of sugar from the pantry and placing it in front of me before she begins folding the clothes she discarded a moment before.

"Did you really just time travel to go buy *sugar*?" I ask. "That has got to be the most boring use of a superpower ever."

"Even more boring than that. I just added it to yesterday's shopping list." She sees my shock and smiles. "It just makes life easier. Surely you've gone back at some point to remind yourself of something?"

I shrug, unwilling to admit she's right. When I've done it, it's only been for important things...or things that seemed important at the time. Missed homework assignments, pop quizzes. But I've never done it without feeling like I was cheating somehow, whereas Marie-Therese clearly suffers no such qualms. As much as I want to look down on her for using her gift so shamelessly, a part of me is envious at the same time.

"Don't you worry you'll depend on it too much? You won't be able to just disappear in front of your husband and children."

"I would not marry a man I was unwilling to tell," she says. "Although I probably won't marry, so I doubt it will be an issue."

Her answer surprises me. As pretty as she is, I'd think her possibilities were limitless, and she's awfully young to have given up anyway. "Why don't you think you'll marry? I'm sure you have your pick in Saint Antoine. There must be *someone* here you'd consider?"

Her gaze drifts away and her cheeks grow rose pink. "There is no one suitable here."

Her choice of words is odd. "Suitable?"

The blush deepens. "The only man in this town I'd consider is not..." she takes a deep breath and looks away. "He is not available."

My eyes go wide. Marie-Therese seems so sweet and inno-cent, so proper. I never dreamed that she'd be lusting after a married man. "And I guess he'll never *become* available?" I ask. "Divorce is probably frowned upon now?"

"Divorce?" she gasps, and then flushes again. "Dieu. He's not married! What do you think of me?"

I throw up my hands. "You said he wasn't available."

She throws an unnecessary amount of vigor into rolling out the dough. "No, no, no. I don't like anyone. I was just saying there's no one here I would consider."

Except that's not what she said, and she is still blushing fiercely. Maybe it's someone Henri would not approve of? Someone poor? Someone Jewish? Of another race? I wish I were staying long enough to help her sort it out.

But, again, I am not.

THAT AFTERNOON, she serves tea on the side porch, which is pleasant in the shade, and forces Henri to come inside to join us. He raises a brow as he eyes the table. "What's the special occasion?" he asks. "Is she leaving?"

Marie-Therese frowns at him. "I thought it might help Amelie feel like she was back home."

His mouth twitches. "Americans don't take tea," he says.

She rolls her eyes. "Yes, so you tell me now."

I take a scone with clotted cream, doing my best to ignore Henri while he ignores me. Poor Marie-Therese is left to fill in the gap in conversation, and begins telling me about Henri as a teen, trying to borrow the car to meet a girl in the middle of the night without making his mother aware. It's hard for me to imagine Henri being *fun* enough to sneak out with the car. He's close to my age and yet he seems a decade older simply because of the weight he carries on those broad shoulders—I see it in his wary eyes every time he looks at me.

"His plan was to push it to the road before starting it, but instead, it went careening into an irrigation ditch," Marie says, laughing. "So he woke me, begging and pleading with me to jump back a few hours to warn him it would happen."

"Which you refused to do," adds Henri.

"Henri was the golden child in our house," Marie-Therese explains. "I thought every once in a while I should not be the only one in trouble. And naturally, he *still* didn't get in trouble, even when my mother found out."

I look toward the vineyard, stretching green and lush as far as I can see, and wonder what it would be like to live in a household where rivalries are merely *amusing*. Where the preference for one child is slight enough that no one minds all that much.

"If you had to live with a sibling who could do no wrong, you'd understand," Marie-Therese says, interpreting my silence as disapproval.

"I did," I reply. Unlike her, though, I don't have any fun stories to share. In my home, after my sister died, I expected nothing from my family other than what was required to survive, and even that didn't seem like a certainty. "My parents didn't approve of our gift, so I never stood a chance."

"Didn't *approve?*" asks Marie-Therese as if she might have misunderstood. "But why?"

I shrug. Though I tell myself it doesn't bother me anymore, at times like this I find it requires a certain amount of effort to act ambivalent. "My mother never liked it, but after—" I stumble over my words, trying to sum up the past without giving any of it away. "After my father left, she seemed to decide it was a little...evil."

The mere act of referencing my mother is sometimes enough to open a hole inside me. I can feel it even now, black and shapeless, filling my head with all her accusations over the years. It's always been as if she knew slightly more about me than I knew about myself, and what she knew was deeply, irredeemably terrible. Even as I struggled to deny what she said, I always found evidence she was right. Every single time.

I look up to find Henri's eyes on me, and for once they aren't narrowed in suspicion or disdain. He's looking at me like I'm something passing by too quickly, something he wants to see and understand before it's too late. And then the expression is gone, leaving me to wonder if I imagined it.

Marie takes a sip of her tea. "Your family must be worried about you, coming here all alone the way you did."

My smile falters a little, and stays in place only by force. I shrug. "No one knows I'm here, actually. Like I said, they wouldn't have approved." I'm sure my mother was relieved by my absence. But once I get home and announce my engagement, maybe she'll start to see me in a different way. Maybe then she'll start to care.

Henri sucks in his cheeks. "So where does everyone think you are?"

"I told them I got an internship in France studying art. My boyfriend was leaving for the summer anyway, so..."

"Boyfriend? I didn't realize you had a young man," says Marie-Therese. There is a tiny wrinkle between her brows. "I suppose you're not allowed to tell him what you really are unless you have children together."

My eyes go wide. "Mark will never, ever know."

"*Ever?*" she asks, flabbergasted. "You must not be serious about him then."

I sit up a little straighter, feeling oddly defensive. "Of course I am. We're getting engaged after I return home. But no, I'm not going to tell him. He wouldn't understand."

She and Henri both look dumbfounded. It's as if I just announced I was marrying a family member or someone in prison. "Wouldn't understand?" Marie-Therese repeats. "I'm sure he'd understand quite quickly once you demonstrated."

I flush. "Not that. I mean he...wouldn't appreciate it. It's complicated."

Henri remains still. His hand rests on his fork, unmoving.

"That's what a woman says when she makes excuses for a man," he says.

I narrow one eye, flicking him with my most disdainful glance. "I'm sure the women you date make plenty of excuses, Henri."

Marie-Therese snickers beneath her hand but Henri glances at me coolly, without emotion. "So tell us, then, how it's so hard to explain."

It feels like even his most innocuous questions are tinged with suspicion, and a thousand responses he'd deem *unladylike* come to mind. Most of them some version of *go fuck yourself, Henri*. I lift my chin. "Fine. He's from a very wealthy family. They just don't...they aren't strange. They would not appreciate a strange ability. He wants a normal wife, and that's fine because I plan to be one. Once I get back home, I'm done with jumping. This is my last trip ever, and then it's behind me."

"Pah," Marie-Therese says with a shocked laugh. "You can't be serious. What if you need something? What if you need to escape? What if you need money?"

I rise and begin to gather dishes. "I won't. Mark's family is wealthy and well-connected. There's nothing I'd need to time travel for that they can't make happen."

Henri rolls his eyes, tipping back in his chair as if the conversation is over. "So you've chosen to marry for money," Henri says. "And he's marrying you for your looks. Apparently some things haven't changed, from my time to yours."

My face heats. "I love Mark," I hiss. "It's a happy coincidence that his background means I no longer have to be something I'm not interested in being." I thank Marie for the tea and retreat. From the moment my mother's name came up I've felt this dark shadow overhead, and Henri's words only compound it. He seems to live to find weak spots in my armor, and God knows I've got enough to make his work easy for him.

I go out to the coop and swing handfuls of feed around. My

mother's voice is in my head, asking what Mark would think if he could see me now—chickens scurrying around my feet, which are clad in Marie-Therese's old shoes, scuffed and two sizes too big. *He'd see that you're a liar*, she whispers. There is no art history internship, no glamorous, can't-miss journey throughout the country.

That's the problem with the things my mother said about me: there was a grain of truth in every single one of them. I *am* a liar. I'm lying to Mark, to my mother. I'm lying to Henri and Marie about not understanding French and by implying that my sister is still alive.

There are so many bad things in the world and I know, deep in my heart, that I am all of them to some extent. And I don't see any way to stop being them aside from starting fresh with Mark when I get home. If I never jump again, once I get back, will it be enough? Or will I always be telling him a lie of one kind or another?

The sound of an opening door draws me out of my thoughts. Henri is walking out of the house but his eyes are on me. I'm never in the mood for his bullshit, but at this precise moment, I feel too fragile to hear a word of it.

His mouth opens and I cut him off. "I spent my entire life raised by a woman who thinks I'm the devil," I snap. "So whether you're about to imply that I'm a thief, or a monster, or a gold-digger, just save it. I assure you I'll hear all that and worse once I return home, and from someone whose opinion I actually care about."

I snatch the milk pail I set outside the coop and turn toward the barn. In spite of what I just said, I feel a sob swell in my throat. I know I'm just tired, but there are days when it feels like I'm not up to another decade or year or hour of being hated for what I am and all the mistakes I've made because of it.

I've just begun to milk the first of the two cows when I hear the crunch of hay underfoot. He stops a few feet away and I ignore him.

"If you pull from the top of the udder," he says quietly, "it'll come faster."

I brush my eyes against my sleeve, wishing he would leave so I could take a deep breath.

But he doesn't. "I'm sorry," he says quietly. "I don't actually think you're a monster, or a thief."

I glance up at him. For the first time ever, he looks contrite. "Then why do you keep saying it?"

He rubs the back of his head. "Because with each hour you spend here, you're making things harder," he replies after a moment. "No matter what you say to Marie-Therese, she's convinced you're going to find out where our mother went. Whether you intended to or not, you've gotten her hopes up."

I stand, wrapping my arms around myself. I liked it better when Henri's objections to my presence seemed ridiculous. But this one isn't. "I thought you agreed that me traveling back to see your mother was a bad idea."

He pinches the bridge of his nose. "I do. I know my mother wouldn't want Marie-Therese following her, and there's probably a reason she left in secret. But my sister can't move on from her obsession while you're still offering some possibility of assistance."

I stare at the ground, trying to gather my thoughts. What he says makes perfect sense. God, I'm tired of getting everything wrong. "And you want me to leave before it gets worse," I conclude.

He runs a hand through his hair and exhales. "I'm sorry. If things were different, I—". His gaze rests on my face, more wistful than I've ever seen it, and then he shakes his head. "Things aren't different though," he sighs, more to himself than me, and he turns to walk out of the barn.

Once he's gone, I lean my head against the back of the stall.

"Kit," I say quietly. "Why the hell am I here? What do you want me to do?"

There is silence, of course. Those nightmares drove me to the brink of insanity, but this was obviously all a stupid mistake. I'm not saving or helping anyone. I'm just making their lives worse, and it's time I left well enough alone.

7

My departure plan is less than perfect. I'm not even close to being ready to jump home yet, so I will sneak out tonight after they've gone to bed and stay toward the outer corners of the orchard until my strength has returned. They don't venture out that far much, and if I hear them, I can always just hide in the woods. The blueberries are ripe and I should be able to sustain myself on those until I get back.

Dinner is simple that night, ham and cheese and bread and fruit. When they are not looking, I push bits of ham and cheese into my pockets. I'm not sure they'll stay good outside in the heat, but I'm probably going to be getting sick of blueberries before I can get home, so it's worth a shot.

Over dinner, Henri is almost pleasant. He's polite and manages not to call me a single name through the entire meal. What a shame that on the one night he's proven capable of behaving himself, I'm too exhausted and worried to appreciate it. I'm worried for myself, of course—the idea of sleeping outdoors with no shelter in particular—but mostly I'm worried for them. The Germans will be here within the next two years, and it's within my power to warn them. I'm just not sure if I should.

"If...something bad was coming," I venture, "would you want to know?"

"No," says Marie-Therese. "Of course not. I don't want to spend years and years dreading something that might not happen."

I glance at Henri. He looks less certain about that than his sister but finally shrugs. "She is probably right," he says. "It's best we just live the lives we were handed."

I wish this hadn't been their answer. *It's already too late anyway*, I remind myself. If they die in the war, I can't undo that.

This fact doesn't reassure me at all.

I RETIRE EARLY, but when the house is finally quiet I sneak downstairs in the borrowed dress, the one with its pockets full of food, and write a quick note to Marie-Therese, telling her I hope we meet again, which is true. If I can find her in my time, perhaps then I can explain why I snuck out the way I did. I slip outside with my shoes in hand, holding my breath as I pull the door closed behind me.

The night is silent. A light breeze and crickets in the distance. There's a bright moon and once my eyes adjust, I think I'll have no problem picking my way through to the orchard's outskirts. Yet as I put my shoes on, the plan feels a lot less simple than it did during daylight. The prospect of traversing the dark fields in the middle of the night has a chill inching along my spine, and falling asleep in them is difficult to even contemplate.

I cross the yard, going around the barn so I don't wake the animals. Even in the moonlight it's hard to see the uneven ground, and I stumble in a small divot, feet sliding a few inches over gravel before I regain my balance.

"In the mood for a stroll?" asks a voice. I jump, heart hammering, and turn toward the sound.

Henri. Sitting against the back of the barn, drowsy but unsurprised to find me here.

"You sleep outside?" I ask. It's all I can think to say.

"Not if I can help it," he replies, rolling the blanket under his arm and walking my way. "But I could only think of one good reason a guest would be shoving food in her pockets all night, and it turns out I was right."

I sigh heavily. "I'm just trying to do what you asked."

"I don't recall asking a half-dead girl to go sleep in the woods and starve while she's trying to return to health." He reaches my side. "Don't worry. I'm not planning to stop you. I could carry you back but I can't watch you all the time. You'd just sneak out again."

His response couldn't be more reasonable. I suppose that's what's so surprising about it. I look up at him in the moonlight, feeling unexpectedly sad that I will never see him again. I swallow. In two years' time will he still be on this farm or will he be off fighting? I don't want to know. I'm glad I'm leaving here before I start to care.

"Well...goodbye. Please tell Marie-Therese I was sorry to leave so suddenly."

I turn toward the orchard, but within seconds I hear the sound of feet behind me, matching my pace, as if the two of us are out here for a leisurely walk, nothing more.

I stop and round on him. "What are you doing?"

"I assume you were planning to sleep near the orchard, but I can't have a dead girl on my property," he says simply.

Oh my God. And to think I was getting all choked up at the idea of him going off to war. "So you're escorting me off your land so I don't *die* here?"

He shrugs. "No, I'll just come with you and make sure you leave in one piece."

I huff in frustration and pick up my pace, but as we approach the orchard, the trees begin to block the moon and it's so dark I can barely see a foot in front of my face. Anger keeps me walking fast despite that fact. "Your presence defeats the purpose. And you can't leave Marie alone. She'll panic."

I stumble and his hand reaches out to grab my arm. "She'll be fine for a few days."

He's making no sense at all. How has he gone from incessantly worrying about Marie-Therese to *she'll be fine for a few days*?

After five minutes of walking, we've reached the orchard. He points to a small clearing near the woods. "This seems like a good spot to sleep?" He's already begun spreading his blanket.

I hate him for ruining this. I was trying to do the right thing and now it feels as if I'm a tantrum-prone child being humored by her dad. "I'm not sleeping with you."

His mouth twitches. "Well, that definitely removes some of the fun from the evening. But there are wolves here, so you might at least want me close by."

Any pride I might have had goes skittering away at the word *wolves*. I slide down to the base of an apple tree across from him, leaning against it with my arms folded.

He spreads himself out on the blanket and glances over. "Didn't you bring something to sleep on?" he asks. "You're not very good at this running away business."

God I hate him.

"I didn't want you calling me a thief for the rest of my life. Just leave the blanket for me and go. I promise to drag myself off your property if I'm dying."

"That's exactly the kind of promise you won't be able to keep if you're being torn apart by wolves," he says, his tone conversational. "They are regrettably less than thorough, wolves are. They'd leave your head and bones behind."

I sort of want to laugh, and I sort of want to throw something at him. His hands fold under his head and he closes his eyes. Wishing I'd planned more thoroughly, I lie down on the patchy grass beneath me. "I wouldn't do that," he says, eyes still closed. "Not if you haven't checked for snake holes."

I freeze. "You're making that up," I hiss.

"Am I?" he asks with a small tick to his lips. "I guess we'll see."

I know he's just messing with me, but within five seconds I'm off the ground and marching over to his blanket. "Move over," I demand.

"Decided you'd like to sleep with me after all, then?" he asks without opening his eyes.

"No, I just figure that you're larger and slower, so the wolves will kill you first," I reply, lying down beside him.

Compared to the bare ground, the blanket feels surprisingly luxurious, and there's a breeze keeping the air almost pleasant when it was stifling in the house. It would be okay if I were here with pretty much anyone else.

I try to picture Mark in Henri's place but I can't. Mark and I would never find ourselves out in the middle of an orchard on a hot night with nothing but a blanket beneath us. His one and only camping experience took place on the golf course of his parents' country club, where a staff provided all their meals and even set up their tents. I'd laughed at the story and he had too, but I remember thinking I wanted that: a life where you could pick and choose your hardships. Where even the worst experiences were shaped into something soft and mild enough that you could survive them.

"I did this once," he says, "as a boy. My mother followed me, just as I've done to you."

"Was she as annoying about it as you are?"

"Worse," he says. "She brought an entire pie and a tub of cream and began to eat in front of me."

The idea of it makes me smile. I'd like to be a mother like that one day, but can you be a good parent if you weren't raised by one? I'm not sure. "I think I'd have liked your mom."

"She'd have liked you as well," he replies. "She had terrible taste in people."

To my surprise, I laugh. "I don't suppose you've brought a pie?"

"Unfortunately, no," he says, rolling toward me and propping himself up on his forearm. "And I don't suppose you'd know how to make one."

I squint up at him. "No, but I think the lack of a stove might be the bigger issue."

"We could always go back to the house," he says. "There's still a bit of pie left there. There are also beds, and pillows. And fewer bloodthirsty animals."

I roll up to my forearm, mirroring his position. "Why?" I ask softly. "You wanted me gone, and it made sense that you did. I even agreed with you. That's why I'm here."

He's quiet for a moment. "I went overboard," he finally says. "I do worry about Marie-Therese, but she'll survive. I realized during dinner that half of what worries me is how sad she'll be when you leave, and it made me feel...guilty."

It's the longest Henri has ever spoken to me without being snide, without insults or sarcasm. It's a side of him I suspected existed, but never thought I'd get to see firsthand. "Guilty? Why?"

"Because it reminds me how much happier she might be in another life. If we could move to Paris, or even into town. If she could go to university."

"Are you sure those things aren't possible? I'm the same thing she is, yet I go to university and I live in a big city and it's never been an issue."

In the moonlight his face grows guarded. "One of the last things my mother ever asked of me was that I keep Marie-Therese hidden here, and safe. I'm incapable of saving my mother. No matter what Marie wants to believe, I know she's dead. But the very least I can do is obey her last wishes."

He blames himself for his inability to save her, and he also blames himself for limiting Marie-Therese. There is no good option for him, no way that he isn't at fault regardless of what he does. I understand that a little too well.

"Perhaps when you marry?" I ask softly. "Then there will be another female in the house for Marie?"

His frown deepens. "A wife would make Marie feel as if this is no longer her place. I won't marry until she's found someone and left home."

Henri is obviously staying here on this farm, alone, to take care of Marie. And she is staying on the farm so her brother won't be alone. How are the two of them ever going to have their own lives if they're so worried about each other's?

"You could marry a terrible cook so Marie feels necessary?" I suggest, half-joking, before I realize it sounds as if I'm offering myself as a candidate. "One from your own time, that is."

He lifts a brow. "So you are not willing to stay here without your air cooling and the thing that cooks a potato in seven minutes?"

I grin. "I might be able to live without microwaves, but television is really cool. You'll have to take my word for it."

He flips on his back, and after a moment he breaks the silence, addressing his next quiet comment toward the sky. "You will never hear me say this again, and I will deny it if asked, but I would like it if you'd stay. Until you're better, that is."

I feel a smile tugging at the corners of my mouth, something soft and warm in my chest. Thank God none of it is visible to him. "Well, since it turns out I know less about wilderness life than I realized, I'll take you up on that. I suppose that means we should return to the house."

"I suppose." He shrugs, as if he's truly ambivalent about the idea. And maybe I am as well. There's absolutely nothing special or fancy about lying on a coarse woolen blanket outdoors on a summer night, but it hasn't been all bad.

We rise and walk silently back to the house. Once inside, I turn to head up the stairs but feel his hand at my forearm, pulling me toward the kitchen, where he grabs the pie off the counter and sets it on the table with two forks.

"Come on, little thief," he says. "I know you want some."

I slide across from him and grab a fork. "Perhaps you could come up with a nickname for me that *isn't* monster or thief?" I ask. "It doesn't even have to be something good. Just something that isn't uniformly negative."

He holds the fork to his lips. "So a neutral nickname then. *Mon petit fromage*, perhaps? Cheese isn't an offensive word, I assume?"

"You'll need to say it in English, whatever it is. Even the worst insults sound cute in French."

"What if I just call you *thief*, but in French? *Voleuse*. You see? Accurate, yet not too harsh."

I raise my chin. "It's not accurate at all."

"Says the woman with pockets full of ham," he replies, but he's grinning, and to my surprise, I laugh. Since I've arrived, for the most part, every word out of his mouth has tapped into this well of shame inside me. *Thief, liar, monster.* But tonight there is no rancor in his words. Instead I hear a hint of begrudging admiration: he likes me better for the fact that I stole the ham, that I tried to preserve myself while doing the right thing. "It was brave," he says softly, as if he can hear my thoughts. "Stupid, but brave."

It *was* a little brave, I realize. And stupid, yes. But brave first and foremost.

I hide a smile. For the first time in ages, I feel as if I've done something right.

8

I spend the morning planting Marie-Therese's pumpkin and watermelon seedlings in the sunny patch of ground to the side of the house.

When I come in at lunch time, Henri is already there. On the surface, nothing has changed between us. And yet I can feel the change before he even opens his mouth.

"Still here then, I see," he says.

"Apparently God has answered your prayers."

"The only thing I've prayed for of late is more wild game to shoot." He looks me over, as if perhaps *I* am the wild game.

I grin. "So we're back to death threats."

He shakes his head. "I've given up on that plan. My day is already too full. There'd be no time to dig you a grave."

"You could always burn me," I suggest.

"Like the witch that you are," he says with a smile, rubbing his chin contemplatively. "I like it."

"*Dieu*," says Marie. "I have no idea what to make of this conversation. And who ate all the pie?"

FOR THE FIRST time that night, my body is not weighted by sleep when dinner is over, which is when I discover how very dull their evenings are: Marie is in the other room, working on a lesson plan, and Henri is reading. I pick up a book, but not only is it in French, it's also about economics, which I wouldn't be willing to read in any language.

"Why did you run away?" I ask Henri.

He looks up from his book. "Pardon?"

"Your mother sounds like she was nice," I elaborate. "I'm just surprised you wanted to run away at all."

"I wasn't actually running away from her," he says. "There was just something I wanted to see outside of Paris, and she refused to take me so I decided to go on my own."

I tilt my head. "What did you want to see?"

"Corbusier had just completed this villa in Garche. He'd used the golden rectangle—this pattern in nature—in its design." He smiles. "I thought I could just head toward the sunset, since Paris is due west, except it turns out the sun doesn't take very long to set. I left late and it was dark by the time I got to the end of the orchard. I was too proud to actually return home, so my mother came to me."

"I had no idea you were so interested in architecture. Did you ever consider studying it?"

He nods, something darker coming over his face. "I did study it," he says. "School was not for me. I prefer to stay on the farm."

I'm not sure what just happened, but I miss the warm, open version of him that was here a moment before. "I understand wanting to remain where you grew up," I say softly. "Lots of people prefer small towns and places they know."

He looks at me for a long moment. "But not you," he says. "You'd hate it."

My childhood has more bad memories than good, and I want to get as far from what I know as I can possibly get. "No," I reply. "Not me."

Marie enters the room, looking a little shocked to see me and Henri actually speaking, free of sarcasm or insults. She picks up her sewing and sits beside me on the couch.

"So this is what you do every night?" I ask with a sigh.

"We don't have to do this," she says, putting her sewing down. Her eyes widen. "I know! We could play hide and seek. Time traveling hide and seek!"

"No," Henri intones. "Absolutely not."

Marie pouts. "You just know you'd lose."

He returns to his book. "Yes, or perhaps I just don't care to repeatedly witness my own sister running around in the dark naked," he replies.

"It must have been so fun, growing up with a sister," Marie says dreamily.

There's a small pit in my stomach. Did I momentarily *forget*? "I was the only time traveler in my family, so it wasn't as fun as you might be imagining."

"But did you play tricks on them at least?" Marie asks, eyes alight. "Once I learned how, I used to jump in and hide things. My mother would be cooking and I'd practice sneaking in to move her stuff." She laughs. "Do you remember, Henri? She used to get so angry with me."

His mouth lifts at the corner. "As I recall it led her to blame you anytime anything went missing."

She sighs. "Well, yes. But it was fun at the start at least."

"My household was very different than yours. My mother doesn't look on time travel as much of a gift."

"But why?" asks Marie.

Because it's the reason my sister is dead, I could tell her. But even that isn't it entirely. My mother hated time travel long before Kit died. For as far back as I remember, it's been as if she could see this evil inside me, something I couldn't alter or eradicate. I'm not sure I'll ever understand it, but I keep hoping that if I can stop using the gift, she'll be able to care a little bit. "She believes it does more harm than good," I reply quietly.

"Nonsense," Marie exclaims. "You and I are like Rapunzel! We can spin straw into gold if we choose."

I glance at her and then around the room. Buckingham Palace this is not. She sees my look and frowns. "We have money. My mother, and now Henri, are just ridiculously concerned with spending it. They think it will draw attention. If it were up to me we'd be living in a mansion overlooking the Seine, and I'd have a servant for every finger and toe. But you could do that, once you're home."

I flush. "That's not how I want to live. Once I'm done here, I'll never travel again."

"That's right," says Henri, with a touch of acid to his voice. "The perfect Mark will meet your every need and time travel will become a thing of the past."

Mark. The mention of him cuts me sharp as a chard of glass. I haven't thought about him once all night, and I should have. He leaves for Nepal tomorrow and this would have been our final evening together, one I'd have loved though he'd probably spend the hours begging me to come with him, begging me to give up my virginity, or both.

"You seem to enjoy making Mark sound like some mercenary choice on my part," I snap, angry at Henri and also myself. "Why is that?"

"Because," he replies, "you've never said anything to imply he's not."

My mouth opens to argue and I close it. I don't have to justify anything to a farmer who's going to live alone for the rest of his life. But thank God I'm nearly ready to leave.

I t's another few days before I feel rested enough for the journey home, the hours enlivened by a constantly time-jumping Marie, who appears in the kitchen without warning, reminding this earlier version of Marie to warn a friend about standing too close to the stove, or to go check on Madame Brun's sick baby and persuade her to take him to the doctor. It had never occurred to me until now that it was even possible for time travel to be used for good, but it doesn't change how I feel about my own ability. I'm every bit as eager as I ever was to be rid of it.

I spend my final day with the Durands doing something no one would consider restful: laundry, which is an unbelievable pain in the ass in 1938. Marie and I are stuck indoors all day long, using a scrubbing board to clean every single shirt and dress and undergarment *individually*. The water is in heated copper tubs and the room is damp as a sauna the whole damn day.

"Jesus," I say, wiping my brow on my sleeve. "Don't washing machines exist yet?"

Marie shrugs, indifferent to the idea. "It's not so bad."

"Marie, we could wash all of this—*all of it*—in one hour

without scrubbing a single thing. You can't tell me that doesn't sound like an improvement."

"I doubt it works as well," she replies.

"It works better."

The next time Henri comes to the pump, Marie walks to the front door and calls to him. "If washing machines have been invented," she tells him when he walks over to us, "I think I'd like one."

"Tell the little thief to keep her suggestions to herself," he replies.

He steps inside just as I'm grabbing the tub of dirty water to dump it. His hands fold over mine as he takes it from me. "Please don't tire yourself today. You'll need all your reserves to make it back safely tomorrow."

"A washing machine would allow everyone to save their energy," I reply with a small smile.

His mouth curves upward. "I'll consider it," he says softly, taking the tub to the garden to dump it.

Marie watches him go and then turns to me. "You're better at persuading him than I am. What other appliances should I demand before you leave?"

My mouth opens, and then closes. She truly has no idea how drastically her life will change in the coming years. If she did, she wouldn't be asking for appliances, she'd be asking for a safe place to live.

If they will die in the war, I can't stop that from happening. But what if they survive? What if they survive *badly*, painfully, because they weren't prepared?

I never had anyone to teach me the rules of time traveling. But I think I'm about to break a very important one.

THOUGH I'M TOO nervous about tomorrow to have much of an appetite, Marie makes cassoulet for my final night here and I eat. Will I be able to hide somewhere in my own time before I pass out, naked and defenseless? If I'd known just how poorly I would fare over long distances, I doubt I'd ever have come here at all.

Henri appears worried too. "Do you think..." he begins, swallowing, "that your trip home will be easier?"

"Maybe," I reply, unconvincingly. Returning to the point where I belong is definitely less work. It's mindless, like the way you can drive all the way home with your mind on something else. But I sort of doubt it's any easier physically, and that's the real problem.

"You were somewhere private when you jumped?" Marie asks.

I nod. "I jumped from the woods. It should be fine."

Henri flinches, imagining it, which makes me smile a little. When I first arrived, I thought he was nothing more than a very handsome jerk. And I still think he's a handsome jerk, but he is also intelligent, funny, driven...and unexpectedly kind. All of these women Marie says he has to fight off when he goes to town —do they see all that in him? Or is he just a chiseled jaw and set of broad shoulders they can pin a couple of romantic daydreams on? Either way, he deserves to choose one and start a family. And with the war coming, I'm not sure he's going to get a chance.

"I'm going to tell you what happens," I say quietly. "Even though you said you didn't want to know." My heart thuds in my chest.

Henri and Marie-Therese look at each other. And they wait.

My hands twist on top of the table. "There's going to be another war with Germany. Not just them. Japan and Italy too."

Marie Therese stiffens, her hand sliding to the base of her throat. Her father died in the last war. Millions of French men died with him. What are the odds Henri will survive if it happens again?

"Hitler's troops come to Paris," I continue. "In 1940, I think.

And there are airstrikes as well. Not just in Paris, but in the coun-
tryside. It doesn't last long. After a few weeks, France surrenders."

"Pah," says Henri. "Never. You're remembering wrong. We beat
them in the great war. They wouldn't dare come after us again."

"They do, and they win. You don't have the troops and you
don't have the weapons."

"We have the entire Maginot Line defending us," he argues.

I bite my lip, struggling to remember the little I know about
France's fall to Germany at the start of World War II. I wish I'd
studied it a bit more. "It doesn't hold. They're going to cut
through the north instead. Somewhere mountainous. Avon?
Ardent?"

"Ardennes," he says quietly, the truth finally sinking it as he
realizes that I only know this because it's become an important
part of the past. "What happens then?"

"France will be occupied by the Germans for the entire war.
They take over your homes, steal your livestock." I could say so
much more right now, but the truth of what will come is so grue-
some it will seem impossible to them. Right now what matters is
that they believe me and do what's necessary to survive. "What
I'm saying is, if you're capable of leaving right now, you should.
Go to the United States, or if you insist on staying in France, head
south. I think that's where the French government went, anyway."

They both look stricken. This *hint* I've dropped was far more
than either of them expected.

"We can't leave," says Marie. "What if our mother comes
home? How will we know? How will she find us?"

I'd expected an argument from Henri, but not *her*. "Marie," I
plead, "be reasonable. Do you really think this is what your
mother would want? You stuck in this house with a bunch of
German soldiers leering at you?"

She raises her chin. "What I know is that until I'm sure my
mother isn't coming home, I'm not leaving this farm."

I look toward her brother, hoping he'll hear what I'm saying and persuade her. But his jaw is locked tight. He knows it's a lost cause.

"Then we need to prepare to fight," he says.

Our eyes hold and I'm possessed by a sudden urge to weep. He will die here. He was a small child during the last war, but he is exactly the sort who dies when his country is attacked, who will climb the roof of his barn when Nazis come to take his home and will care about nothing beyond killing as many as he can before they catch him. He has no sense of self-preservation.

"Not just fight. Hide food. Hide money. They are going to take everything."

He nods, a weight on his shoulders that wasn't there when the evening began. It hits me hard for the first time, just how much danger he's in. Many of those graves in Normandy belonged to American and British soldiers, but so many of them belong to the French as well, and I can't save him. Their future is already written, already in the past. It's not that Henri *might* die during World War II. It's that he might already be dead.

But Marie, at least, is likely to survive. And might avoid a great deal of suffering if she could just be reasoned with.

"What would persuade you to leave?" I ask her quietly, desperately.

"If I knew for certain about my mother," she replies. "Then I might consider it."

The gauntlet is thrown down. I refused to go back to see her mother when it was simply about satisfying her curiosity, but this is different. How can I possibly say no when it could change the course of the next decade for her?

My stomach begins to churn. It's time for me to return home and put my days of jumping behind me for good, but it looks like that isn't going to happen just yet.

"Then I'll go," I tell Marie. "I'll go talk to your mother and find out where she went."

"No," says Henri harshly. "You won't."

Marie turns her wide eyes from me to him. "How can you say that?" she demands. "Don't you want to know?"

He runs a hand through his thick hair and grips it hard. "What I want is for my mother to not realize, through a series of questions, that her death is imminent," he says. "And what is supposed to happen when you get your answer? You try to follow her, put yourself into the precise situation far more experienced travelers haven't survived? Wherever she's been, she's been there too long. She won't be able to travel forward to us."

"I just need to know where she went," Marie pleads. "I'm not saying I'll follow her."

"Amelie is *not* going," says Henri. "I forbid it."

Wrong words, Henri.

I smile at him. "I'd like to see you try to stop me."

10

M adame Durand disappeared just after Marie's birthday, so Marie has decided I should appear right around that point.

"My birthday was November 12th, and my mother had just given me the most beautiful coat—aubergine with fur cuffs. If I'm wearing that coat, it means you haven't gone back too far," she says. "Henri will be away at school, so if he's here, you've not gone far enough." She gives me a few other landmarks, but they are less reliable, based on the state of a weathervane, a broken door —so I hope I'm not going to be forced to use them.

She's so excited about my trip she can hardly contain herself, whereas I feel mostly dread. Traveling back by years is not hard— you just count, like jumping squares in hopscotch—but landing in a particular week requires more specificity, and that is not my strong suit.

Actually, I'm not sure I have a strong suit where my gift is concerned.

I time my departure fairly early in the morning, so that if I land in the right place I'll be there to see Marie leave for school in the coat. I walk to the barn with Marie and, to my surprise, Henri comes too.

He looks as if he might not have slept, and he definitely hasn't shaved. I imagine placing my palm over his rough jaw and telling him to go back to bed, imagine the feel of my lips brushing his skin as I say it, and then I blush, shocked at where my mind goes at the strangest times.

"I wish you wouldn't do this," he says gravely, shoulders slumped.

"I won't let her know what's coming," I whisper. "I swear it." My plan is to introduce myself as a friend of Marie's from the distant future, one with whom Marie has discussed the circle of light, and explain that my aunt disappeared searching for it, and I'm hoping to track her last days.

He holds my gaze. "Be safe," he says. He actually looks like he means it.

I force a smile. "I guess that's better than a few weeks ago, when you were planning to shoot me."

I close my eyes, needing to shut out Henri's worried face and Marie's hopeful one in order to focus. In my head I look back, the way I might if I was just remembering the past. There are small hints when you are about to travel—a slight breeze over the skin, a weightlessness—I feel those hints now, and I allow them to come. The breeze is barely noticeable, and then it picks up as my body grows lighter and lighter. With the rush of wind and darkness closing in, I can feel time around me, almost like a rope I cling to. My body wants to fly forward, toward home, but instead I force myself backward, estimating the way I might if I were measuring a small distance in my yard. I go slowly, given the need for accuracy, counting by months rather than years, and when I reach what I believe is November of 1935 I take a deep breath and land on the other side of the barn, up to my knees in snow.

Marie never mentioned snow, and surely snow in early November would be memorable? I can't see the broken weathervane from here so I creep through the barn's back door, jerking to a stop when I see Henri in the distance, standing beside their car. He's younger, dressed in much finer clothes than I've seen him in. He looks like a handsome prince, one of those carefree rich boys who attend Eton and worry about nothing more than sports and girls and gambling. Except there is utter grief on his face.

I've arrived after their mother is gone, I realize. A part of me wants to continue to watch this version of him, so handsome and stricken and lost as he stares blankly at the fields, but it's dangerous, and my legs are growing numb. I close my eyes once more and move further back, this time creeping along—moving by inches, rather than feet.

When I land the snow is gone, but it is still chilly. The weathervane and the shed door are broken, because Henri is not home to fix them. This may not be the week she left, but it's probably as good as I'm going to get. I grab the horse blanket off the hook and huddle in the barn's corner, waiting for Marie to leave on her way to school. I'm tired. It's not the obliterating exhaustion of traveling from my own time, but it's worse than I should feel having gone back only a few years. I'm contemplating curling up in the hay for a minute when Marie finally appears, looking very young and happy, wearing the new aubergine coat she told me about. I wait one more minute, and then I cross the yard and knock on the door, saying a silent prayer that Madame Durand likes strangers a little more than her son.

The woman who answers does not look old enough to be a mother of teenagers, but I see Henri and Marie in the slope of her cheekbones and the shape of her eyes, which widen at the sight of me.

"*Bonjour*," I begin in halting French. I know she speaks English, but it seems rude not to at least begin in her language. "*J'espère que vous pouvez m'aider.*" *I hope you can help me.*

Her eyes narrow just a touch. I see Henri's keen intellect in irises that are brown, rather than green. His guardedness too.

"What do you need?" she asks in English. "You should not be here."

I take a deep breath. "Marie told me you might be able to help me find my aunt." At the sound of her daughter's name she softens just a bit, and then, with obvious reluctance, she opens the door and asks me in.

I don't realize how cold I am until I've followed her inside, but as the warmth reaches my frozen feet I begin shaking with it. She looks at me and hesitates again. "I shall get you some clothes. Go stand by the fire."

I sit on the hearth and she returns with a blanket, a sweater and a pair of trousers. "These belonged to my son when he was much younger. We do not need them back."

She goes to the kitchen while I pull on Henri's things, which drape over my frame, making me feel like a child. When she returns with a tea tray, she gestures to the seat across from her and pours a cup for me, more dutiful than willing. As a time traveler, she is unsettled by my presence, but with a daughter not much younger than I am now, she can't bring herself to let me freeze.

"So what is it you need?" she asks, frowning as she hands me the cup.

I find, when lying, that it works best if you stick as closely as possible to the truth, and that is what I do now. "My aunt disappeared searching for the circle of light. I told Marie, and she said you might be able to give me some information."

She lifts her head, fastening me with those questioning eyes, so like Henri's. "She would not have discussed this with just anyone," Madame Durand says. "In fact, I'm inclined to think she wouldn't discuss it with anyone at all, and that leads me to suspect that you are lying."

I take a nervous sip of my tea. "I'm not," I reply. "But I guess a liar would say that too."

"You must finish your tea and warm up," she says, "before you

go on to your next destination." There's a finality to the words—
which means I've failed. Marie is going to be so disappointed and
I realize that I am too. I did want to give her some closure, if
nothing else.

I pick up the framed photo of a very young Henri and Marie
that sits on the side table and smile at Henri's chubby little
cheeks and mischievous eyes.

"That's Marie-Therese, who you claim to know, and my son,
Henri, who is away at university now." She laughs almost to
herself. "He would very much have enjoyed meeting *you*."

I seriously doubt that. Though I should probably just finish my
tea and leave, I can't help my own curiosity. "Where is he in
school?" I ask.

"Oxford," she replies.

I blink. *Oxford?* Even back in 1935, it must have been an honor
to be accepted there. So why did he leave? "Does he...does he like
it there?"

She smiles, her suspicion of me lost in a cloud of adoration
for her son. "He is in love with it, with all of it. My son was never
cut out for a small life here with us, I'm afraid. The top student in
the village."

It's almost the opposite of what he said the other day. I think
of his youthful obsession with architecture, the fact that he was
willing to run away from home just to see some architectural
principle at play. How exactly did I convince myself he was just
too provincial for life in a big city? That he preferred being a
farmer? Something changed, and I wonder what it was.

"This is him now," she says, reaching for another frame on the
mantle and handing it to me. Henri grinning in rolled up shirt
sleeves, a rugby ball tucked beneath his arm and other smiling
boys around him. He looks so handsome and carefree, but the
sepia of the photograph and the clothes remind me how long ago
this all actually was. That Henri, in my time, is old. It's hardly a
revelation but it hits me now with a sharpness it didn't before.

"You must miss him," I say faintly. Weirdly, it feels as if *I* miss him. As if I miss this carefree boy in the photo, so different from the man I just saw in 1938. I can't seem to take my eyes off the picture.

Her smile is fond and sad at once. "He has much greater dreams than a small farm, I'm afraid. His friends have already invited him to stay with them out in the Cotswolds next summer, and what can I say?" she asks with a shrug. "All you want as a parent is for your children to love their lives. He does, and if it means I see less of him it's a small price to pay."

It hits me at last: he didn't return because he missed the farm, because he preferred home. He came back because his mother disappeared, and there was no one to protect Marie.

I look at this beautiful, beaming woman across from me and wish to God she hadn't left. The odds that she's still surviving somewhere are so slim, but I find myself praying for it anyway. If we could save her, Henri could have his life back, and so could Marie.

She's watching me carefully again. "Do you *know* my son?" she asks softly.

We are getting into dangerous territory. Telling her I *know* Henri would indicate that he and Marie-Therese are probably in the same place—which runs counter to what she will expect, given that she just told me she doesn't think he'll return home. But I don't feel capable of telling an outright lie.

"Yes," I reply. "A little."

Her brow furrows. A single moment of uncertainty and worry. "He is well, where you're from?"

"Very."

She smiles and tips her head again. "And is he still very handsome?"

I'm willing to admit to myself that Henri is attractive, but saying it aloud is something else. I'm not sure why—I've told Mark a thousand times about my crush on Sean Connery. But that's different. It's not real. Which I suppose means my crush on Henri sort of...is.

"We should probably not speak too much of the future?" I suggest gently, and she nods in agreement, but worry creases her brow again.

She has guessed, or is at least wondering, if I'm describing a future in which she does not exist. She's asking about the son she adores and she wants to know that he's okay.

"He's the most handsome man I've ever laid eyes on," I tell her quietly, looking once more at his photo before I set it on the table.

When I glance up at her something has changed in her face—as if I just gave her the critical clue in a mystery she could not make sense of until now. She refills my tea. "You were asking about the circle of light," she says. "What did you want to know?"

I blink in surprise. Two minutes ago she was politely asking me to leave, and just as suddenly she appears to have changed her mind. I lean forward, eager to get an answer before she rethinks the decision. "I'm trying to figure out why my aunt went after it and where she would have gone."

She tsks. "*Why* she went after it? Because it's what we all crave, of course. Surely your mother explained all this to you?"

"My mother can't time travel. And if she did know, she wouldn't tell me." I swirl my cup in my saucer. "She thinks time travel is a bit of a, um, curse."

She gives me a sad smile, one that reminds me of Marie. "That must have been very hard for you," she says. "People can be very ignorant sometimes. If she were capable of it, she'd feel differently."

I can't say I agree. What good has time travel ever brought into my life? Could a few trips backward to warn myself about pop quizzes and a paper I was going to botch possibly be worth all the terrible things it's been responsible for?

"I can do it, and it seems to have led to more bad than good for me."

She holds my gaze for a moment. "Without it, I'm not sure what we'd have done after the war. It's saved my life and my children's lives on more than one occasion. It's how I was able to visit my husband during the war," she adds with a small, wistful smile. "Which is the reason your friend Marie exists."

I grin. Madame Durand time traveled to have sex with her husband during the war. Henri seems like the type who would hate knowing that. It's going to be so tempting to let it slip.

"Anyway," she continues, "you know the prophecy, I'm sure."

I sip my tea. "Only the outlines."

"*In France there will be a hidden child born of the first family, conceived during a great war and born on the other side of it,*" she recites. "*In her our hope shall rest, for she will produce the circle of light, and within that circle, our past and present will be safe from those who would do us harm.*"

Marie got most of it right, but she left something out: *a product of the first families*. I'm not sure who the first families *are* exactly, and I don't dare draw her suspicion again by asking.

"None of us are certain what the circle of light is," she continues. "To be honest, I always thought it would be a *person*. But there were reports of something that sounded like it just after the war—a mysterious golden circle people saw just behind Sacré-Coeur."

My stomach sinks. The war ended in 1918. If that's where she went, twenty years have passed. She'd have gotten home by now if she were going to.

"A mysterious golden circle doesn't seem like much to go on," I reply. "That could be anything."

"It was all over the news. For weeks there was chaos in Paris— the city was flooded with visitors, entirely female. Clothing and food disappeared to such an extent that it became international news. And in Paris they began calling it *le plus beau mois,* the most beautiful month, because of the loveliness of the women. It's suspicious, do you not think?"

I sigh. It's very suspicious. An object straight out of a prophecy, and an influx of what very obviously sounds like time travelers coming to check it out. "And no one found it?"

"Not as far as we know," she says, her mouth tipping up at the corners. The way Henri smiles sometimes when he's trying not to. "Not *yet*."

Don't go, I want to plead. *Don't do this. How could it possibly be worth what you'll lose?* "What would make anyone believe they could find it when no one else has succeeded?"

She smiles again. "Haven't you ever heard the legend of King Arthur?" she asks. "Only the chosen one could remove the sword. Perhaps the circle of light is the same."

There is something she is not telling me, but what is it? She clearly doesn't realize there's such a risk involved in going back for this thing, but she isn't a naïve woman. Why would she think she could do what no one else could? And why wait seventeen years if she thought she could?

"I'm surprised you didn't go try to find the circle at the time," I suggest.

She looks out the window, seeing nothing. "I was a widow with a newborn and a toddler. I was in no position to go anywhere. And there'd have been no point—it's not as if *I* am the chosen one."

It makes even less sense, then, why she'd be going to see it now. But I'm not here to understand it. I'm here to know where she'd have gone.

"So if I were to go looking for my aunt, where and when should I go?"

"Fall of 1918," she says. "The circle is seen in the evening, in a small square called Parc de la Turlure. The war ended on November 11th, so the day after might be best."

November 11th, the day before Marie's birthday. It seems significant somehow. I let the facts rattle around in my head like spinning coins, waiting for them to fall. The dates. Madame

Durand's decision to go look for something she already knows isn't for her. And the prophecy: *in France, a hidden child*. Hidden. It's a word Henri has used multiple times, discussing Marie and their life on the farm.

Marie, who was conceived during the war, and born one day after it. For some reason, this has led Madame Durand to think Marie is the prophecy's hidden child. And Henri thinks so as well.

I LAND in the barn no more gracefully than usual. It was only a few years but—perhaps because I'm still not in my own time—I'm not sure I have the energy to put on my clothes. I grab the blanket and wrap it around me, taking one step toward the house before I change my mind.

"Just for a few minutes," I say aloud, curling up in the straw. My words are slurred as if I'm drunk. I hear the sound of footsteps approaching but I'm too tired to open my eyes.

"Amelie," Henri says, his voice husky, concerned even. I force a single eye open. He is crouched beside me, and indeed looks very worried.

"Just need sleep," I slur. "Five more minutes."

"Ridiculous girl," he says with a soft laugh. A moment later I feel myself scooped up in his arms and carried. I'm more than half asleep, but some distant part of my brain registers everything. His smell: hay and sweat and soap. His warmth, his size, the bulge of his bicep beneath my head. How gentle he is when he lays me down on the mattress.

I want to tell him what happened. I want to tell him how proud his mother was of him, how she glowed at the very mention of his name, but my brain is short on words. "You went to Oxford," is all I can manage. He's pulling the blanket over me, his face a mix of pleasure and sorrow.

"My mother was talking about me," he says, forcing a smile.

It's so unfair. She adored him and now she is gone. I can't understand why it causes this pain in my heart, why I ache so much more than I should for what he's lost.

I'm falling back into the darkness, drifting away from him, and I wish I could stay. "She loved you so much," I whisper.

I don't realize I'm crying until I feel his finger on my skin, brushing a tear away. "Yes, I know," he says with a quiet laugh. "It's only you who dislikes me."

I don't dislike you anymore, I think as I drift to sleep. *I'm not sure I ever did.*

WHEN I WAKE, hours later, he is there, sitting in the chair by the bed with a book in hand.

I yawn, stretching like a kitten and begin to rise. "I'd be careful about that," Henri says with a brow raised. "You're naked under that blanket."

Oh, right.

I clutch the quilt to my neck and sit up. My clothes have been laid out for me on a chair, with my underthings sitting atop them. I flush.

His eyes track mine and he laughs. "Very pretty."

"If you are expecting me to act embarrassed you'll have a long wait. I'm not the one who entered a sleeping girl's room and sat there like a creep."

There's an amused set to his mouth, but it fades quickly. "We need to speak...before you talk to Marie."

He rises and shuts the door behind him, sliding his chair next to my bed. "I need to know what my mother told you," he says quietly.

"She told me all about you at Oxford," I reply, watching his face. "You didn't leave because school wasn't for you. You weren't even planning to come home for the summer because you loved it there so much."

His eyes meet mine. "Someone needed to watch Marie. If she knew why I really came home she wouldn't stand for it."

"Except she's an adult now," I counter, "and could easily take care of herself, yet you stay."

He gives an ambivalent shrug. "I'm used to how things are. Until she's married, I'll remain here." He's hoping that's the end of it. He's about to be very disappointed.

"Even *you* aren't quite that selfless," I reply.

He grows still. "What are you talking about?"

I hold his eye. "You think Marie's the hidden child."

He runs a hand through his hair, and gives a particularly forced laugh. "That's crazy."

"Is it? Because she was conceived during the war and born after it, in France. You've referred several times to hiding Marie, and your mother said she thought the circle of light might be like Excalibur...something only a *chosen one* could access, but she knew she wasn't the chosen one. But you can pretend I'm wrong if you want. I'll just discuss the theory with Marie and see what she thinks."

His jaw grinds. And then he exhales slowly, unhappily. "Fine, yes. In the last letter my mother wrote me, she told me what she believed and asked that I make sure Marie stays hidden here."

I'm glad he's admitted I'm right, but the whole thing still doesn't make a lot of sense. Hiding Marie here because of a theory about who she could be is a little extreme, and Henri is usually level-headed. "But she might not even *be* the hidden child. I mean, lots of families probably conceived daughters during the war and gave birth to them afterward."

"Yes," he says, "but of the first four families to ever develop the gift, only one resides in France. Mine."

"How could you possibly know that?" I ask.

"Nothing is certain, of course, but on my mother's side it's all been pretty thoroughly documented. Since so few of you can carry the ability, it's pretty straightforward."

I sit with that a moment. If he's right, it pretty much has to be Marie, doesn't it? So maybe it's not extreme after all. "So when I first arrived here, when you were so awful to me..."

He looks away again. "I thought you'd found her. I meant to shoot you but I just couldn't."

"And here I was just thinking you were an aggressive jerk."

He gives me a lopsided smile. "I wouldn't rule that out either."

"I won't tell anyone about Marie when I go home," I say. "I assume that's why you were worried about me visiting your mother in the first place."

He shakes his head. "No, I already knew you wouldn't. My concern was that you'd tell Marie."

My eyes go wide. He can't expect to hide this from her? "But—"

He holds up a hand. "Yes, she deserves to know," he says, "but first I think she deserves to have a normal life. This circle of light, if she's this hidden child of the prophecy—we have no idea what it really is. How does she follow her heart with that kind of pressure? I want her to make the decisions she's going to make, free of it. That's what my mother wanted for her too."

I put myself in Marie's shoes. You'd think this circle of light she's supposed to produce is probably a child, but even if it isn't, the responsibility of it could freeze her in place. Because how will she ever know if her next decision is the one she's *supposed* to make. One bad choice—turning the wrong corner, choosing the wrong mate—could ruin it all.

"You'll need to tell her eventually," I reply.

"I will, but not yet. Let me give her a few more years. Let her fall in love, decide on the life she will have."

Meanwhile, he puts everything he wants from life on hold in order to protect his sister, to preserve her ability to choose a direction for herself.

"I won't tell her," I say. "But I'm going to give her the information she seeks...about where your mother was headed."

He stiffens, his head bent low as if he's waiting for a judge's sentence. "What year?"

He has stated before that he's certain she's dead, but I still wish I wasn't the one who had to confirm it. "She went back to 1918," I reply. "I'm sorry."

He nods, his head still bowed. "I already assumed she was dead," he says quietly.

I think of the moment they found Kit in the lake. The sight of the policeman carrying her tiny frame, her long hair a waterfall over his arm. Until that moment, it remained possible she was simply lost or playing a prank.

I lay my hand over his. "There's a difference between suspecting something and knowing it for sure."

HENRI LEAVES me to dress and then I slowly walk downstairs. My speed has less to do with exhaustion and more to do with dread. I wish I didn't have to be the person who destroys Marie's hope.

She smiles at me when I enter the room. "Back safe and sound," she says, so casual she could be mentioning almost anything—the weather outside, the amount of sugar in my tea— but her hands tremble as she places a plate in front of me. I glance up and in her face is everything: she remains a girl who longs for her mother. She is envious of the time I just had with her. And I envy her for having the mother she did, even for a short while. "I already know about your trip, to some extent," she says. "You weren't even back yet when I suddenly had this *memory* of my mother telling me about your visit, as if it was something I'd known but buried. Isn't that amazing?"

I frown. "I'm sorry. I wasn't trying to change your memories."

She shakes her head. "It was a good memory and I'm glad to have it. Meeting you reassured her about the future."

I can't imagine how that's possible, but I'm glad if it's true. "She was lovely. I was able to enjoy her company despite the resemblance to Henri."

His mouth tips up at that but Marie seems like she hasn't even heard it.

She takes the seat across from me and clasps her hands on the table. She appears calm but her hands are twisted so tight they're nearly bloodless. "And she didn't have any clue what was to come?"

I shake my head no, although, to be honest, I'm uncertain. I saw something in her quiet appraisal of me that was both happy and sad at once. "No. And she didn't want to tell me anything, but once I got her talking about the two of you she opened up." Marie holds herself still, braced for bad news, and I can't put it off anymore. "There were reports of the circle of light being seen behind Sacré-Coeur, just after the war," I say gently. "I think that's where she went."

"But that—" She closes her eyes as the color bleeds from her face. "That was twenty years ago."

"I'm sorry," I whisper. "I know you were hoping…"

She shakes her head, brushing tears from her face. "It's okay," she whispers.

Henri has been silent, brooding, throughout this conversation. "It's for the best that we know," he says. "At least we can finally put it behind us now."

Marie's head jerks up. "Put it behind us?" she exclaims. "She could still be out there somewhere, trapped. Maybe she has amnesia. There's nothing *behind* us."

Henri and I exchange a stunned glance. I don't think either of us imagined Marie still hanging on to her hope at this point. "Marie," says Henri, shoulders sagging under a sudden weight, "there's nothing to be done now. You have to realize that."

She turns to me. "My mother said you'd be important to us. Maybe you and I are supposed to go back to 1918 and find out what happened to her."

"Absolutely not," growls Henri, and though his edicts typically inspire a desire to rebel on my end, I hear the panic that rests just behind his words. "Our mother and Amelie's aunt both disappeared going there. The two of you risking your lives to find out what happened would be insanity. Our mother would kill you herself for even suggesting it were she here."

I agree with him. And while I still question if I've done enough for them, if I've done what my sister wanted me to do, there's no way *I* could be the best person to travel to 1918 with her. I'm the worst time traveler I've ever heard of, while Marie can flit from place to place and time to time as easily as she breathes. If two people far more skilled than myself got trapped there, it'd be a death sentence for someone like me.

"I'm not saying we do what they did," Marie argues. "They had no idea it was dangerous, and we do. We can just travel there and watch from afar. See who's responsible."

"Marie," I plead, "I can't possibly be the person your mother claimed was coming to help. My abilities are ridiculously limited, and I'd be so exhausted by the journey you'd need to spend a week nursing me back to health in 1918 before we were on our way. If someone is meant to help you with this, it is not me."

She nods, looking down at the table. "Someone else will come then," she says, and then she looks at us both with a forced smile. "And for now I will simply enjoy your company. You will stay with us, yes? Another week or two, perhaps?"

I glance up at Henri. At his shoulders straining against the linen of his shirt, that lock of hair falling over his forehead. *I will miss him*, I realize. I adore Marie but it's him I'm truly sad to leave. And that is so, so wrong. None of this is real. He's an old man and I'm practically engaged.

I avert my eyes. "I'm sorry," I reply. "I really think it's time I went home."

"You aren't ready," says Marie-Therese. "You are swaying on your feet even now."

"I'll rest tomorrow and leave the day after. What's the worst that can happen?" I ask with a forced smile. "If I can't make it all the way home, you'll just host me 20 years into the future."

The idea makes my stomach swim unhappily. I picture the two of them still here, alone. No children. Their faces lined with years and hard labor. Or perhaps Marie-Therese will be gone and Henri will be here with a wife and children. I don't much like that image either.

Neither does Henri. When Marie goes into the other room, he looks at me, his face a little sad. "When you return home, I'll be an old man," he says. "I don't want you to see me that way."

I shake my head, the smallest possible movement. He will be lucky to make it to old age, to survive the war. I don't want to care. And I already do, more than I ever imagined possible. It makes me wish I'd never come here in the first place.

"Doesn't it seem...unfair somehow?" I ask. "People who are older than us always seem different, almost a different species. As if they were always old and faded and cared about the wrong things. I wish there were a way for us all to see each other exactly as we would like to be seen. To freeze ourselves at a certain age and stay that way if we choose."

"There is a way," he says. "You already have it. All you time travelers do. My mother was 39 when she left but she could have passed for 18. She came to see me at school once. My mates all assumed she was my sister."

"What good is staying young if the people you love can't stay young with you?" I ask.

His gaze holds mine. For one moment, and then another. "You're right," he says quietly. "It would be nice if we could all be young at the same time."

WHEN I FALL ASLEEP, I dream about weddings. A wedding in my apartment, which I'm not prepared for, and guests are knocking on the door while my roommate and I frantically hide all the dirty clothes.

Then I dream I'm at Mark's parents' estate in Westport. From the window I can see the white chairs set out on the hill overlooking the river, the guests milling around already. Mark is there greeting everyone, his gold hair catching the light, million-dollar smile flashing. But my mother is out there too, walking toward him, and my stomach drops to my feet.

I need to find him, I think. *I need to tell him the truth before she does.*

I go downstairs, pushing my way through the crowd, and then find myself alone, standing just at the river's edge. *No, not alone*, because Kit is here too, flailing in the water a foot away. Her small hand latches around my ankle, the grip strong as an adult's, trying to pull me in. "Kit, stop," I beg. She only pulls harder, glancing behind me at Mark, who is coming toward us with eyes that are wide and shocked, staring at her muddy hand, at the hem of my dress turning black.

"He doesn't even know who you are," Kit says. She tugs again, harder. Both my feet sink into the mud and the water rises around my calves. My breath come in tiny, shallow bursts.

"Kit," I beg. "Please stop."

"Promise you'll help Marie."

I'm sinking now and Mark is just watching, as if he knows exactly what led us to this point, as if he'll never forgive me for it. *It was insane to think I could tell him the truth. He will never understand what I am, or what I did.*

"I'll help her," I cry. "Just please don't pull me in."

"I will drown you if you don't," she replies, in my mother's voice. "Mark and I will drown you."

I wake crouched in the corner of the room, weeping. I can still feel Kit's grip on my ankle. And I can still feel the promise I made in that dream like a brand on my skin. It's a promise I'm going to break, though, and I wonder exactly how she'll make me pay for that once I'm home.

11

I'd hoped my last full day here would be pleasant, but when I wake the rain is coming down in sheets. Henri drives Marie into town to teach her class and I'm stuck inside, alone and bored out of my mind.

I pace aimlessly, trying to ignore my anxiety about returning home, as well as my anxiety about Kit.

Last night's dream is never far from my mind. *Mark and I will drown you if you don't.* Was it just metaphorical—my own subconscious telling me I'm going to drown in guilt if I don't tell Mark the truth? Except telling him is not an option. He would never accept me. He would never accept what I've done. Whereas, I can live with being drowned by guilt. I've survived it ten years already.

I continue to pace, biting my nails and wandering closer and closer to Henri's room. I've never been inside it. Under normal circumstances, the very idea of snooping gives me hives—I can barely even stand to watch it on TV because I'm always waiting for the person to get caught.

But I need something to take my mind off the return home, and cars in 1938 are far too loud for anyone to sneak up on anyone. The truth is, I just want to see his room. Henri is like a song you want to hate yet find yourself humming, ears straining for even a hint of it. Even if I'd never admit to my curiosity openly, a part of me wants to know who he really is.

I push the door open, feeling a trifle guilty but mostly curious. It's fairly austere, as I'd have expected. He's not exactly the needlepoint-and-flower-arrangement kind of guy. Mostly what I notice are the books—lining the shelves, stacked on his nightstand, piled on the dresser.

Yesterday's clothes hang over the back of a chair. I'm not sure what compels me to do it, but I let my fingers run over his trousers. They are heavy, like military fatigues. His shirt lies just under the pants, a coarser material than I'm used to. It smells like him. Like lye soap and skin and something male I sort of like.

I picture him dressing in here alone, and undressing, climbing into that neatly-made bed at night. Who does he think of when he slides between those sheets? My heart gives a single, hard *thud* at the idea of it.

I run my hand over his pillow, then pick up the book on the top of the large stack near the bed. Baudelaire. *Poetry*. It's hard to imagine Henri reading anything but farming journals, but it reminds me that he wants things he'd never dare say aloud. A small and very wrong part of me wishes I could be the one to discover what they are.

I hear the rumble of a car on the road and quickly duck out of the room, closing the door behind me. It feels as if I'm leaving a mystery behind, one I'd very much like to solve.

MARIE RETURNS LATER in the day, but there is no sign of Henri, despite the weather, until he appears at dinnertime, pissed off and covered head to toe in dirt.

He bathes and changes clothes before dinner, but it does not seem to improve his mood. Marie is doing her best to make my last night here a cheerful one. Henri is making no such effort.

"I do wish you would stay," Marie says. "With one more week, I could definitely teach you how to cook. In spite of microwaves, wives should know these things."

Henri looks up from his plate. "Personally," he says, "if I were Mark I'd prefer a wife who could tell me the truth."

I roll my eyes. "Are we really back to this? I already told you I'm not jumping again once I get home. So it *will* be the truth."

He sits back, pushing his nearly-full plate away from him— something I've never seen him do before. "No, it won't, because that's not who you are," he replies, a dangerous light to his eyes. "You're giving up everything for a man who doesn't even love you."

His words shouldn't hurt, but they do. "What fascinating theories you concoct with absolutely no basis."

Henri's eyes raise to mine—darker now, like the forest at dusk. "You're deluding yourself if you think otherwise. How could he possibly love you? He doesn't even know you."

I once again see Kit's hand around my ankle. *He doesn't even know who you are,* she said.

I feel a sob swelling in my throat and I refuse, refuse, to cry in front of him. I just won't do it. I jump up from the table. "Excuse me," I say, but my voice cracks on the last word, ruining the effect entirely, and I bolt out the front door. The rain is coming down so hard I can barely see an inch past my face but I just need to get away from him. *I'll leave now,* I think. *I'll leave right this second and Henri will never know he made me cry.*

I run toward the barn, soaked to my skin, ignoring the sound of him shouting somewhere behind me.

But just as I arrive, I find myself airborne. Plummeting down, down, a fall that seems to occur in slow motion. Long enough for me to wonder if I will survive it.

I land feet first. Hear the snap of a bone and the sharp shot of pain above my foot. I crumple, flailing as I fall to the ground.

Above me somewhere a match is struck. A torrent of profanity, all in French. Then a ladder slides into the hole and Henri is scrambling down it faster than I ever dreamed someone could. He drops to the ground beside me, and his hand reaches out to hold my face. In the dim light his golden skin appears pale for the first time.

"Are you alright?"

I squeeze my eyes shut. I don't want to cry but the pain makes it nearly impossible not to. "It's my ankle. I think it's broken."

"I'm so sorry," he whispers. "This is all my fault. I was being awful tonight and I don't know why. I didn't think you'd take it to heart like that."

I'm still not sure why I did. Perhaps because, as always, there was a grain of truth in the ugly things he said, and I was able to find it.

"Please don't cry," he begs. His thumb brushes a tear away, and he continues to hold my face, looking at me like I'm the only thing in the entire world that exists for him. For a moment, I wish that I was. I wish he would pull my face to his and kiss me, and I wish for it in a way I've never wished for it from Mark.

A spark of pain from my ankle jolts me back to the present, reminding me that what I'm thinking is insane. Henri, in my time, is a 72-year old man. And it's that, more than anything else, that has another sob swelling in my throat. "Why is there a hole here?" I ask.

"You told me we'd need to hide food and weapons," he says. "I never dreamed you'd run out here tonight like this."

"*Mon Dieu!*" cries Marie, standing at the edge of the hole. She speaks French so quickly I can't understand a word she's saying, but I know she's angry, and it seems entirely directed at Henri.

"*Je sais, je sais,*" he replies. *I know, I know.* Finally, he holds up a hand. "Enough, Marie. You can yell at me later. Right now I'd like to get her out of here so we can set the bone."

I shudder a little at that last bit...*set the bone* has me picturing Civil War hospitals, biting down on a rag as limbs are fixed, or amputated. Will it be any more advanced here, with these two French people my own age in charge of the repair? I doubt it.

"I'm going to carry you over my shoulder," he says. He lifts me as carefully as possible and begins to climb the ladder, holding me with one hand and the rungs with the other. He's trying not to jolt me but even the tiniest movement around my ankle is intolerable.

"Hurry, Henri," urges Marie Therese.

"She's heavier than she looks," he grunts, ruining what might have been a decent moment between us.

"Or maybe you're just not as strong as you look," I reply between gritted teeth.

"So you think I look strong," he says in response as he takes the final steps out of the hole. "Good to know."

He puts me down and I take weight on the good ankle, which doesn't feel all that good. Marie's arm comes around me.

"Poor Amelie," she whispers. "It looks like you may be stuck with our company a little longer than planned."

I almost laugh when I realize how simple the solution to this problem really is. "No," I say. "Wait. If you just time travel to earlier tonight, you can warn me it's going to happen and I won't run out of the house. Problem solved. I'd do it myself except I can't jump backward without landing on my ankle."

The answer is so obvious and so easy, but there's something strange going on with her. I expect her to readily agree, but instead her eyes slide from me to her brother, and then rest there, her mind both on us and also somewhere very far away. "But then *I* might fall in the hole," she argues.

Henri exhales loudly. "For God's sake, Marie. You know how to land well. You've never injured yourself once. And if you're so worried, just go back a few days, before it was dug."

She folds her arms across her chest. "No."

My jaw and Henri's drop at the same time.

"You cannot be serious!" Henri yells. "She's in pain! What the hell is wrong with you?"

Marie's arms fold tighter. "I think perhaps it was fate. And I am not one to interfere with fate."

The pain in my ankle makes it hard to argue and harder still to think straight but I do my best. "Why could fate possibly require I stay in 1938 for *months* while my ankle heals?" I demand. "I'm not even supposed to be here." I suppose I could jump on my own but the idea of it makes me wince, when I can hardly bear standing right now on my *good* ankle. But I'll have to, if she can't be reasoned with.

Henri sees the look on my face and scoops me up again. I want to weep with relief.

Marie shrugs. "I guess we'll know once your ankle is better," she says simply. "I'll go call the doctor."

She walks ahead of us and Henri follows with me in his arms, careful to avoid jolting me. "I know you're planning to jump backward yourself if she refuses," he says. "Please don't do it."

I would laugh at how well he knows me if I wasn't in so much pain. "Why not?"

His eyes close. "Think about how poorly you land under the best of circumstances. I knew you were in the barn both times you arrived here because I heard you falling. If you jump back on your ankle, in addition to how unbearably painful it would be, you're likely to break something, and then what? Or what if you land in another place, or another time? You'll survive a broken ankle. But it could be so much worse."

I sigh. He makes a good point. Knowing me I'd wind up with a shattered spine in the wrong year. But if I spend two months here, two months will pass at home as well, and that can't happen. "I guess it just depends," I reply. "I have to be home by August, no matter what."

He carries me inside, placing me on his bed rather than my own. I'd probably find this all pretty exciting but the pain in my ankle is getting worse and Henri seems to sense it. He pushes both hands back through his hair, gritting his teeth.

"The doctor won't drive at night," he says, dropping beside me. "I'll go get him but it might take a while. Thirty minutes at most. But first, let me try to talk some sense into Marie."

He leaves the room and begins yelling at his sister in French, so quickly I can only grasp a few adjectives here and there—*cruel, insane, thoughtless, selfish.* The more urgent he grows, the more stubborn she becomes.

I know he's given up when I hear the door slam behind him.

She comes to my side then with a bottle and a spoon. "Open wide," she says. "I don't trust Doctor Nadeau to give you enough for the pain. He's quite stingy."

The fact that I'm going to *need* a lot of pain medication just angers me more. First, because it never works for me the way it's supposed to. Mostly, because I shouldn't have to take it at all. I move my head away from her. "Would you trust him more if he could fix my ankle with a simple blink of the eye and *refused*?"

She frowns. "I know what I'm doing does not make sense. I just have a feeling about these things sometimes, and I'm not often wrong. It's not so bad here with us, is it? You've been happy."

"You're right. It doesn't make sense." It's just so unlike her. Marie has been my ally for weeks, and now she's actually making *Henri* seem like the pleasant, reasonable member of the household. "This isn't my home," I cry. "And I need to get back. Mark is expecting me."

She shrugs. "Then you stay here eight weeks and return as if you've been gone two."

I groan. "You know that doesn't work." I've done it before, on a smaller scale—reclaiming weeks you've already spent feels *off*, like jet lag that never quite goes away. My teeth grind as I force myself to appear cooperative. "Look, if you want me to stay, I'll stay, but don't make me go for weeks and weeks in a cast. It's just cruel."

She hesitates, as if she's actually considering what I've said, and then shakes her head. "*Non.* We already know you don't mind lying. And sometimes fate is cruel." She pats my knee with a smile that is either sweet or psychotic, depending on the context. "Now, open wide or it will hurt a great deal when your ankle is set."

A SHORT WHILE later the doctor arrives to pronounce what we already knew—I have one broken ankle, one sprained. He says it will likely take me six weeks to heal, and I once again consider the situation. I don't want to stay here that long, but I *could*. I'd still be out of here by late July, which is weeks before I'm due to meet Mark in Paris, and means I'm not jumping backward on a broken ankle and risking a broken spine in its place.

The doctor gives me pain medication but—true to form—it doesn't make a dent.

Henri stands in the doorway with his arms folded across his broad chest. He looks as if he could burn a hole through Marie, but she hardly seems to notice. She's right at my bedside, pretending my ankle is her greatest concern.

"I'm going to set the bone now," the doctor warns. "This will hurt, but only for a moment."

Marie grips my hand and I glare at her. "It doesn't *need* to hurt at all."

The doctor twists something and I gasp, meeting Henri's gaze over the doctor's head. He's flinching, brow damp with sweat though the room isn't especially warm. *This is harder on him than it is on me*, I realize, just before the doctor twists again and the world goes black.

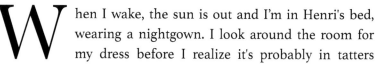

12

When I wake, the sun is out and I'm in Henri's bed, wearing a nightgown. I look around the room for my dress before I realize it's probably in tatters from that fall.

Before I can begin worrying about poor Marie and the dress I've ruined, I remember that *poor Marie* has the power to go back and fix my ankle, yet refuses.

A single crutch is leaning against a wall. It's too tall for me but I grab it and hobble out of the room. Henri sits at the kitchen table. His eyes go wide before he averts them. "You need a robe," he says, rising. "You can borrow Marie's."

I look down. The nightgown covers twice as much skin as any school uniform I've ever owned. "You refused to give me clothes the day I arrived here and now you're acting like the sight of my neck and arms is too much for you."

"The day you arrived I was too worried to notice much," he says, walking away.

Which means he *is* noticing now? I hate the way something in my stomach goes soft and gooey at the idea of it.

He returns a moment later and hands me the robe, which I dutifully wrap around myself. "Where's Marie?"

"Teaching. Or perhaps just hiding in town to avoid my wrath." He glances at the crutch I've leaned against the wall. "I'll have better ones for you by the end of the day. And we'll switch rooms since you won't be able to manage the stairs for a while. I'll clear my things out once the crutches are made."

I shake my head. "You don't need to do that."

He laughs, but there's more misery than joy in the sound. "Of course I do. You're stuck here now for weeks because of my sister. And also because of me. I goaded you into what happened last night."

I give him a half-smile. "You realize you're stuck with me for weeks now, right? That seems like punishment enough."

"Yes, I suppose it's a punishment for us both," he replies. He's smiling but just behind that smile I see something else: he's worried. And I wish I knew why.

THAT AFTERNOON, Marie comes home both wary and unapologetic. She's brought me chocolate.

"You don't think you can buy me off with a candy bar, do you?" I demand. "I live near the world's largest chocolate manufacturer, but instead I'm here and I can't even *move*."

She shrugs and pushes the chocolate off to the side. "Henri is making you crutches. They're nearly done."

"Henri should not *have* to make me crutches!" I climb to my feet, as if I plan to march off somewhere, except I can't even stand without clinging to the table. "Jesus, Marie. Why are you doing this?"

"I'm sorry," she says airily. "Some things don't make sense until after they're done."

I slap a hand to my forehead. All this time, Marie has been so mature, so logical. It's as if she developed multiple personality disorder last night, and the personality that emerged is a freaking sociopath. All, undoubtedly, because she thinks if I remain here she'll convince me to go with her to 1918. "This is never going to make sense. I need to get home. I told my mother I wasn't going to jump again. If you keep me here, she'll know when she sees me at the end of the summer. Please, *please* don't do this."

She looks at me with sympathy. "I'm sorry," she says. "Someday she'll need you to use your gift, and when that day arrives, she'll see her mistake."

I sigh heavily. She clearly doesn't understand my mother, a woman who hasn't viewed time travel as a gift for any of my twenty-one years and is therefore unlikely to so in the future.

"If I'm not there soon, Mark is going to worry."

"You can fix that."

I huff out a breath in anger. "I don't want to *have* to fix things. Don't you see how complicated you're making all this?"

She smiles. "Yes, and I apologize for that. Now what shall we make for dinner?"

"*We* won't be making anything," I reply. "Not until you fix my ankle."

She gives a one-shouldered shrug. "It's no matter. You weren't likely to be much help. I picked up some books in English for you at the library, by the way. They're in my bag."

I can barely even reach her bag. I have to hobble toward it, clutching furniture to get there. I'm not even trying to make her feel guilty; between the one ankle in a cast and the other sprained, every movement is awkward at best and agonizing at worst.

In the bag is *Mansfield Park*, my least favorite Jane Austen, and *Tender is the Night* by F. Scott Fitzgerald.

"*Tender is the Night* is quite new," says Marie, flouring the butcher block like she's Betty Crocker. "I couldn't believe they had the English translation in our library."

It's not new, I think, annoyed. Nor is it a *translation*. And if I didn't get the hype about *The Great Gatsby*, I seriously doubt I'll love Fitzgerald's *least* popular novel.

I push myself out toward the stone porch, collapsing into the same chair I sat in a week ago, having tea. If I was a better person I'd appreciate the fact that I'm here in France with good weather and a gorgeous vineyard for a view. Instead I let my eyes shut, wishing I was anywhere else, wishing my ankles didn't hurt and the weather was mild. I find myself thinking of the night I laid on a blanket with Henri in the orchard—a pleasant breeze, moonlight flickering through the branches overhead, him with that ever-present smirk on his face. His response when I said I wasn't sleeping with him out there: *Well, that definitely removes some of the fun from the evening.*

I'm smiling, remembering it, when my body lightens, and a breeze rustles around me. My eyes fly open suddenly to find that my arms are translucent. Half here and half gone. I force myself back into the terrible present, my heart beating hard. If I hadn't stopped myself, I'd have landed somewhere on my bad ankles, the cast left behind with my clothes. So it's absolutely critical that it not happen again, but what's shocking is that it happened at all. I haven't *accidentally* time traveled since I was young—twelve or thirteen, perhaps—and I can't believe it nearly happened now.

And happened when I was thinking about *Henri*, of all things.

TENDER IS the Night deserves to be Fitzgerald's least popular novel. If I thought all Americans were as annoying as his characters, I'd avoid the country entirely. I'm forcing myself to read it when Henri comes out to the porch with the crutches in one hand and two small glasses of wine in the other, one of which he hands to me.

"My sister said you were churlish this afternoon and need loosening up."

I groan, loudly. Churlish? *Really*? "Did you suggest she might be churlish too if she had a life-threatening injury I refused to fix?"

His mouth turns up at one corner. "Life-threatening? Is that what we're calling a broken ankle now?"

"Maybe it's not *my* life that's in peril," I reply, glancing inside at Marie while I take a sip off the glass he's handed me. I don't even like wine, but I need something to take the edge off my anger. "I don't know what I'm going to do if my ankle isn't healed when it's supposed to be."

He takes the seat across from mine. "What precisely do you need to rush home for?"

I sigh. I'm sure the truth will only confirm what he already thinks about me—that I'm a liar, a fraud. Whatever. "My pretend internship is ending on August 12th—I said it to buy myself extra time here just in case—Mark is supposed to be meeting me in Paris right after that and I might not even be there."

He takes a sip of his wine. "I still don't understand why you felt you had to lie to such an extreme," he says. "Especially to your mother. She already doesn't approve of you, so why keep trying?"

I'm not sure if I'm frustrated by his lack of understanding, or if I just don't like that there's some truth to what he's saying. "Because I still have a chance of fixing this," I reply. "I'm trying not to use my gift, and once I stop...she'll know. She'll be able to tell. And then maybe..." I don't complete the sentence because it's too goddamn pathetic to be said aloud. "I don't know."

"Your parents won't be suspicious when you go through the entire summer without calling them?"

I flush. That I can't make my parents care still feels like a personal failing, no matter what I tell myself. "My father left when I was twelve and I never heard from him again," I reply stiffly. He contacted Steven, but never me. More proof that I was flawed and that what I did was unforgivable. "And my mother... well, she'd prefer not to hear from me. When I call, she just tries to get off the phone anyway."

He's watching me again, and before he's even opened his mouth, I know I'll regret having told him so much. It's more than I've ever said to Mark, and I have no idea why I suddenly decided to be so regrettably *open* about my family.

"Is she really worth all this, then?" he asks. "All the lies, just trying to earn her respect? She doesn't sound like much of a mother."

But she's all I have, I want to say. It's not true, of course. I have Mark. I have my brother. But that's different. Mark has no idea what I am, and Steven only has the vaguest understanding of it. It's my mother who knows, who was raised among time travelers and truly realizes how much harm it can do. Persuading her that I'm not evil might allow me to persuade myself.

"Her respect is the only thing I've ever wanted."

His nod is small and in his eyes I see what looks an awful lot like pity. I wanted him to agree with me and it scares me that he doesn't. Maybe there's absolutely nothing I can do to win her over —no job, degree or spouse capable of fixing it. Perhaps even giving up my ability won't be enough, because what I want even more than her respect is her love, and there might be something inside me that just makes that impossible.

He runs a hand through his hair and releases a heavy sigh. "I'm sorry. I know this isn't how you would choose to spend a summer."

For the first time in hours, I manage to feel bad for someone other than myself. I know he feels guilty about what happened and I'm not going to make him feel worse. "It's not that," I reply.

"I'm just going crazy, sitting here like this all day. But the crutches will help. Thank you for those."

He's lost in thought for a moment and then glances at me. "Do you ride?"

"Horses?"

He laughs a little. Of course he means horses. "Yes. I could take you riding. You just have to promise you can keep your seat."

"I grew up on a farm. I can keep my seat."

"You said you could milk a cow too, as I recall," he counters. "But tomorrow then, we will ride, though only *after* Marie-Therese is gone. I wouldn't want to give her the impression that you're enjoying this."

We both glance inside at her, still humming and working on her pie. I never thought I'd see the day when Henri and I were united against something. And I definitely never thought that thing would be Marie.

13

The next morning after Marie has left for the school, Henri returns to the house, handing me a small pair of trousers and a shirt he's dug out of the trunks in the attic. Once I've struggled to pull the pants over the cast, I hobble to the door where Fleur, the calmer of their two horses, awaits.

I lean the crutches against the door as he comes to lift me into the saddle. "Are you sure you're up to this?" I ask. "As I recall, you said I was heavier than I looked."

"And as I recall," he says, lifting me high in the air, seemingly without effort, "you said you thought I was strong."

His hands, firm and gentle at once, stay in place until he's certain I'm stable, though his proximity makes me feel far more unstable than the weight of the cast. I swear I can feel the press of his fingers through my clothes, and it makes my breath come short. "I'm okay," I say.

He releases me and jumps onto Napoleon—so named, he says, because as a foal he was "little but mean"—and heads toward the vineyard, trusting me to follow.

The vines are lush and green, dotted with tiny purple clusters. I've never been in a vineyard before, and it's beautiful, yet my eyes want to lock on Henri instead—on his broad shoulders ahead of me, or on the nape of his neck, where the hair is shaved close and would feel rough to the touch. Like his jaw might, this late in the day.

I picture pressing my mouth there for a moment and flush when I catch my own thoughts. I've been away from Mark too long, is all. I force my eyes back to the vines.

"So the wine we've been drinking," I say, "did you make that?"

He shakes his head. "Mostly, no. We have a few Beaujolais vines here, but we're too far north for them to grow well. On the nights when we've had a good wine, I can assure you it wasn't ours."

I shrug. "I don't really like wine anyway, so I can't tell the difference."

He glances at me with a furrowed brow. "You don't *like* it?" he asks, as if he thinks he misheard me.

I like daquiris and margaritas, which are essentially slushies for adults, and that's about it. Mark teases me about my unsophisticated palate, but I hadn't even turned twenty-one until the month before I left, so it's not as if I've had a lot of exposure to anything but beer at this point in my life.

"I'm starting to get used to it." I look around. "So what are these if they're not the Beaujolais?"

"Champagne. You're in the champagne region of France. Didn't you know?"

I guess that explains all the champagne bottle-souvenirs in town when I arrived. I give him a rueful smile. "I didn't read up much before I came. The only thing I wanted to know was when the Germans would arrive."

He looks at his vines and his smile fades. "As much as I wanted to study architecture, I love all of this too. It would be hard to watch the Germans destroy it."

I follow his gaze, looking out over the acres of green in the bright sun. "The Germans like champagne too, so I can't see why they'd ruin it. But when they come..." I swallow. "I hope you don't plan to try to fight them for it."

He laughs. "You're not serious? You really think I'm just going to hand my home over to them?"

If I'd given it any thought before I spoke, I probably wouldn't have suggested it. That's not who he is. "No, but you should. You know why Paris falls so quickly once it all begins? Because they're completely outmanned, and they've got to choose between total destruction or possibly surviving the war and preserving the city. There is absolutely no chance they can prevail, and there's no chance you can either. Your single gun won't last you an hour against a couple dozen well-armed Nazis."

"That's not the point," he mutters. "It's the principle of the matter."

"Your *principle* will get you killed."

He glances at me with a small smile. "A horseback ride through a French vineyard and all you can do is scold. What a lucky man Mark is."

I roll my eyes. He doesn't want to discuss it and there's no point anyway. He's too stubborn to listen to anyone but himself. I suddenly notice we're heading toward the woods. "Where are we going?"

"There's a lake at the border of the Bousonne Wood you might like."

I stiffen. "That's okay."

He turns to look at me. "You're getting tired?"

"No," I reply. "I just don't like lakes."

He looks at me for a moment, waiting, perhaps, for me to explain. Saying you don't like lakes is like saying you don't like good food, or comfort. Who doesn't like lakes? When I say nothing, he just shrugs. "We can ride to the eastern meadow. It's a sea of wildflowers at the moment."

We turn and head north, picking our way through the vineyard and then the woods, until the trees clear and a hill stretches in front of us. "Just to the top," he says, hovering close to me as we proceed.

When we finally ascend the hill, my breath releases in one long, contented sigh. It's not merely a field of flowers. It's a field of lilies, so densely packed it's hard to believe they're real.

He climbs down and before I can stop him, he's grabbed me by the waist and set me gently on the ground. "The horses will graze and we will rest."

I have far less faith than he does in the animals' obedient nature. "What happens if they run off?" I ask.

"Then I will walk home and leave you for dead, of course."

I laugh. "It was probably your plan all along."

He nods, rubbing his chin contemplatively. "I do wish I'd thought of it sooner."

He helps me lower myself into the grass and I lie back, letting my face turn toward the sun. We sit in silence for a few minutes, and when I open my eyes, he's watching me with a hint of a smile.

"What?" I ask.

"I'm wondering if you've realized yet what happened the day before yesterday?"

"That I broke my ankle? No, I didn't realize it at all. No wonder it's so painful and encased in plaster."

He laughs. "Always so sharp-tongued. I was referring to the fact that you asked—no *begged*—my sister to use a gift you your-self claim to neither need nor want."

"I certainly realize she *refused*."

"That's not the point. The point is that some part of you desperately wanted this thing you claim you hate. What makes you think you won't need it again, just as badly?"

"I won't. Mark's family is very well connected. There's nothing they can't access."

"They can heal a broken bone with the blink of an eye, then?" he asks. "Money can accomplish that in your time?"

He has a point, of course, but I refuse to consider it. "No, it can't. But a bit of suffering is part of life, and using time travel constantly—it becomes a habit, an addiction, to avoid things you'll live through just fine. Maybe you'll even grow from them."

"But you didn't want to grow from the experience of this broken ankle, it would seem."

I've come around to Henri, but his constant harping on this topic is getting old. I frown at him. "This is different. It's a special situation. I'm not in my own time. I'm ready to be a different person, and I can't do that until this is all behind me."

He's silent for a moment while the lilies rustle in the fragrant breeze. "I don't think you need to be a different person," he finally says.

"What about my unladylike behavior?"

He grins at that. "True. I'll amend what I said. You don't need to be an *entirely* different person."

BY THE END of my first week in a cast, I've finally realized my sulking does not seem to be changing Marie's mind in the least.

I take over baking the bread and help her make preserves of the strawberries she's picked for days and days. It's hard to do much else, however. I can milk the cows, but I can't carry the milk. I try to feed the chickens, but I'm not coordinated enough to do it while holding onto the crutches. And no matter how hard I try, I can't stop feeling resentful—of her freedom, of her mobility, not at all helped by the fact that she's now busier than ever. Between her language classes and all the things she does for the church, she's never home. I'd suspect she was doing this hoping a romance might blossom between Henri and myself, except it's just too absurd. Surely she must realize that even if I didn't have someone waiting at home, I could never give up my own time to stay here.

Though I'd be lying if I said I never thought of Henri that way.

We're spending so much time together it would be hard *not* to. He's been coming in from the fields early on the days when Marie is gone and we spend those afternoons together on the porch, reading or playing chess. I reread *Mansfield Park*, which isn't as bad as I remember, and finish *Tender is the Night* out of desperation. I find a new stack of books on the porch a few days later, better books. Some that I've read—*Sense and Sensibility, Gone with the Wind*—and some that I haven't, such as *A Handful of Dust, Decline and Fall*, and *Howard's End*.

It's not a bad way to spend a summer, yet I can't get past being annoyed that I'm confined while Marie's not. When I enter the kitchen the morning after I've found the new books, she is packing her bags to leave. The rain is going to start at any moment, yet I still envy her ability to go at all, to control her life in small ways I cannot. I should be home right now, doing the only thing I can to win my mother over, and every minute I stay here puts that off, which is aggravating because I've already waited a lifetime. How could Marie possibly think this situation will persuade me to do *anything* for her?

I have to force myself to be polite. "Thank you for the new books."

Her brow furrows. "I didn't get you any books. I haven't been back to the library this week."

I bite my lip. It's strange that Henri would have done it. And that he'd have chosen so well.

"I'll be out until after dinner," she continues. "You and Henri won't kill each other while I'm gone, will you?"

The animosity between Henri and me has grown into an odd thing. He still routinely acts like it's an unpleasant surprise to find that I'm here, and I still ask if he's thinking of killing me. But almost anything he says to me, no matter how terrible, just makes me laugh.

"I'm small and I don't know how to handle a gun. Also, you

might not be aware of this, but I have a broken ankle. So I think your brother is safe. No promises on his end, however."

A small smile turns her full lips up at the corners. "I suspect you're safe. And you've forgotten you do have a weapon or two."

I glance down. "Are you talking about my breasts?"

She explodes in laughter. "*Dieu*, Amelie. I meant your cooking, but if you think your breasts can kill also, by all means use those if necessary."

HENRI DRIVES HER INTO TOWN, and I find myself at loose ends. On crutches, I'm mostly too inept to help with much. I could cook something, but my best-case scenario is wasting a lot of their food and my worst case is burning their home to the ground.

I'm tired of reading. I'm tired of my own company. I while away the time by swinging my body around the living room on the crutches, trying to see how fast I can cross the room. It's a stupid and potentially dangerous game, but I don't know what to do with myself today.

When Henri walks in, he is drenched to the skin but stops, looking over at me with suspicion. "What are you doing?" he asks.

"Absolutely nothing," I reply. "Perhaps you should entertain me."

He laughs, brushing wet hair off his forehead. "I have a fence to mend."

The rain is coming down so hard I doubt he could even see a foot in front of his face. Why does he never give himself a day off? "You can't mend a fence in this weather. It's pouring rain. You'll get sick."

"Better a cool rain that a hundred degrees and sun," he says.

"Come on," I wheedle. "Stay in. It'll be pleasant on the porch."

He gives me a half-smile. It's enough to light up his whole face. "So you want me to entertain you? Shall I sing? Dance?"

"*Can* you sing or dance?"

"*Non*," he says, mouth still turned up.

"And you're not funny, and you don't say all that much, which really makes you a poor choice on my part, but I don't see a lot of options."

He leans back against the wall with his arms folded over his chest. "So I'm to struggle to entertain you while you insult me today. This sounds better and better."

"I won't insult you," I promise, holding up my hand as if I'm taking an oath. "Not more than usual, anyway. And I'll even...I'll make you hot chocolate."

"*You* know how to make hot chocolate?"

I shrug. "Sort of."

"Fine," he says. "Let's see you *sort of* make hot chocolate. Then, perhaps, I'll stay."

"Go get on dry clothes, first," I order.

A single brow raises. "You're worrying about me now?"

I flush. Why *do* I care that he's in wet clothes? "No," I reply. "I just don't want you dripping all over the floor."

He goes up to his room to change and I stand at the counter, struggling to remember the recipe for cocoa. It's always been a skill of mine, this bizarre ability to recall things when I need to— I just have to focus on the memory and it's almost like I'm there again, seeing what I need to see. I close my eyes and try to picture the back of the Hershey's cocoa box. It's been ages since I've made it from scratch. Probably not since Kit died.

My eyes are squeezed shut, but I hear him come back into the room. "What are you doing?" he asks.

"Remembering the recipe for cocoa," I reply, pressing an index finger against my lips so he won't ruin my concentration.

I see myself as a child, in the kitchen with Kit after a day of sledding. Her cheeks are pink and her hair is soaked through. *How long will it take?* she asks, jumping in place. She always had so much energy, a constant blur of movement from the moment she woke until she collapsed into sleep. I'd forgotten that about her, and remembering hurts. I guess it's why I try so hard to avoid thinking about her.

I pick up the Hershey's container and begin to read from the back of the box.

"I need sugar," I say to Henri, my eyes still closed. "Half a cup. Four cups of milk. A teaspoon of vanilla—the recipe calls for slightly less but we like it with more. A third cup hot water, a dash of salt, and a quarter cup of cocoa."

I take one last look at Kit. *I'm sorry*, I think. *God I'm so sorry. If one of us had to die, it should have been me. Not a single member of the family would say otherwise.*

And then I open my eyes and find Henri standing across the counter, staring at me. His eyes are all pupil. "What was that?"

"I *told* you I was going to make cocoa. I was just remembering the recipe."

He shakes his head, slowly. "*Non.* You didn't just *remember.* You seemed to flicker in and out like a candle. You were...shimmering. I saw it."

My breath stops for a moment, and then releases. It's not possible that I time traveled. I'm not even good at being in *one* place at a time for God's sake and being in *two* places at once...it's just not a thing my kind does. "You were seeing things."

"Then how did you recall that recipe verbatim?" he challenges.

"I just have a good memory."

He tilts his head. "Tell me again how much cocoa you need then."

I blink, searching my head for the answer. When I was reading the ingredients, it's as if I was channeling it all. "I told *you.* You were supposed to remember."

He gazes at me, still with that assessing look, like I just escaped from a locked cage wearing a straitjacket, and he wants to know how I did the trick. "I do. A quarter cup. My point is that you *don't*. So don't try to tell me this was your fabulous memory at work."

I sigh loudly. "I didn't time travel, if that's what you're trying to say. I was standing right here the entire time."

He tips his head, as if he's conceding the point. But it's clear as day in his face that he doesn't quite believe me.

FIFTEEN MINUTES later we are seated on the porch with our cocoa. While he sets up the chess board, I gaze out over the fields, surprised by how oddly content I am right now. I love the colors of the farm on a sunny day, but I think I almost like this more: against the charcoal gray of the sky, all the colors seem deeper. The grass and vines a lush green, the air pleasantly balmy rather than sweltering.

We begin to play. Slowly, carefully. Even a week ago, I wouldn't have done this with him solely because I couldn't stand to see him win. Now, oddly enough, I'm not sure I'd even mind. Perhaps I'm giving him too much credit, but he's surprisingly easy to be around at the times when you'd expect him to be unbearable.

As the game carves its way through the afternoon, we put the mugs of cocoa aside and replace them with glasses of wine, which I'm starting to come around to, although perhaps I merely like that it's accompanied today by salty olives and fresh bread.

We finish the bottle and he opens another. "You must have a hollow leg," he says. "Marie-Therese would be falling out of her chair right now."

"I suppose that's unladylike, according to you?"

He grins. "Not at all. Though it would be unfortunate if I were *trying* to get you drunk."

Butterflies flutter in my stomach at the mere suggestion of it. "Is that your strategy on dates?"

He gives me another half-grin. "I have a few others I try first."

I'll just bet he does. He probably doesn't even need to get a girl drunk. He can just smile at her the way he's smiling at me right now and she'd pull her dress up to her waist.

"Do you and Mark do this?" he asks.

For a second I think he's asking about sex. I blink. "What? Oh, chess? No, we..." The truth is that I'm not sure what we do. We haven't lived in the same place since the summer we met and our time together has always been in short bursts of togetherness, jam-packed.

When we see each other, it's always a reunion, and therefore a celebration...a slightly exhausting one. I sleep for a full day when I come home from a trip with him. I've been looking forward to the time when we could have a day like this, yet I'm hard pressed to imagine it. Mark never wants to stop. The idea of staying home on a rainy day might drive him insane.

For so long, he's represented how I will grow, how I will become the person my mother wants me to be, once we're together. But now it occurs to me for the first time that I might be giving something up in exchange.

14

A s the weekend approaches, Marie attempts to demand that I attend church.

"She can't," Henri argues. "She sticks out like a sore thumb." *Trust Henri to find the most unflattering light to put me in.* "Just let her stay home."

"We had an excuse last week. She'd just broken her ankle," says Marie. "We no longer have one."

I swing forward on the crutches—I've gotten pretty adept at getting around on them as long as there is level ground. "I'm on Henri's side for once," I tell her. "I have no desire to go to church."

Marie raises an eyebrow. "What about heaven?" she counters. "Do you desire to go there, or would you prefer somewhere a little warmer?"

I ignore her. "Can't you just tell everyone I went to Paris for the day? Surely when people visit here, they sometimes go elsewhere?" God knows I'd be on the first train to Paris right now myself, if it were a possibility.

"I will very reluctantly stay home with her," Henri says with a gallant bow. "Otherwise they'll wonder how she got there."

Marie shakes her head vehemently. "And how do we explain it if someone stops by, or sees the car here?"

"We could actually go?" I venture. "To Paris, I mean. I'm dying to see it before the war."

Henri shakes his head. "You're on crutches and I can't be responsible for two of you in Paris. You'll attract too much attention."

"I can't go anyway," says Marie. "I'm helping Father Edouard set up the small social after mass. But the two of you feel free, since you're so ambivalent about where you'll spend the afterlife."

Ignoring this, I turn to Henri. "I've gotten so much better on the crutches," I say eagerly. "I think I'll be fine."

I fully expected him to object and am delighted when he shrugs in agreement instead. "A day in Paris always beats a morning at church. Yes, little thief. Even one spent with you."

THE NEXT MORNING Marie wakes me early, giddy with excitement on my behalf. She makes me wear a different dress – baby blue serge, with a v-neck and collar. "I took up the hem a bit last night after you went to sleep," she says. She forces me to wear hose and garters with it, acting like going into Paris without hose would be the equivalent of going there nude, and also insists I put my hair up.

Because I refuse to cut it, which is the style here, she uses curling tongs to roll it under at the nape of my neck so it *looks* as if I have shoulder length hair, along with a few waves on top. When she's done and she's got me in the dress, she claps her hands together. "You look like a movie star," she says with a dreamy sigh. "Henri, look at our Amelie," she says, turning me to face him. "Does she not look like Carole Lombard?"

I find I am waiting for his response more anxiously than I should. How could his opinion possibly matter, especially when it's bound to be negative? He reluctantly glances up from his newspaper, and I see something on his face I can't quite read—as if he's looking at me and thinking hard at the same time—before he looks down again. "Yes," he says. "Perhaps a little."

Marie grins, turning me back toward her as Henri walks out to start the car. She fixes a bobby pin in my hair and beams at me. "Did you hear that? He said you looked a little like Carole Lombard! He thinks she's the most beautiful woman alive."

I laugh. "Yes, because you specifically asked him if I did. What else was he supposed to say?"

She gives me a look. "Are you seriously under the impression that Henri wouldn't have said *no* to that question if he could have? Have you found him to be a man who minces words?"

Hmmm. I suppose she has a point.

WE LEAVE for Paris down an unpaved road which, I realize with a sudden start, is the same highway that ran alongside the train tracks for much of my trip to Saint Antoine. I struggle not to bounce in my seat, like a child headed to the circus. Here I was, merely hoping to see pre-war Saint Antoine and now I'm getting Paris in its place, with almost no begging or wheedling. I'm still a little shocked by the ease with which it's all happened.

"What would you like to see today?" he asks.

"Everything. I came straight to Saint Antoine from the airport so I still haven't set foot in Paris. And I do need to get a few things."

He snorts. "You get the chance to see the most beautiful city in the world and you want to *shop* while you're there."

"If you had to wear a bra that's several sizes too small, you would too," I reply. The tiniest hint of color grazes the top of his cheekbones. "Oh my God. Have I made the impenetrable Henri Durand blush?"

"In my time, a lady does not discuss her undergarments in mixed company."

I roll my eyes. "You're very hung up on this whole *being a lady* business."

He gives me one of those smirks that makes me want to laugh and punch him at the same time. "You might benefit by becoming acquainted with it."

"Being a lady is just one of many ways you subjugate women," I reply. "It's an unequal paradigm for behavior."

"*Unequal paradigm for behavior*?" he repeats with a small laugh. "Where did you come up with this theory?"

"I learned it in a women's studies class last semester," I admit.

"Women's studies?" he asks incredulously. "It must have been a very short class. Marie Curie, Mary Cassatt, Mary Shelley. There, I've provided you a nearly comprehensive list of women who've made any kind of contribution to the world, if you really want to consider *Frankenstein* a contribution."

I lean my head against the window. "God, you're such a dick."

"Dick?"

I cast him a withering look. "It means penis. And before you start in again about my unladylike mouth, let me ask you: Why should I be held to a different standard of behavior than you? Why is it okay for you to go to a bar and tell dirty jokes with your friends, while the women must stay home, making sure their voices are hushed and all their words are appropriate?"

He shrugs. "Because it's how we were created. A woman's gentler nature is what inspires man to move beyond his basest instincts, makes him want to protect and care for something other than himself. It's an exchange, beneficial for both genders."

There's a certain sweetness to the idea, but mostly it just strikes me as naïve, and I don't love the implication that a woman would also *need* a man to care for her like a child. "In the future, life is safer. A woman no longer needs a cave man to protect her from wild animals and war."

"No?" he asks, smirking again. "Is that not the appeal of your rich boyfriend—the protection he offers?"

"Of course not," I snap.

"I've just never heard you provide a single other reason you're with him," he says.

Before I can react to this, he changes the topic. "What would you like to see first?"

I'm so irritated by his last comment about Mark I can barely focus on his question. All I know is that the things I'm dying to see—the Louvre, the Orsay—I don't want to experience with *him*. Not when he's there nattering on about my relationship and other things about which he knows *absolutely nothing*. I'll wait until I'm back in my own time so I can truly focus on them. I'd rather see them with Mark anyway.

"I don't know. The Eiffel Tower?"

He actually *sneers*. "With all the amazing architecture in this city, it's a monstrosity that excites you?"

"It's kind of...the emblem of Paris. Maybe even the whole country. In my time."

"Dieu," he says with an unhappy laugh. "Keep your television and your microwaves. I don't care to live in any world where the *Eiffel Tower* is the emblem of Paris and women's studies is actually a course at university."

"Fine," I sigh. "You decide."

He weaves through the city while I gawk at pedestrians. Everyone is so nicely dressed, and the roads are not clogged with cars the way they would be in my time, but it doesn't feel entirely real. I can't shake the sensation that I'm in some kind of 1930's-themed Disney attraction instead of a real place.

Eventually he parks in a neighborhood just off the Seine. "Put on the gloves," he says. "And the hat."

The hat with the small veil in front, pressed into my hands by Marie just before I left. "Is this really necessary?" I ask. "I feel like a widow."

His eyes flicker over my face for the space of a heartbeat. "Yes, *time traveler*. It is."

With a sigh, I open the door, slapping the hat on my head as I do it.

"Amelie, for God's sake," he says, rolling his eyes, jumping from the driver's seat. "Wait. You're not supposed to get your own door."

I ignore him. I'm not going to sit here like a child waiting for her father's permission to exit the car. "Why can't I?" I ask, climbing out and shutting the door with a satisfying *thud*.

He looks appalled, rather than amused. "It's not that you can't. It's that you shouldn't *have to*."

He gets the crutches from the trunk and hands them to me. "You certainly don't treat me like a fragile little flower when you're criticizing me, or when you were watching me sweat my ass off doing laundry last week, so let's not pretend you suddenly believe I need you to open my door."

He releases a small groan. "Do all women where you're from object to everything the way you do? It's quite tedious."

"Not at all," I reply. "I just didn't realize I needed so much protection. I hope this means you'll be escorting me every time I go out to milk the cows?"

His mouth edges up. "I probably should, given how poorly you do it."

Before I can reply, I see the awning on the corner and stumble to a halt. We're standing feet from Les Deux Magots, one of the most famous restaurants in history. "Oh my God." The words emerge wispy and high.

His brow furrows. "You've heard of it?"

"Of course!" I say with an excited little jump on the crutches. He fixes my hat, knocked slightly askew by the jumping. "It's where Hemingway wrote! And Sartre and Simone de Beauvoir! Everyone was here."

He's looking at me blankly.

"You must have heard of them?" I ask. But even as I pose the question, it occurs to me they might not have become famous until later. Maybe these were the glory days they'd only recall with fondness years hence, glossing over poverty and hunger and nights without heat.

He scratches his neck. "Hemingway. I just read a book by him not long ago. It was garbage."

"He's one of the most famous writers of all time," I reply. "What book did you read?"

"*A Farewell to Arms*. Romantic drivel," he says, his lip turning up into a sneer. "Please tell me you don't associate Hemingway with Paris too. He's not even *French*."

I laugh. "Sorry, *mon ami*. He's one of your most famous former citizens."

"*Dieu*," he mutters. "I've never been so grateful to live in my own time."

We turn a corner and Notre Dame rises in the distance, just a short walk away. Henri nods at it. "I hope our cathedral is at least as well known as the Eiffel Tower," he says.

Something perverse in me demands I provide the answer that will bother him most. "They made the book into an animated children's movie, so that helped get the name out."

"A *children's* movie?" he says. "Everyone dies in the end!"

"Not in our version," I reply. "It's super cute."

He likes my answer about as much as I'd have predicted, but his irritation disappears once we get close. He points to the arching wood at its front. "This was one of the first places in the world to use flying buttresses. They were added after the fact when the upper walls started to crack. The gargoyles and chimeras as well."

I glance up toward the gutters. "I thought the gargoyles were just some medieval bullshit about protection from demons."

He laughs begrudgingly. "There's a little medieval bullshit, as you so charmingly phrase it. I still can't believe they made *The*

Hunchback of Notre Dame a children's movie. You know Hugo wrote the entire book to call attention to the cathedral's gothic architecture? He was disturbed by the way it was being destroyed."

"And did it work?"

He turns his head back to the flying buttresses. "Those still stand, so I suppose it did, to some extent."

As we enter the cathedral, Henri begins pointing out things I would not have recognized on my own—all the structural changes they made to free up the space for stained glass, the Romanesque architecture of the tower and nave versus the Gothic elements, the arches and rib vaulting. He is unguarded and enthralled, two adjectives I'd never have used to describe him until now. But he suddenly stops himself.

"Sorry," he says, with a faltering smile. "I'm telling you far more than you're interested in hearing, I'm sure."

"I'm an art history major," I reply. "Architectural history isn't so different. Why would you think I wouldn't want to hear it?"

He looks at me for a long moment, before he glances away. "I suppose because the women I know aren't like you."

"Right, because I'm unladylike."

"No," he says, shoving his hands in his pockets and starting forward without me, "because you're interesting."

When we leave Notre Dame, we take a circular path through town, cutting through the Luxembourg Gardens on the way. People stroll, children play, and there are painters everywhere I turn.

"You keep staring at those painters like you know them from home," he quips.

"Because they could be anyone!" I whisper. "I know some of the great artists came here to paint—Picasso, Matisse, Monet—

and some of them could actually be here. Right this minute. Some of them not even known yet."

He laughs. "They are all quite famous here. And Monet is quite dead."

I groan. "I know that, but you're missing the point," I reply. "Imagine you went back 52 years from now? So..."

"1886," he says, before I can do the subtraction.

"You're better at math than I am. Don't get too cocky. A child of five is better at math than I am."

"And speaks better French," he returns. "But yes, I see your point. I saw it long before you made it. Unlike you, I've always thought the ability to travel back in time would be an amazing gift to possess."

We turn back toward the Seine, and once we find ourselves in the center of everything again, I push to eat at Les Deux Magots and he ignores me, insisting it's not appropriate, and instead takes me to a small restaurant nearby, the kind with silver and white linen and waiters in tuxedos. Even Mark's parents don't dine like this, at least not that I've seen.

"This doesn't seem like the dining establishment of poor farmers," I say once we are seated.

A smile plays at the corners of his mouth. "You're forgetting I don't have to pretend to be a poor farmer when I'm here."

He orders what sounds to me like a stunning amount of food, but it comes out in small courses, each served with tiny glasses of wine. And as the meal winds on, Henri grows warmer, less guarded. We talk about art and architecture and school. He asks what I would do if I were forced to remain in 1938 and I laugh.

"You mean the way I'm being forced right now?"

"Even worse," he says, raising a brow. "I mean permanently. If something happened—if you stayed for so long you couldn't go home again—what would you do?"

I take a sip of my wine, considering the question. "I think I could do here what I hope to do at home anyway—find strug-gling artists and help promote their work."

He grins. "You mean discover someone who's famous in your day before they are discovered by someone else and *profit* from their work?"

I make a face at him. "Of course not. That would be cheating, first of all. Secondly, it's not about the money, obviously. I could have plenty of that if I needed it. It's just about helping people who deserve to be helped, though I'd have plenty of staff to make my life easier while I did it."

He gazes at me over the rim of his glass. "That sounds almost altruistic, little thief."

"Despite what you think," I retort, "I'm not evil."

He takes a sip of his wine and shakes his head. "I'm not the one of the two of us who believed that anyway."

Our meal continues in this way—some teasing, some arguing, a great deal of laughter—until the bell rings four o'clock and my jaw drops. "We've been here for *two hours*?"

He laughs. "Perhaps my company is not as terrible as you previously believed. But we should go to your shops before they close so you can get your, um, things," he says.

I grin. "You mean the *bra*? For my *breasts*?" I'm not sure why I love baiting him as much as I do.

He closes his eyes as if praying for patience. "My God, you never stop. But yes, that. And get yourself some dresses too," he adds. "Since you'll be staying a while."

For the first time, he doesn't sound like he's sorry that's the case.

THE RIDE HOME IS QUIET, but it's a companionable silence. I think about the tentative plans Mark and I made for our meeting in Paris—he'd mentioned Saint-Germain-des-Pres specifically. And

I'm sure if we do wind up there, it will be great. Just not the same kind of great.

"Thank you," I say, as we pull up to the house. I think back over our day—lunch, Notre Dame, the gardens—and can't pick out a favorite moment. Even bra shopping was fun, particularly the moment when I caught Henri—standing just outside the lingerie department—trying to see what I was buying. "Today was...magical. I never in a million years thought I'd get to see Paris in the 1930s and eat in the same restaurant Picasso dined in the night before."

He considers me for a moment. "You do realize that it was possible because of your gift? That a million other adventures beyond this one are still possible. Even if your ability is not strong enough to go much further back, surely there are things you still want to see?"

"Why are you constantly on me about this?" I sigh. "Why can't you just respect my decision and let it go?"

"Because you seem to willfully ignore all the good it can do. All the good it's done. Your gift made today possible—how can you wish that away?"

I feel emotions spinning inside my chest: confusion and anger and sadness. He isn't wrong, but he also isn't right, and I can't explain that to him.

"Because," I reply, climbing from the car, "there's no amount of good that can make up for the harm it's already done."

15

"So," Marie says to me over dinner, wincing, "Madame Beauvoir has given you a job."

My head jerks up. "*Me?*"

Henri glares at his sister. "This had better be a joke. She is not taking a job, I can tell you that much right now."

Marie ignores him as she turns to me. "Madame Beauvoir heard about your ankle from the doctor. She's decided you should come read to her mother, Madame Perot, until you're back on your feet. Her sight is troubling her, and she thinks reading in French will help you learn the language."

"*Non*," says Henri. "She couldn't care less about the reading. She's just hoping to throw Amelie in the path of her dolt of a son, André."

Marie's shoulders sag. "We can't afford to alienate the Beauvoirs, Henri, especially with a war coming. And reading a book aloud doesn't typically result in marriage."

I could assure her it *definitely* won't result in marriage, but that doesn't mean I'm not worried. "But what if...I slip up somehow? I've done it here, with you, several times."

"You're more relaxed with us. It's not necessary to hide who you are when you are here," says Marie. "And if you mess up badly, I can always travel back to warn you so it doesn't occur."

I groan, letting my head rest against the back of the chair. "So you'd warn me about a misspoken word, but not about an ankle break that will immobilize me for another five weeks?"

"Yes," she says, unapologetic as ever. "Things having to do with Madame de Beauvoir are not fate."

I still don't think it's a great idea but at least it will give me an excuse to see Saint Antoine. "I suppose I can just tell him I'm married. It'll be true soon enough."

"So that...that's actually a plan?" Marie asks. "You're really getting married when you get home?"

I shrug. "Not right away, no. Mark wants me to move to New York next year to live with him and finish my degree there. I want to stay where I am, so I'm not sure what's going to happen...but either way, there's no rush. People in my time live together before they get married usually anyway."

"Live together?" gasps Marie. "As a couple?"

I laugh. "Yes. It's not a big deal. Things—everything, really— is much...looser. People don't wait for marriage to have sex. They live together. Sometimes they even have kids together before they marry, or they just choose not to marry at all."

Henri's jaw shifts a little at that. "In my time, there's a name for women who give themselves away before marriage."

I feel irritation inching upward. "But no name for the men, I assume?" I ask. "It's okay for you to sleep with whoever is agreeable and then look down on her afterward for it, yes?"

"Not necessarily, but look at it from an evolutionary perspective," he argues. "Women are driven to find the best provider for their young, and men are driven to procreate. Women must keep the gate closed in order to ensure men hold up their end of the bargain."

I can't believe he's defending this nonsense. I thought he was smarter than that. "Maybe men are just better at keeping promises in my day."

His jaw grinds. "Maybe women just aren't desperate enough to accept any lie in mine."

Marie rubs her temples. "The two of you will find anything to argue about, won't you?"

"She started it," says Henri, flushed and angrier than the situation calls for.

"Me? I don't argue with anyone! Mark and I have never argued once. It's you."

"How could you argue?" he asks, heading for the door. "You're too busy letting him walk all over you."

The door slams behind him and the windows rattle in his wake.

"It's both of you," says Marie. She says something in French as she heads for the stairs, too quickly for me to understand.

"You know I don't speak French."

"It was your Emerson," she says, turning to me from the landing, raising a single brow. "*Thou art to me a delicious torment.*"

THE NEXT DAY, once I've donned the hose and one of the better dresses and Marie has rolled up my hair, Henri walks me to the car, holding the door for me, taking my crutches once I'm in. It's silly, but also kind of sweet. I suppose the 1930's code of chivalry is helpful if your ankle is broken.

The two of us have barely exchanged a word since last night's argument, so I'm not surprised it's what he decides to lead with. "You only have a year left of school," he says abruptly before he's even started the car. "Why would he ask you to move with him?"

My shoulders tighten. "I'm nervous enough about going to the Beauvoirs. Can you not pile on by starting another fight with me right now?"

His tongue darts out, tapping his lip. "I'm not trying to start a fight, I swear it. I'm just trying to understand. If I say the sky is blue, you insist it's green. But this man wants you to drop out of college and you're okay with it?"

I let my head fall back against the seat. Obviously I can't even do a job I don't want to do without first having a discussion I don't want to have. "I didn't say I was going to drop out. I said he asked and I was thinking about it."

"You're missing my point. It's less about whether or not you do it, though that's certainly another issue to discuss. It's about the fact that this man, who in theory cares about you, is asking you to give up the main thing in your life and you don't blink an eye. If what was best for the woman I loved was for her to stay where she was, the one thing I'd *never* do is ask her to give it up. And I'd go to her if it was at all possible."

"Well, he's got a job in New York so he can't come to me," I say, feeling my stomach tense. "Can we please go? I just want to get this over with."

Henri starts the car. "Times must change dramatically, then," he says, pulling onto the road. "Because in my day, there are jobs in Philadelphia as well as New York."

I ignore him, leaning my head against the window. I could argue that the jobs in New York are better...but then again, I'm at a much better school in Philly than I would be in New York. He would probably ask me why the quality of my degree matters less than the quality of Mark's job. And I guess he'd have a point.

When we get to town, I look around in wonder, remembering the day I arrived at the train station. Henri watches my face. "Is it very different in your time?"

"No...no, but also yes. This is the historic section, and the buildings are pretty much the same, but everything is also different." I point to the butcher shop. "That sells macarons now. It's very bright and pretty, and there are these rainbow-colored boxes in the window."

"An entire store that sells only macarons?" he asks. "*Why?*"

"A lot of tourists come here," I tell him, but I stop myself before I go further. How would it feel to learn your entire way of life will, in not so many decades, be a novelty? That people will soon laugh over the idea of buying paper at a *paperie*, of needing a specific shop just to buy cheese? The consolidation of everything won't seem like a good idea to him, it will seem like an uncivilized one. "It's really not so different, though," I conclude.

He looks relieved by that, and continues to drive through town, cutting down several side roads before he arrives at a large, regal home, with a wrought-iron fence and a massive garden off to the side.

"Here we are," he says unhappily.

I search his face. "Is André like your sworn enemy or something?" I ask.

"He's too inconsequential for me to consider him an enemy." He gets my crutches and then walks me to the front door, looking more and more unhappy with each second that passes.

He rings the bell and a servant answers, blushing and tipping her head at the sight of him. A reminder of the way women must react to him every time he comes to town.

"Hi," I say sharply, with what is probably a somewhat menacing smile. "I'm here to read to Madame Perot."

"*Désole*," Henri tells her. "*Elle ne parle pas un mot de français*."

I bristle at that, at the snide way he tells her I don't speak *a word* of French. Like the meanest guy in high school laughing at the class nerd.

The girl's brow raises. *Not a word?*

She doesn't even know how to say hello, he replies, glancing at me with such a smirk on his face I'd have to be an idiot *not* to realize he was mocking me.

He asks her what the plan is for the afternoon and she tells him I'm to read to *Grandmere* Perot in her room, before I have tea downstairs with Madame and her son.

Henri's teeth grind at that last bit, and he translates for me with a tight jaw, completely failing to mention the way he threw me under the bus about my lack of French. "And they apparently want you to stay for tea," he concludes.

I refuse to act like I think it's the trial he does. Especially since he seems to hate André.

What's the expression? *The enemy of my enemy is my friend.*

"Oh, tea!" I say brightly. "How fun!" I flash him a wide smile over my shoulder as the door shuts behind me.

The house is magnificent. It reminds me of something you'd see on a historic tour, like Mount Vernon or Monticello, a place where whole rooms are cordoned off and you're scared you might accidentally touch something and get yelled at. The girl leads me upstairs, over gleaming, newly polished hardwood, and I struggle to follow her on crutches. Then we head down a long hall with high ceilings and more crown molding than I've seen anywhere outside of a museum. Even Mark's parents' mansion in Westport would look a little slipshod next to this place.

We enter a room where an extremely old woman lies on a canopy bed, snoring. The maid shrugs at my questioning glance.

"*Les livres sont là,*" she says, pointing at the books on the nightstand.

I survey the pile. *Ivanhoe.* God, it was boring enough in English. I can't imagine trying to read it in French. Beneath it is *Middlemarch,* also in French. Undoubtedly chock-full of 18th century syntax. My French definitely isn't up to *these* books.

Which leaves, beneath it, Baudelaire. A book of poems similar to the one I saw in Henri's room. I open it and begin to translate, painstakingly. The old woman's eyes fly open. She looks irritated to find me there.

"*Lisez le-moi, si vous devez,*" she says. *Read it to me if you must.*

Awesome. The rude maid works for a rude old woman.

With a slow exhale, I begin reading. I was never anywhere near fluent in French, and I'd expected to feel even rustier now that I've been forcing myself not to use a word of it, but it seems all these weeks of eavesdropping on Henri and Marie have had some benefit. The words flow off my tongue, less stilted than they'd have been before I arrived, but I'd enjoy it more if the old woman didn't sneer at me each time I pronounce something wrong. Toward the end of the hour, she's even begun to slap my hand when I mess up, and I'm worried if it continues much longer I'm going to slap her right back.

She's in the midst of a tirade about *les gitane*, whatever that is, when the girl who answered the door arrives to tell me it's time for tea.

I follow her to a parlor where Madame Beauvoir waits with a man not much older than me. He must be André, who is, at first glance, not quite as odious as Henri made him out to be. Though he lacks Henri's size and looks, he's handsome enough and wearing a very nice suit. He kisses both cheeks.

"A pleasure, Mademoiselle Durand," he says. "André Beauvoir. I believe you've already met my mother?"

Yes, when she burst into Marie's home bitching about the chickens, and then demanded to know who I was. Was that really only five weeks ago? It seems like so much longer. I force myself to smile at her before she leans in to do the customary kiss to the side of my cheek.

We sit at a table covered in heavy damask and laid out with cutlery and fine china. Mark and I once had tea at a table just like this, only at the Ritz Carlton—memorable because I felt the same sort of anxiety I do now, maybe even worse. It was early in our relationship, the days when he still wanted to know everything about me, and I'd had to spend hours and hours pretending I was someone else entirely—a woman who had normal problems, who suffered only the regular amount of parental disapproval. I had to create a new reason for my father's departure, for my avoidance of home. Everything I was and everything I wanted seemed to touch back to my sister's death and the role I played in it—and if I couldn't tell him that, I couldn't tell him anything.

The tea is poured and André proceeds to ask me polite, generic questions: how I'm enjoying Saint Antoine, how long I plan to stay, how I broke my ankle.

I tell him I tripped on uneven ground and he looks at me with utter sympathy, translating for his mother.

Poor girl, says Madame. *That farm is a disaster. They live like animals.*

I thought it was hard to feign a lack of comprehension around Henri, but this is much worse. My nails dig into my palms as I try to silence myself.

You're being uncharitable, Mother, André responds. I smile at him, though I'm still supposed to be feigning ignorance of what was said.

The servant reappears to tell Madame she has a call and she excuses herself, exchanging a quick, meaningful glance with her son. It feels an awful lot like a set-up, but as far as set-ups go, it's not a bad one.

He watches her leave the room and then smiles at me. "You were very kind to read to my grandmother. And brave. Did she yell at you the whole time?"

I laugh. "She yelled at me a little. Mostly she was yelling about something else. *Les gitane*?"

He laughs low, glancing over his shoulder before he turns back to me with a conspiratorial smile. "The Gypsies. One of my grandmother's many dislikes. They stole her car at the end of the war, or so she claims. The police found it almost immediately, but she's never forgotten it. I'll try to make sure I'm home the next time you read so I can intervene if necessary. I'd have been here sooner today, but work called me away."

It's kind of nice to be around a man who wants to help me, instead of one who's always lecturing me. "What do you do?"

"I manage my family's company," he says. "We own a manufacturing plant on the outside of Reims. It's not what I dreamed of doing when I went to university, but I can't complain, obviously. Times are hard and we're lucky to have the company to fall back on."

I tip my head, wondering how Henri can possibly object to this man. Is it jealousy? It must be. I can't imagine André being anything but pleasant, while I can easily imagine unpleasant behavior from Henri.

"What did you dream of doing when you were at university?"

He gives me a sheepish smile. "I studied engineering. I was always fascinated by airplanes. I don't think they've come as far as they might—if they were streamlined and their engine size increased, I believe they could hold perhaps fifty or sixty people at a time. But Maman disagreed, and of course, she needed someone to manage the company," he concludes with a forced smile, "so it fell to me."

He and Henri have more in common than either of them realize. They both gave up their own dreams to take care of their families. And why is Marie not interested in this guy? He's good looking, he's sweet, he's well-off. Yes, it would involve dealing with Madame Beauvoir, but if she married André, she'd live a much better life than she does now. No more Saturdays spent doing laundry. No more hours in the kitchen.

"Do you know Henri and Marie well?"

He gives me a cautious smile. "I don't. I went to boarding school as a child, so I never got to know anyone here in town until I finished university two years ago. And right now, I'd rather get to know their beautiful American cousin."

I can understand why he'd rather flirt than become friends with Henri, but Marie is stunning. He should be flirting with her, and I can't imagine why he is not.

"Except I'm leaving in a few weeks," I reply. "And I'm seeing someone back home."

He reaches for my hand, grazing my knuckles with his lips.

"Perhaps, with a few weeks' time, I can change your mind about both."

HENRI ARRIVES NOT long after that, and André sees me to the door. He is perfectly polite to Henri, who returns his handshake with obvious unwillingness.

"How was it?" Henri asks when we get in the car.

I think of the old woman, yelling at me and hitting my hand. "It would not be my first choice as a job, that's for sure."

He turns to me, his jaw tight. "Did something happen? Was André inappropriate?"

I can't imagine why this is the conclusion he'd jump to. "No, no, of course not," I say, waving him off. "I just don't like reading. The crazy old woman was yelling at me about talking to Gypsies and hitting me when I pronounced poorly and I...I just didn't enjoy it."

"I didn't realize she spoke English," says Henri.

Shit.

"She doesn't," I stammer. "Well, you know, just a few words. Enough to make her point."

"Ah," he says, resting in his seat more easily. "Well if you don't like it, you should not go back."

I didn't mind tea with André at all, and if I could just shift his attention from me to Marie, perhaps some good will have come from my visit. Maybe *this* is how I save Marie, by freeing her from a lifetime of domestic servitude.

"I have to go back. What would we tell them?"

"I don't give a shit what we tell them," he says.

I smile. "Henri, you just cursed. How unseemly."

He starts the car and pulls into the road. "Congratulations, little thief. You've stolen my good manners." He looks over at me.

A muscle in his jaw flickers. "And you haven't mentioned tea yet. How was that?"

I could downplay it, since he obviously doesn't like André, but then I remember the way he gossiped about me to the girl who answered the door. "It was delicious. I can't imagine why you don't like André. I think he seems very nice."

His frown deepens. "Don't judge a man until you've seen him without an audience," he replies.

16

～

Marie begins packing her things to leave almost as soon as I get home, and I sigh heavily. "This is ridiculous," I tell her. "If you are so desperate to avoid me, just fix my damn ankle!"

Her eyes widen. "Avoid you?" she repeats. "No. I'm not. I promise. I suppose it's a little selfish under the circumstances, but with you here, it means I can go do things. Normally, I stay in during the evening so Henri's not here alone. I just thought if he had you for company it would be okay, but if you want me to stay I will."

"It's fine," I sigh. As much as I resent the whole situation, I don't really care whether or not she's home and I do want to see them both move on with their lives. Although the idea of Henri *moving on* bothers me a bit more than it should.

～

"So it's bread and cheese for dinner," I tell him when he gets in that night. "It's all I can do with the ankle the way it is." I don't feel particularly bad about this. His bullshit this morning at the Beauvoir's house is still irking me.

His mouth goes up on one side. "I was under the impression it was all you could do anyhow." He looks at the food I've taken out and begins to gather it, throwing everything in one of Marie's baskets hanging from the copper rack overhead, and adding a bottle of wine. "That dinner was meant to be for us both," I say.

"Yes, I know," he replies, heading for the door. "Come with me."

He walks outside with the food and I follow, more slowly and far more unsteadily on the crutches than he is on two good feet. He looks over his shoulder at me. "You're okay?" he asks. "It's not much farther."

I nod and we continue on, past the barn, to a hay bale that sits at the top of a hill, facing west. He spreads a blanket on the ground and helps me sit, before pulling the food from the basket.

"A picnic?" I ask. It seems kind of odd to have a picnic forty yards from the house, but it's not a terrible idea. The view of the valley from here is amazing and at least we can get a bit of a breeze.

"You do this, where you're from?"

I shake my head. "No, not really." We did it once or twice, driving into the Alleghenies, when I was small, but that was before Kit died. Afterward, my mother went out of her way to avoid any time spent as a family if she could help it.

"I suppose you have better things to do, what with your televisions and drive-through restaurants."

Diplomacy requires I assure him a picnic is every bit as satisfying as watching television, but as my mouth opens to say something polite and meaningless, I realize the truth of it: this *is* as satisfying as television. Probably more.

"We don't have better things to do."

He gives me a sidelong glance, a doubting one.

I struggle to explain what I mean. It's nothing I thought about, before I began to spend time here with Marie and Henri, but as the words emerge I know they are unequivocally true. "At home you can watch TV for hours and hours, but when you leave it the time has gone and you have nothing to show for it. You don't even feel rested. You just feel tired, a little empty. And it's not memorable at all. All the hours you spend blend together."

"This will be memorable, at least," he says, nodding at the sun as it begins to set. The light retracts, sinks into itself until it looks like an orange ready for picking, just over the next hill. Sitting here, with the sun almost close enough to touch, a light breeze blowing, is an experience no show or movie could possibly replicate.

"We don't do this at home either," I say quietly, unpacking the basket. "Watching the sun set, I mean."

He glances at me. "For all your inventions, I think I'm glad I'm not from your time."

I might believe he was better off in 1938 too, if I didn't know what lies ahead for him. "It's much safer."

"I think you value safety far too highly," he says. "What use is it, if you have to give up the things you love in exchange?" I'm about to ask what precisely he thinks I'm giving up when he hands me a glass of wine. "Are you going to be okay with this?" he asks, nodding at the wine. "Walking back on the crutches?"

I laugh, holding the red liquid up to the dying light. "As you've stated, I have a hollow leg. I've never been drunk once in my life. And a glass back home is four times this size."

"Perhaps that's why there's so much free love in your day."

I roll my eyes. "Rumor has it sex is enjoyable. Isn't that reason enough?"

"*Rumor has it?*" he repeats. "What does that mean? I thought in your time sex 'wasn't a big deal'?"

I feel my cheeks heat and stare out at the vineyard to avoid his eye. "I was raised in a very religious household. Waiting for marriage...it's just one of those things my mother was very focused on."

He leans back. "For someone raised by a woman as awful as your mother, you certainly seem to care a lot about what she thinks."

I look at the sun without really seeing it. "She's my mother. It's not something I can help."

His arms cross, broad shoulders straining the fabric of his shirt. "I think I'd try, in your case," he says, not unkindly. "I certainly wouldn't allow her to dictate my behavior if I were you."

"She's not," I argue. "Mark and I...this summer when I get back, we're...never mind."

The tendons in his forearms are suddenly visible. "What do you mean?"

I flush. "I mean that part of the deal with me leaving this summer so suddenly was...*that*."

Henri's jaw drops. "You had to agree to sleep with this man solely in order to go on a trip?"

It irks me, the way he always manages to spin Mark's behavior into something evil. "No, of course not. You're twisting what I said. We're getting engaged once I'm back, which is as good as married, for one thing. But also it was shitty, the way I cancelled on him. So I ...promised to make it up to him."

His jaw draws tight. "A good man would not accept that offer. And a woman who knew her own value wouldn't have made it."

I roll my eyes. "I'm not giving away a kidney. It's sex. I assume I'll enjoy it as well."

"*That's* not how you decide to sleep with someone. You choose it when you can no longer stand *not* to choose it, no sooner."

It all sounds good, but I've never felt like that and I don't imagine I ever will. I've sometimes wondered if I'm just missing some hormonal impulse I'm supposed to have, although given how I react to the sight of Henri without a shirt, it certainly seems to be making an appearance now.

"Like I said, in my time, we don't take everything quite so seri ously. You're allowed to just enjoy what you enjoy without it having to mean something."

He is watching me again. "You're so busy defending the atti-tudes of your time, but you agree with me that it should mean something, or you'd have done it already. And if you've been with him for two years, it probably should have meant something by now."

I stare at the wine in my glass, as something rises in my throat, a lump that clogs it and makes me anxious I might cry. He's wrong, of course. I'm certain of it.

I'm just not quite as certain as I was.

"How did it go tonight?" Marie asks when she gets home. "Henri was not awful?"

I blink. The truth is that Henri has not been awful in a while, but it feels like something I don't quite want to admit. "No more so than ever."

"How did you keep the kitchen so clean?" she asks. "You can't sweep with the crutches."

A surly voice in my head retorts *yes, the crutches I need because of you,* but I no longer feel quite as much rancor about it. "We ate outside, actually."

Her eyes go wide. "You did?"

"At that hay bale on the far side of the barn, where the sun sets."

She is speechless for a moment. And then, finally, a small smile. "A *picnic*? Well," she says. "Well."

17

The following weekend, Marie-Therese and Henri decide there's no way I can avoid mass again, as telling the village I'm not Catholic—my suggestion—would apparently be far worse than skipping mass.

So on Sunday, instead of sleeping in—not that there seems to be much sleeping in here ever—I rise early to don the hose and the blue dress and curl my hair. All the effort—plus wearing garters, gloves and a hat—no longer seems strange to me. I feel frilly and girly, but as long as no one from home can witness it, I don't mind.

When I leave my room, Henri is waiting, lean and handsome in his suit, comfortable in his skin and the fine clothes. He looks like a man who attended Oxford: intelligent and arrogant and confident, certain of his place in the world. I envy him that.

He stands when I enter the room, eyes tripping over the dress to the shoes. He swallows. "I suppose you'll do," he says with half a grin.

I'm beginning to think that the more he approves, the less willing he is to say so. But would it kill him to compliment me just *once*? "You're such an asshole."

A brow raises as he heads toward the door. "I know it's asking a great deal, but if you could perhaps restrain your foul mouth and sharp tongue during mass, I'd greatly appreciate it."

I slowly raise my eyes to his. "Just because you don't curse much doesn't mean your tongue is any less sharp than mine."

His mouth tips up in an arrogant smirk. "Except I've had no complaints about my tongue so far."

I slide my gloves on and flash him a smile. "The only females I've seen you near since I arrived are livestock. Just because you can't understand them doesn't mean they're not complaining."

He walks out the door, choking on a laugh.

Marie comes downstairs just then. "You look like the cat who got the cream," she says with narrowed eyes, observing me.

I exhale. "I'm always a little happier when Henri leaves the room."

"Hmmm," she replies, still narrow-eyed. "So you claim."

HENRI DRIVES into town and parks on the street. When I reach for the door, he casts me a warning glance. "Open that door yourself and I'll break your other ankle too."

He grabs my crutches from the trunk. "What a strange world you live in," I say, when he finally reaches me and performs the *heroic* feat of turning a handle to release me from the car, "where it's not appropriate for me to open a door, but it *is* appropriate for you to threaten me with bodily harm."

"Have I ever touched a hair on your head?" he asks, opening Marie's door next.

"That would be a more convincing argument if you hadn't held me at gunpoint."

Marie groans. "Will you two not even stop on a Sunday?"

She marches ahead of us and Henri comes to my side. "You started that one," he says.

"You know, I'm not argumentative by nature," I reply. "You just bring it out in me."

"Likewise." He glances my way. The sunlight hides his expression. "So you and Mark never fight?"

I sigh, wondering where he's headed with this. I'm sure he can find a way to turn *anything* I say into an anti-Mark rant. "Almost never."

He grins triumphantly. "It means you will have no passion in bed," he says.

I roll my eyes. "Then I guess that means you and I *would*?"

He's so stunned by the question that he stops in his tracks. I feel burned alive by his gaze, by the way his jaw shifts and those eyes of his dip to my mouth before veering away. As if he allowed himself, for a moment, to consider it. "What a question to ask just before I walk into mass," he mutters. He turns toward the church steps and places a hand on my back. "Prepare yourself," he says.

"For what?"

He nods to the crowd ahead, already turning toward us. "This."

It feels as if every single person here is staring at me, and by the time we reach the first step, we are enveloped. His hand is on the small of my back, friendly to all who approach, but using his shoulders and the occasional menacing smile to make sure I get up the stairs safely, which is easier said than done with so many people stopping us to talk.

Ma cousine Americaine, Henri says again and again. And then he apologizes for the fact that I don't speak French as if it's a serious flaw, as if I'm a child who's spitting everywhere or won't stop hitting people.

Nearly everyone who approaches wants to meet me, aside from the young females, who only use my presence as a ruse to come hit on Henri. It's grown tiresome by the fourth step and by the time we reach the top, I'm tempted to start swinging my crutch.

We are nearly inside the church when we are waylaid by yet another pretty girl named Claudette, all dimples and shiny eyes. Her wide smile is only for Henri, although Henri introduces us anyway, making sure, as always, to mention I don't *speak a word of French*. I see something calculated enter her eyes upon learning this. She rests a gloved hand on his arm and moves in closer, casting a quick, mildly hostile glance at me. *We barely see you anymore*, she says to him in French. *She's stayed a very long time. It must be getting tiresome.*

The bitch is talking shit about me right in front of my face, and I clench every muscle not to react, praying, *praying* that Henri puts her in her place.

She's only here a few more weeks, he says mildly. Hardly the vigorous defense I'd hoped for. Disappointment twists a small knife in my stomach, and I turn away from them and begin heading inside, wishing I'd just refused to come.

Within seconds Henri has caught up with me, his hand once more on the small of my back. "Where are you going?" he asks.

"To sit," I say between clenched teeth. "I don't need your help, so don't let me get in the way of your flirting."

"I wasn't aware that I *was* flirting," he replies, steering me toward a particular pew. "And you have no idea what we even said."

"I don't have to speak the language to know flirting when I hear it," I reply coolly. He takes the crutches from me as I slide sideways into the pew. "Are you dating her?"

He raises a single brow. "What?"

"Dating, courting, wooing...whatever stupid expression you use. Are you doing it with her?"

He gives a low laugh. "How can I, when I spend all my free time bickering with you?"

Heat climbs in my chest and I face forward, knees pressed tight, pretending he is not there. That's when I see Marie, sitting to the left of the altar with the choir. She looks eager. Flushed and happy. Different than she is at home.

Her eyes flicker toward the door of the church and my head turns, wondering who she's looking for. The crowd is pouring in. What was it she said just after I arrived? That there was someone she wanted but he wasn't *suitable*. Is that who she's looking for? I glance back at her and am suddenly certain it is. The longing comes off her in waves.

Her eyes drop to the book in her hand, and then back toward the door. Whoever he is, she likes him a lot more than she's let on. She said he wasn't suitable. Does that mean he'll come in here with a fiancé or a wife? Or perhaps he's a different race, though it seems unlikely—a Klan meeting is more diverse than the membership of this church. I peek around Henri a second time.

"Do you always fidget so much?" he asks.

"I'm just wondering where all the handsome men are."

He raises a brow. "Being so near me all the time has been like staring at the sun, hasn't it?"

"Painful? Ill-advised?"

"Blinding," he corrects. "My looks make it impossible for you to appreciate lesser men."

I roll my eyes. "You may very well have ruined men for me, but not in the way you think."

The choir begins the first hymn and the congregation rises. I can hear Marie's voice, as angelic as her face, which is a quality we do not share. And she is *still* glancing at the door.

Henri holds the hymnal open for me.

"I don't sing," I tell him, and he smiles. A somewhat blinding smile, I reluctantly admit.

"Not enough profanity in the hymns for you?" he whispers.

I laugh quietly against my will and glance once more at Marie, who is watching the doors of the church now with something like reverence on her face. Except everyone is seated and she doesn't seem to be looking at any particular person.

She's still waiting, I realize.

Two altar boys enter, followed by an old man carrying a bible and a middle-aged woman carrying a chalice.

And behind them, the priest.

He is young, tall and extremely handsome, with the kind of broad shoulders that don't come from baptizing babies and hearing confession. *Father What-a-Waste,* my friend Rina would have called him back home. Marie's eyes lower as he passes, as if the whole world will see what's in her heart if she doesn't. And maybe they would, because I see it even with her eyes closed.

I wonder what it all means for the future—hers and Henri's. If she's truly the *hidden child* of the prophecy, and if the circle of light is related to her giving birth, which is certainly what it seems, how will she ever fulfill her destiny if she's so hopelessly in love with a *priest*?

And if she doesn't ever move on with her life, how can her brother move on with his?

I glance up at Henri, who looks sleepy and mildly bored. Completely unaware of the whole thing. I wonder if he'd be so open to Marie spending the time she does here if he realized why she was doing it.

AFTER MASS ENDS, we make our way toward the back of the church where a small refreshment table is being set up—with Marie's assistance, of course.

André is the first person who steps in our path. He bows his head. "I was hoping I might see you today," he says.

Henri makes a small noise of disgust, placing his hand on my arm and giving it a small tug. "We can't stay. We need to find Marie."

André arches a single brow at this, and I don't blame him. Henri is generally not rude to people other than me, but André appears to be the one exception.

"I'd be happy to take Amelie home," Andre offers. "My day is quite empty and I'm sure you have things to attend to on the farm." It's a masterclass in posturing, the subtle reminder that Henri's *peasant* labor is never done, while André is free as a bird. And though I'm annoyed with Henri, I can't say I especially like it.

"We have plans," my unhappy host growls, his hand still on my elbow.

Just then, the girl who accosted Henri before mass comes up to us, wide-eyed and delighted, as if it's so very unexpected to find us here when she *already saw us here.*

I meant to ask earlier, she says, *if you'll be at the dance next weekend.*

Henri glances at me. *I'm not sure yet*, he tells her.

You should come, the girl replies. *There will be plenty of men to entertain your cousin. Though she's a bit old for a babysitter.*

You obviously don't know my cousin well, he says.

André frowns at them both. "They're talking about the town dance," he says to me. "I hope you plan to come. It's still a week away—I don't suppose you'll be out of the cast by then?"

I glance down. "I have three more weeks, so if I come, I'm not sure how much dancing I'll be doing."

Henri shoots me a hard look. "You won't be doing any dancing. You'll probably fall over and break the other ankle too."

"Do you treat all your cousins as if they're made of glass?" asks André.

Henri straightens. He's several inches taller than Andre and for the first time, I get the sense that he's trying to make a point of it. "Just the ones who tend to break easily. Excuse us," he says abruptly, and with his hand firmly pressing on my back he all but pushes me to the left, toward the refreshment table where Marie is talking to Father Edouard.

Her eyes are shining, her cheeks are flushed. And, I notice, so are his. Father Edouard is looking at Marie with a sort of reverence I did *not* see on his face during mass.

I push back against Henri's hand. "Leave them alone," I say quietly. "Marie can come home later if you're in such a rush."

He glances at me. "*Why?*"

I sigh heavily. Even though I can't begin to imagine how this infatuation could turn out to be a good thing, I can't bring myself to ruin it for her. "She's busy."

He shrugs. "It's just Father Edouard. And we need to leave."

He steps forward and shakes the priest's hand, and then Father Edouard extends a hand to me. *You must be Amelie*, he says in French. *Marie speaks of you often.*

"Not often enough to tell you she only speaks English," says Henri, and Father Edouard laughs.

"Apologies," he says. "I forgot. But as Marie will tell you, I enjoy getting a chance to speak something other than French." His English is as perfect as Henri's, not even a hint of an accent.

"Are you British?" I ask.

He shakes his head. "Just raised by a British mother. And Marie says you're from Pennsylvania—I studied in Massachusetts for a while. That's close, I believe?"

I smile. "It depends on your definition of close. Were you in—"

"I'm sorry," Henri interrupts, "but I do need to get home. I think I may have left the paddock gate unlocked."

Marie's head tips, as confused as I am by his behavior. He's never once left that gate unlocked, and the horses are too docile to run even if he had. "I need to help with the children's classes," she says. "I'll walk home later."

Henri practically pushes me out the door, his hand heavy on my back even as we reach the stairs.

"Stop pushing me!" I hiss. "You're going to make me fall!"

His hand leaves my back, but he remains unhappy, some kind of weight on his shoulders that wasn't there when we arrived. He's silent on the walk to the car, his mind somewhere else.

He opens the door without even looking at me, grabs my crutches in the same manner.

"What the hell is wrong with you?" I demand once he's in the car.

His jaw flexes and he stares straight ahead. "I told you I was in a hurry to get home."

"And what was that about anyway?" I ask. "You never leave the gate open."

"I'm sorry," he says, a touch of acid in his tone. "If it's any consolation, you'll apparently have plenty of time to throw yourself at the men in town during the village dance."

"*Throw* myself? I didn't say two words to anyone but you!" I cry. "You were the one..." *making fun of me in French*. "Flirting," I finish.

His nostrils flare. "I saw the way you smiled at him. Don't deny it."

"The priest?" I ask. "You are *insane*. I was being polite."

"You were more than merely polite, but I was talking about André," corrects Henri. "Is it your goal to win over a rich man for every decade? I suppose that's one way to make sure you have a place to stay during your travels."

I press my palm to my forehead. "Are you serious right now? I wasn't flirting and if I was going to marry someone in another time, it sure as *hell* wouldn't be this one!"

He ignores me. "You are not reading to Madame Perot again. I don't like the way he looks at you."

I have no desire to read to Madame Perot, obviously, but he is not going to be the one who decides that for me. "Sorry, Henri," I reply crisply, "but where I'm from women aren't property that gets commanded around."

"No?" he asks. "Then why is it your boyfriend believes you should drop out of college and give up your dreams to move with him?"

"That's different," I reply. "He's not forbidding me to do anything and he's not commanding me either."

"No, he's just acting like your goals and desires are not equal to his own," Henri replies. "While I'm thinking about your safety."

"Well, I'm thinking about the fact that I'm an adult and can make my own decisions," I retort. "And reading to Madame, or spending time with André, are both decisions I don't need your help with."

MARIE COMES HOME BRIEFLY around lunch. There's been no sign of Henri since we arrived back here this morning. I help her prepare the *coq au vin*, one pan going to the bible study class held at the church this evening and one pan to stay here. I'm browning the onions while she chops vegetables behind me.

"I didn't realize priests were so attractive," I say casually. "I see now why your mass is so well-attended."

"Father Edouard?" she asks, shocked. "That's sacrilege."

I laugh. "You don't actually expect me to believe you haven't noticed? Just because he's a priest doesn't mean he's *invisible*."

She flushes. "It's inappropriate to look at him that way. He's chosen his path and we must respect his decision."

She's giving up too easily. I *saw* the way he looked at her. "I think he'd make a different decision readily if you gave him an opening."

Her beautiful face clouds over. "He's a man of God. He'd view what we do as witchcraft."

Perhaps I'm too willing to give up time travel, but Marie is very much the other extreme. It's as if the idea is impossible to her.

"Is being able to time travel really such a wonderful gift? I see how you use it mostly—to add to a shopping list? To fix a broken chicken coop before the animals get free? I can't believe you'd lose the man you love in order to keep doing it."

Her eyes flash as she glances over her shoulder at me. "It's not a gift. It's what I *am*, and unlike you, I do not plan to deceive the man I will marry. So, even if he were to decide he wanted to leave the church, I would still never choose him."

MARIE IS LONG GONE when Henri finally comes in. He says nothing to me until he's gone into the bath to wash up and change clothes, and then he emerges with damp hair and a contrite expression that has me ready to forgive him before he's said a word.

"Come to the hay bale," he says. "It's almost sunset."

Correction: I'm *almost* ready to forgive him. "Hmm," I muse, holding a finger to my lips, "that didn't sound like an apology."

He gives me a small bow. "I'm deeply sorry I accused you of throwing yourself at André. I'm certain that if you choose to throw yourself at him, you'll at least have the decency to do so in private."

I raise a brow. "That still doesn't sound like an apology."

"It was," he corrects. "I just paired it with an insult. Come on."

MARIE'S COQ-AU-VIN is too difficult to transport to our normal picnic spot, so we just grab odds and ends for dinner instead. By the time our meal is complete, the sun has set. He pushes our things off to the side and leans back against the hay bale.

"Close your eyes," he says.

I do as he says, leaning back just as he did. It's silent, and suddenly I'm aware of things I wasn't the moment before. Perhaps things I was trying hard to ignore: the heat of Henri beside me, the rise and fall of his chest moving his sleeve against my bare arm with each breath.

"What do you smell?" he asks.

I smell him—soap and freshly cut grass.

"Cow dung," I reply. "Is that not the only possible answer?"

He elbows me. "Keep trying. There are other things too."

"I smell your soap," I admit. I love the smell of his soap. I wonder if it still exists in my time. If it does, I will buy it just to remember him.

"I smell you as well," he answers. "When you arrived it was one of the first things I noticed about you, your smell. Like roses and sage and summer. I thought it was your soap, but I smell it even now."

"Is *that* why you held me at gunpoint?" I tease.

"No," he replies. "But it might be why I failed to shoot you on the spot. Let's pray that when the Germans come they haven't just bathed."

I laugh, but as I take in his perfect face and his broad smile, something cracks inside me at the same time. He is so many things, too many things. He can't die in the war, can he? Thirty million soldiers did, but it feels as if he deserves some special protection they didn't receive. I guess this is how every woman alive feels when her husband or son goes to war, except he's not my husband and he's not my son and I shouldn't care quite as much as I do.

"If your mother had known about the war," I tell him, "she'd have begged you to escape, you know."

He raises a brow. "Shall I leave some sort of welcome basket for the Nazis then, when I hand them my farm?"

"Better than handing them your sister."

"I can't hit her over the head with a club to make her leave," he says. "Despite what you think of me, I have my limits."

I close my eyes, willing myself to stop feeling upset. I can't make them do what they should and it might not make a difference anyway, but I can't stop wishing things were different.

"I'd agree to let you hit her over the head, just this once."

"You worry an awful lot about my sister for someone who never mentions her own," he replies.

I don't want to talk about my sister. At the moment I don't want to talk about anything. "We aren't close," I reply. "And my childhood isn't full of happy memories like yours. So there's not much to say."

His index finger glides, for a single breath, over the back of my hand. "Not everything you tell me needs to be happy, you know. Just give me one good memory, and one bad."

I swallow. I have to reach back pretty far to get to the good memories of Kit, and even those are laced with bad. "When we were little, we used to go swimming. We'd pretend we were mermaids and we'd lay on top of the water and compete to see who had better mermaid hair."

"What's mermaid hair?"

I laugh. "I don't even know. Long, and very wet. You'd get it good and soaked and then just kind of let it splay out over the surface of the water. Kit won," I say, my laugh smaller. "Every time." It's something I haven't let myself think of in years. And it's not a good memory. Telling him now doesn't make me happy. It makes me feel sick to my stomach.

He reaches out to pull a lock of hair free from this morning's updo. "She had more beautiful hair than you?" he asks, brow furrowed. "That's hard to imagine."

It's the closest he's ever come to paying me a compliment. I would like to point that out but hold back. "Our hair was identical, actually. Pale blonde, never got a real haircut."

"If your hair was identical, then how do you know she won?"

I shake my head. "I don't know. She just did. She always won everything." I begin picking up the remnants of our dinner. "We should go. Marie will be home soon."

His hand wraps gently around my wrist. "Now give me a bad memory."

I glance up at him. His face is earnest, but he has no idea what he's asking.

"Let's just leave it at the mermaid hair," I reply. "My bad isn't like other people's bad."

His hand is still on my wrist, keeping us connected when I want nothing more than to pull away and curl up somewhere.

"I don't care how bad it is," he says, sounding irritated. "I just want it to be something *real*."

My temper finally frays too thin. I'm so tired of the implication that I'm fake somehow simply because I want to keep some things to myself. My mother thinks I'm evil for being what I am, and he thinks I'm evil for trying to pretend I'm anything else, and the fact that I can never win exhausts me.

"Fine, you want real?" I ask. My voice is hard. "Here you go: Kit had to have her tonsils out and my mother stayed in the hospital with her. And when she finally came home, I told her I hated her and wished she had stayed away. She was just a little girl, and I was awful to her. There's your bad memory."

He tips his head. "I doubt you were some kind of demon child who said and did terrible things to the innocent. Something must have prompted it."

I swallow. "I don't have some pretty excuse for it. I was jealous. That's it."

"Why?"

I stare at my lap, at the tiny roses dotting the dress I changed into after mass. In truth, it was a lifetime of slights both great and small that led to my jealousy, but it's too much detail for the question he's asking, so I choose the most relevant.

"When I was seven I got meningitis, which is usually fatal. I was in a hospital about an hour from home for two weeks and my parents didn't come see me once. My mom told me afterward that all she felt when the doctor called to say I'd pulled through was disappointment. Seeing how different things were for Kit..." My voice breaks and I stop talking, shocked that even now, all these years later, I'm still upset. I rise and grab the crutches, desperately needing privacy. I've never told anyone that story and I have no idea why I shared it now, but I just want to be alone.

He's in front of me before I've even raised my head. "Where are you going?"

I glance away, feeling overwrought and humiliated by my disclosure. "Inside."

He pulls my crutches away from me, throwing them behind him. "Hey!" I shout. "What the—"

He pulls me hard against his chest, arms bound around me so tightly I can barely breathe, my nose pressed to his sternum.

"I'm sorry," he whispers. "I'm so sorry it was like that for you."

There's a lump in my throat. Something that happened ages ago shouldn't have me so upset, but it does, and I'm torn between wanting to be alone until this feeling goes away and wanting to stay right where I am, my head to his warm chest, breathing him in, feeling his heart beat against my cheekbone.

"I didn't tell you that story so you'd feel sorry for me."

"You told me because you were mad," he says.

One arm still pulls me close, but the other is on my chin now, forcing me to look him in the eye, and suddenly it feels like I can't get a full breath. I feel too much...and I think it has as much to do with him as it does the sister I lost. Because I am going to lose him too, whether it's because I'm leaving or because of the war that looms. I'm back where I've been too many times in my life, desperately wishing there was a bargain I could strike with God when I know it won't work.

"I'm sorry I pushed you so hard," he says. "I just think you've got secrets that will poison you if you keep holding on to them the way you are."

"What about your secrets?" I ask, my voice cracking. "Marie still has no idea why you came back. And if she did, she wouldn't insist on staying here, which she shouldn't because you—" My voice breaks. "You are going to *die* here if you don't explain to her what's really going on."

He holds my gaze. "I didn't think you cared."

Tears roll down my face. "I don't. I don't care at all."

We hear the sound of bike tires over gravel and step apart. Marie is walking her bike into the barn, but he continues to hold me there, as if he's trying to capture something before it passes.

"Oh," says Marie. He's finally let me go but her eyes are wide, taking the two of us in. "Were you crying? Is everything okay?"

Henri hands me my crutches and I propel myself forward, passing her on my way to the house. "I'm just tired," I reply. "But everything is fine."

I'm lying, again, of course. I'm lying about so many things to so many people I don't even know what the truth is anymore.

18

K it hits the water with an unimpressively small splash. It's our favorite game these days, swinging on the rope to see who will land farther. I hold my breath, waiting for her golden head to emerge, and when it finally does she is laughing. Her little arms paddle furiously, propelling her back to where the water is shallow enough to stand.

When she's finally near me she flips onto her back and floats, pulling her hair up so it is flat along the water's surface. "Look at my hair," she says. "Do I look like a mermaid?"

Yes. No. There's a small bite of unhappiness inside me as I decide on an answer. Kit is adorable, everyone's favorite. I can't blame them for it, really—she's my favorite too. But at the same time I can't help the small sting of envy I feel toward her. Why couldn't any of it be shared, all the love and attention that gets sent her way?

"Yes," I reply, swallowing down my envy.

She dives under water and heads for the shore again while I paddle listlessly, sulking over thoughts Kit will never understand. She grabs the rope again and begins to swing, pushing herself off the tree again and again, trying to gain momentum.

It isn't her fault. I could be the *only* child and I still wouldn't be the favorite. But sometimes it feels as if she's stolen what she has from me. If Kit and Steven didn't exist, I might be able to convince myself the problem was my mother. But they do, which leaves no doubt that the problem is me. I never saw it more clearly than when my mother stayed with Kit at the hospital as summer began. Such a small thing, but even now the sadness I felt wells in my throat, clogs it.

Kit continues to swing, going higher and higher, but her joy suddenly makes me mad.

"If you go too far, I'm not coming after you!" I shout and she sticks her tongue out at me, knowing good and well that I'll come for her if she can't swim back on her own.

I cleaned the house top-to-bottom on the day they came home from the hospital. I had visions of my mother smiling, looking pleased, or maybe proud of me, for once, but even an hour after they arrived, she still hadn't noticed. She didn't even seem to notice *me*.

I picked up, I finally whispered, and that's when she looked at me with her flat eyes and her mouth a thin, bitter line.

"You know what would be more helpful?" she asked. "If just once you would not stand there looking like a beaten dog."

Maybe she was right to be irritated. It's not as if I'd cleaned the house out of an honest desire to help. I did it merely hoping for a single crumb of the attention she showered on Kit.

Now, watching Kit swing on the rope, I wonder why I bothered. *Why did I try to make her happy when nothing I do ever makes her happy? I shouldn't have. I should have just asked why she hates me so much, why she never visited me in the hospital.* I picture it hard, hard enough that it feels real.

I hear Kit land in the water but the world has turned dark and air seems to rush around me. I have no idea what's happening, or how to make it stop. I land hard in the kitchen, naked and dripping water. My mother stands there, talking on the phone. Her eyes widen and I panic, as if I've been caught in a terrible lie. I scramble into a ball, waiting for the sting of her hand, for her raised voice, wishing desperately I was back in the lake...

And then I am. I'm back in the lake.

And I'm alone. Kit is gone and I'm completely alone.

The world is silent, empty.

And I begin to scream just to fill it back up with something.

"Amelie," pleads a voice. "Wake up. You're dreaming."

My eyes open. Henri is sitting on the edge of the bed beside me, his hands gently shaking my shoulders.

My sister is dead. When will I wake and not be surprised by this? My sister is dead and it's still my fault, all of it. And this secret I've kept for nearly a decade suddenly feels too heavy to carry on my own anymore. I don't feel capable of lying about it anyway—not to him.

"My sister is dead," I whisper. "I should have told you." I roll to my side and begin to cry. He sits with me, his hand on my shoulder.

"It was just a dream," he says gently. "Just a nightmare."

What's he going to think of me when he knows the truth? I came here not because I was brave but because I was such a damn coward I couldn't continue to face my sister in dreams. Such a coward I couldn't bring myself to admit to Henri I'm the reason she drowned.

I take a shuddering breath. "No," I whisper. "It wasn't. My sister is dead. She kept coming into my dreams, telling me to find Marie."

He pushes the hair from my face. His jaw is open, confusion and doubt in his eyes. "I don't understand. She died...recently?"

I look away. "No, she died when I was eleven. It was my fault. I was supposed to be watching her, but I time traveled by accident and she drowned."

Instead of pulling away, he sinks to the floor so we are face-to-face. He looks horrified, and sad, and then he pulls me against his chest and holds me there, tightly. I'm frozen, relishing the feel of him and the steady thump-thump-thump of his heart while I wait for the other shoe to drop, for what I'm telling him to sink in: my sister is dead and it's all on my hands.

"If you time traveled by accident, how does that possibly make this your fault?" he asks.

There are ways to spin almost anything to make yourself sound blameless, but I am definitely not that. Just ask anyone in my home town.

"When Kit died, my mother let people think I did it because I was jealous. And she was right. I was. It happened because I was jealous. That's why I time traveled."

He pulls back just enough to see my face. "An accident is an accident," he says. "Regardless of the reason it happened."

"My mother doesn't see it that way," I whisper.

His brow furrows. "Your mother was the adult. And she should have known that at such a young age time travel is out of your control. She made a poor choice, and continues to make a poor choice, by telling you you're to blame."

I want to believe him. I do. But there's a decade of recrimination behind me, insisting I shouldn't get off so easy. "But if I hadn't time-traveled, it wouldn't have happened."

His face is inches from mine. He gives me a sad smile as he pushes the hair off my face. "My mother blamed herself when my father died," he says quietly. "She went to visit him where he was posted, arranged a weekend pass for him. His regiment deployed while he was there, so he got sent to another one going to Caporetto, which is where he died. Would he have been killed anyway? Probably. But my mother felt as if his death rested on her head...just as I feel her death rests on mine."

I meet his eyes for the first time since the conversation began. "How could your mother's death be your fault? You weren't even *here*."

He stares at his hands, now entwined with mine. "If I hadn't gone away to Oxford, I might have convinced her not to leave. And if I die in this war you claim is coming, Marie will find a way to blame herself. She will be convinced there was something she could have done." His eyes search mine, darker, urging me to understand. "So if some of the guilt must rest on your head, if you refuse to see that you were an innocent little girl given a task that was beyond you, so be it. But you need to know that it doesn't make you evil. It just means you're human. Each of us is presented with infinite choices, and we never know whether they were wrong or right ones until it's too late."

I nod, swallowing around this lump in my throat. What he's said...it doesn't relieve my guilt, but it normalizes it. It gives me a single moment or two in which I can believe it's possible I'm not a monster, not something inherently evil and cursed. Maybe, like his mother, I'm just someone who made the wrong choice.

"Thank you," I whisper.

He rises from the side of the bed and I have to resist the impulse to reach for his arm.

"You'll be okay?" he asks.

I nod, but the dream is still too recent. I don't want to see that empty lake again. He pauses and then goes to the chair across the room.

"Close your eyes," he says. "I'll stay until you fall asleep."

I shouldn't accept this. He rises early and he's going to be exhausted. But I don't want him to go. "Thank you, Henri," I say settling into the pillow. "You can ridicule me for this in the morning. I won't get mad."

His mouth lifts. "You take all the fun out of it by giving me permission."

"Well since you're going to ridicule me anyway, can you pull the chair closer?"

He laughs but he does it, coming right up beside me and resting his palm on my forehead. "Sleep, little thief. I'll make sure you're kept safe."

"I know," I say quietly. "You've been doing it since I arrived."

And with his hand on my head, I float off into a dreamless sleep.

19

W hen I wake in the morning, the sun is pouring
through the windows and Henri is gone, though I
know he stayed because when I woke just before
dawn he was asleep in the chair, his hand still on my head. No
one's ever done that for me before, but I guess I've also never
been able to bring myself to ask for it either.

There's no sign of the sweet version of Henri when he comes
in that day at lunch. He hasn't shaved and there are circles under
his eyes. I blame myself for both.

"Amelie needs a dress for the dance," Marie-Therese tells
him. "Can you drive us to Reims in the morning?"

I glance up from the peas I'm shelling. Marie hadn't even
mentioned the dance to me prior to now, but suddenly it's as if
we've spoken of nothing else for days on end. I can't say I particularly share her interest, since I imagine the evening will be spent
watching her dance while every other girl within twenty miles
throws herself at Henri.

His eyes linger on me for just a moment. "No," he says. "I'm
busy this week. And she has dresses."

I shrug. "I don't need a dress. I'll wear the blue. And it's not like *I'm* trying to win anyone over," I remind her with a knowing look.

"Nor I," she replies primly. "But the blue is not good for dancing and nothing else you have is fancy enough."

Henri's fork lands on his plate with a *clang*. "She won't be doing any dancing, Marie."

I frown. I'd come to the same conclusion, but whether I dance or not will be my decision, not his. And why shouldn't I dance? Is he worried I'll get in his way with *Claudette?*

"I might," I say sharply. "And it would be nice to get a new dress."

"Good luck walking, then," says Henri. "Because as I already told you, I don't have time."

He's not that busy, he's just being an asshole for some reason I can't fathom. Fortunately, I'm pretty good at being an asshole too.

"That's fine," I say with a smile. "I'll see if André can take us instead."

By some miraculous feat of scheduling, Henri decides he has time to drive us to Reims after all. I try hard not to gloat but he's surly the entire trip anyway, muttering about a wasted morning and making it sound as if the entire fate of the vineyard will be determined by the hour or two our trip will take.

Reims is a true city, busy and vital, not that I'm given much of a chance to see it. Henri pulls up to one clothing store, helps me out of the car and informs Marie-Therese we have thirty minutes or can walk home.

The shop is different from shops back home, or even Le Bon Marché, where Henri took me in Paris. Instead of racks of clothes, a shopgirl brings you dresses to look at, based on your size. Though it's supposedly elegant, I find it irritating, especially when she pushes me to consider a dress that looks like something a toddler would wear on Easter.

Fortunately, Marie is hell bent on finding the right dress and sends each of them back with the dignity of a queen until, just before the thirty-minute mark, one finally meets with her approval—a bright poppy red, with a gathered bodice that cuts low across the chest and tiny cap sleeves. She smiles at me in the mirror. "He won't know what to do with himself," she says.

I raise a brow. "*Who* won't?"

She schools her features. "André of course," she replies innocently. "Who else?"

THE FRIDAY before the dance is the first evening Marie has been gone all week. Henri asks if I want to come outside, grinning in a way that makes me suspicious. He heads out and I follow on the crutches. After nearly four weeks with a broken ankle, I've almost forgotten there was a time when I could barely manage on them. He spreads a blanket in front of the hay bale and helps me lower myself to the ground. I let him, even though I no longer need help.

The sun is already on its way out, solidifying into a fixed ball of color, far to the west.

"I've brought you a treat—a very large chocolate bar—but you need to earn it."

I glance up at him. "That sounds dirty."

He gets a slow smile on his face. "For a woman who's never been with a man your mind certainly goes in that direction a great deal. Do you want to hear about the very large chocolate bar or not?"

I roll my eyes. "*You're* the one making this dirty. Talking about the *very large* chocolate bar. So how *large* is it?"

He meets my gaze. "Shockingly large. Far more than you can fit in your greedy little mouth."

Your greedy little mouth. My stomach clenches, an unexpected spike of want deep in my gut.

"Anyway," he continues, "do you want to learn how you will earn the chocolate, or do you want to continue to drive this conversation in a very inappropriate direction?"

In truth, I'd like to continue sending this conversation in an inappropriate direction, but I suppose I've already passed into the realm of *unladylike* and shouldn't push it. "Fine, how do I earn the chocolate?"

"By eating it with me down by the lake." He pulls the bar out of a saddlebag and opens it, letting the smell waft my way. I've always had a somewhat ambivalent relationship with chocolate, or did until I arrived in 1938, where sweets have been extremely hard to come by. Now I think I might punch a small child to get my hands on it.

I narrow my eyes at him. "I'm not going to the lake."

He shrugs. "Fine. Then I guess the chocolate is mine." He waves it in front of my face and I breathe it in. I can almost taste its scent on my lips.

"Wave that thing in front of me one more time and I will snatch it right out of your hands."

He breaks off a small piece, relishing it as it melts against his tongue. "Such good chocolate too."

"It's not that big anyhow," I reply. "I've seen much, much larger."

"Next you'll tell me size doesn't matter," he says, laughing as he breaks off another small piece.

He waves it in front of my face and I'm done. I lunge for it, landing atop him, scrambling, without a thought in the world about whether my dress gets filthy or the weight of my cast bruises his shins. It lasts all of two seconds before I find myself flipped onto my back, his weight pinning me down in the dirt.

He grins, triumphant. "Did you really think that would work, little thief? I'm twice your size." We are both laughing, struggling like children. There's nothing sexual about it, but my pulse is racing and I feel set free, abandoned from my normal restraint. Nothing matters more than winning. Even if I wind up shoving that chocolate bar in the dirt.

My hand snakes out and I pinch his side hard, the way I once did with Steven. Somehow I'm certain he's as ticklish as my brother once was—and I'm right. His body jerks sideways in surprise and I use the momentum to flip him on his back straddling him with my hands pressed to his chest.

"Give me the chocolate," I demand.

His expression has changed, eyes glittering with something dark and determined I haven't seen there before, mouth slightly ajar.

"No," he says. His voice is rough.

I reach for the chocolate, my face hovering just over his when I feel it. Only his pants and a bit of my bunched-up dress separate us, but there's no denying the size and the status of the thing directly between my legs. His face, an inch below mine, looks tortured and when I shift he flinches, releasing a small sound that contains so many things—pain and restraint and defeat and hunger, all rolled into one.

He uses my surprise to flip me again, and when I'm under him he holds some of his weight off me, but not all of it. His breathing is heavy as his eyes brush over my face, resting on my mouth. I'm fairly certain my breath has stopped entirely.

I want what will come next so badly that I swear I can feel it happening. My lips swell with that future kiss, my body taut and tormented, skin eager for the rough press of his unshaved jaw. I already know how soft his mouth will feel, what it will be like to slide my hands through his thick hair and pull him closer. It's all I can do not to arch into him to make it happen faster.

He flinches. "You may have the chocolate," he says, removing himself.

His absence feels like rejection, and it is knife sharp. It makes me want to lash out at him somehow, or merely have a tantrum I can blame on him.

"Too much excitement for you?" I ask.

His eyes lower to my chest, where my nipples are poking against the thin material of the dress. "Not just for me, it would seem," he says, and then he saunters away, completely at ease with the entire exchange while I am left with some combination of furious and confused and so excited it borders on pain.

And I should be none of these things. I scoot back to the blanket and lean against the bale of hay, looking for any possible way to justify what nearly happened, justify how much I *wanted* it to happen.

Mostly I'm just astonished it happened at all. I've never reacted to Mark in that way. Granted, we've never fought over a chocolate bar before—Mark wouldn't act like Henri did, taunting me with it like a child. But still, I wanted that kiss more than I've ever wanted anything in my life. I wanted it like a drowning man wants something to grab onto—desperately, gaspingly. I still do. I've been so proud of my restraint all this time but now I have to wonder if I've managed to hold onto my virginity simply because no one ever made me want to lose it.

In that moment with Henri just now? I wanted to lose it.

20

On the night of the dance, after bathing, I slide the dress over my head. It's the most beautiful thing I've ever owned and the color suits me perfectly, a swirling red flame that sets off the pale yellow of my hair and the gold in my skin from these weeks in the sun.

All I can think of is Henri's reaction to it. I picture a repeat of last night—of his hands around my wrists and the feeling of him pressed against me. It shouldn't matter what he thinks, but I've never hoped for a reaction more in my life.

Will he ask me to dance? Will things be different between us? As hard as it is to imagine, it's even harder to imagine that they *won't* have changed after last night.

"*Dieu*," says Marie-Therese when she enters the room to do my hair. "No one will even look at poor Claudette Loison with you in the room."

"And they won't look at me with *you* in the room," I reply as she pushes me into a seat. In an amethyst dress, her eyes look impossibly green and her black hair shines, standing in perfect waves to her shoulders. It seems nearly impossible that André would choose any girl in the country over her.

"Pah," she says. "I'm not interested in anyone there."

"And I am?" I ask in the mirror.

Her eyes meet mine. "Aren't you?" she asks. "Just a little bit?"

I blush. Is it so obvious, my crush on her brother? God, I hope not. "No, I have a boyfriend, remember?"

She raises a brow at that but wisely chooses not to say anything. When she's finished with my hair, she insists on mascara and red lipstick. I've never worn red lipstick in my life because the last thing I need is to call more attention to my lips, but she insists it's the style and I'll admit that it's a nice effect, the red lips with the red dress. If it weren't for the cast, I'd be feeling pretty elegant right now.

We exit the room just as Henri comes into the kitchen, looking extremely handsome in his freshly pressed shirt. He tells Marie she looks nice and then turns toward me and does a double take—exactly what I'd hoped for, except the surprise of the first glance is followed by unhappiness upon the second.

"I'll be outside," he says, turning on his heel. "Let's get this over with."

Marie hasn't noticed the slight because she's busy gathering things, but I feel it deep in the center of my chest. I walk outside, directly to the trunk of the car, and throw the crutches inside myself, ignoring his hand when he tries to help me. All this effort, I realize with a sinking stomach, was put forth on his account. And for a moment when he first walked in the room, I thought maybe he was going to make it worthwhile. Instead he's acting like it pisses him off.

THE DANCE IS HELD in a mansion which was once, apparently, the palace of some lesser prince. Though the decorations are meager, the place is already so adorned with crown molding and frescoes and gold filigree that adding anything to it would have been overkill.

We enter the ballroom to find the dance floor completely full. Most of the couples are full-on swing dancing, something I doubt I'd be able to manage even without a cast and definitely not with one. In my head I'd pictured 1938 as a dark time in the world, a time in which people began tightening their belts and preparing for war. But it isn't that way at all. These people are my age, for the most part, and they are all so *alive*, so silly and happy and enthusiastic, just like twenty-somethings anywhere. They still believe this year, this time in their lives, is a big, fabulous beginning and they are exuberant about it. It makes what lies ahead for them that much more heartbreaking.

We get five feet into the room and Marie is whisked away by some friendly boy who waves to Henri as they go. Henri remains by my side, looming over me with those broad shoulders as if I'm something highly fragile, likely to shatter if touched. We move into the room with his hand on the small of my back, his eyes daring anyone to get close to us.

Claudette, however, doesn't heed the warning. The moment she spies him she's moving toward us, and he doesn't seem to mind when *she* gets too close.

You look lovely, Henri tells her, and my heart begins a long slide to the floor.

He couldn't say a single word to me tonight—not when he walked into the house nor on the entire drive here—but two seconds into seeing *Claudette* and he's got a compliment at the ready. It stings more than I can begin to admit.

She grabs his hand, begging him to dance with her, and he demurs with a polite smile, telling her he needs to get me situated first.

"If she wants to dance, go ahead," I tell him, gritting my teeth. *By all means, Henri, if she's so fucking lovely, you should dance with her.* "I'll be fine."

He opens his mouth to argue and I turn to hobble away on my crutches, making the decision for him while I try to persuade myself coming here wasn't a colossal mistake. So what if I wind up alone in a corner all night, watching Henri dance with his future wife? I get a firsthand view of a 1930's dance in pre-war France.

"You're not ditching me that easily," says Henri behind me.

I look back at him, feeling inexplicably upset. "Go ahead. You obviously wanted to dance with her and I'm perfectly capable of finding a chair for myself."

"You don't seriously think I want to swing dance?" he asks with a brow raised. He grabs a chair at an empty table and holds it for me.

"Why not?" I ask. "She's very pretty. I'd think that would induce you to dance whether you wanted to or not."

His brow furrows. "I'll get us cocktails," he says. "Perhaps that will improve your mood."

He walks away, but no sooner has he left than a man I don't recognize drops into his seat.

"Exactly who I was hoping to talk to!" he says. "I thought I'd have to wait until Henri was in the bathroom before I got my chance."

He's young and handsome in a slightly more polished way than Henri. More like Mark, actually. To my surprise I find I don't prefer it.

"Have we met?" I ask.

He smiles. "From what I've heard, the Durands only let you leave home to attend mass, and since I try to make sure I'm still *asleep* during mass, meeting you has proved difficult. My name is Luc. What would you like to drink?"

"I think Henri—"

Luc waves his hand. "Henri will come back with something dull. Have you ever had a sidecar?" He grabs someone passing by and pushes some francs in his hand, before clapping him on the back. "There. He'll be back with our drinks in a moment, but hopefully I'll have persuaded you to run off to Paris with me before he returns. I doubt your cousin is going to let me linger long enough to see you finish a drink."

"Paris?" I ask.

"Yes," he says with a crooked smile. "We're heading there once they've run out of booze here. I promise you a night you'll never forget." He gives me such an unapologetically lecherous look that I can't help but laugh.

"Got Durand away from her already?" says one of two men approaching the table.

Luc leans toward me. "Here come my friends, trying to move in the moment I've got you to myself. They're very bad people. I don't know why I like them." He turns to them as they take seats at the table. "Go away. I got to her first."

They both laugh, introducing themselves to me in English, though they don't speak it with Luc's ease.

Henri is near the bar with drinks in hand, surrounded by a half circle of females vying for his attention. I'm sure he's told all of them they look *lovely* too, though he appears to be trying to get away from them. I accept the drink from Luc when it's delivered, taking some small amount of consolation from Luc's conversation in French with Jean and Marc, rude though it is.

No wonder Henri's been keeping her to himself, says Jean.

Can you marry a cousin? asks Marc.

No, but I bet you can fuck one if you keep it quiet, replies Luc.

Luc turns to me, asking about my trip here and how long I plan to stay and if I'm ready to leave for Paris yet because the dance is already boring him. Suddenly Henri is looming over us both. He sets a drink in front of me with an irritated glance at my half-empty sidecar.

Trying to get my cousin drunk, Barbier? he asks Luc.

I was hoping I might, Luc replies. *No luck thus far, however.*

I've never seen Henri smile in quite such a threatening way

before. *If I see you near her again, I'm going to smash your pretty face wide open,* he says quietly, still smiling as if his words are pleasant, *and there won't be enough liquor in the world to get you laid. Now get out of my seat.*

Luc raises a brow and shrugs, leaning over my hand with a broad smile. "Your cousin is telling me I need to leave. But if you want to come to Paris with us, let me know. I'll help you escape." He moves away with a wink, and Henri drops into the chair he vacated.

"Stay away from Luc," he says. "He's not a good person."

I finish my sidecar. "Tell me something, Henri, who *are* the good people in Saint Antoine? Because as yet I've only heard you mention the bad."

He glances over at me. "There aren't any."

"Except for you?"

He picks up his glass and empties it. "Not even me," he replies.

We watch Marie dancing, flushed and happy. I envy her mobility and feel sorry for her at the same time—this is who she could be and should be all the time, if their lives were less closed off.

"She should be at university," I say.

"I know," he says. "She deserves far more than a quiet life on the farm."

I glance at him. "So in spite of all your garbage about a woman's place and being ladylike, you'd be okay with her working, maybe doing something that isn't traditional for females?"

He looks at me incredulously. "I can't believe you feel you need to ask me that. Of course I would. I'd want her to do whatever makes her happy."

"Then you must see that it's not right, keeping her stuck here."

His jaw tightens. "I'm doing it to protect your kind and your way of life. And a lot of things aren't right, but we're all going to have to learn to live with them."

The music changes, and everyone on the dance floor begins doing a particular dance I don't recognize. "What is that they're doing?" I ask him.

"The Lindy Hop," he says, as if it's obvious. "It's named after your compatriot, Charles Lindbergh. I'd think you'd know that."

I lean toward him, still watching the dance floor. "He died not long after I was born. He's only a compatriot to me in the way Joan of Arc is one to you."

He laughs. "You do realize Joan of Arc lived 500 years ago, yes? It's not as if she and I just graduated a few years apart."

I don't laugh, the way I normally might. Disappointment has left me feeling dangerously unstable. If I wasn't on crutches I'd already have left.

"You seem unhappy tonight," he says quietly, but the thought goes no further, because another set of girls is approaching the table to talk to Henri. He rises, kissing their cheeks, telling them both in turn how beautiful they look tonight. I must be the only female in the entire damn room he can't say it to, and I've had it. I will walk home on the crutches, or perhaps I'll even go to Paris with Luc. It's a feeling I've experienced many times at home, this misery so deep that I'll grasp onto anything to keep myself afloat.

He's talking to them about some fair in Eperney and I grab my crutches and begin striding away without even excusing myself.

I've only made it two table lengths away before he's at my side again, placing his hand on my forearm to hold me in place.

"Where are you going?" he asks. "Come back to the table before some drunk knocks you over."

I snatch my arm from his grasp, turning my head to meet his eye. "Fuck off, *Henri,*" I hiss. "I don't need a babysitter."

His jaw drops. "What the hell is wrong with you tonight? It's as if you want—" he cuts himself off mid-sentence, glaring at a boy standing just behind me. *She's not here for your viewing plea-sure*, Henri snaps at him. *Look away if you'd like to keep those eyes the rest of the night.*

"What was that about?" I ask.

"He was about to knock into you. I told him to be careful of your ankle."

I hold his eye. "Really? And what did you say to Luc?" I ask.

He shrugs. "I told him you are engaged. Was I wrong?"

"Yes," I reply, getting ready to move again. "You were wrong because I don't need you speaking for me as if I'm a child." I set my crutches in another direction but am stopped by Marie, who skips toward us, flushed and smiling.

"I've found you at last!"

Henri raises a brow. "We've been here over an hour and you were on the dance floor the entire time, so don't pretend you've been looking for us."

"Who were you dancing with?" I ask.

She waves her hand lazily. "Just Xavier. He was in Henri's class. But I need to rest. Can we sit?" She turns to Henri. "And Claudette is looking for you. You'd better dance with her or there will be hell to pay."

He frowns. "You'll keep an eye on Amelie?" he asks.

I roll my eyes and begin moving through the crowd again. I'm twenty-one for God's sake. I can't imagine why Henri's decided to act like I'm some three-year-old he's saddled with for the night.

Marie is by my side a moment later. "Can we sit?" she asks. "I'm exhausted."

I'm tempted to mention that I'd be exhausted from dancing too if my ankle wasn't broken, but I already know what she'll say in response: *you wouldn't be here at all if your ankle wasn't broken.*

We grab two chairs and she fans herself with a program of some kind. "Are you having fun?" she asks.

I force myself to smile, watching Claudette pull Henri onto the dance floor. "Yes," I reply. "It's a very nice dance."

For someone who claimed to have no interest in swing danc-ing, he does it quite well, and that doesn't surprise me. Henri's one of those men for whom athleticism comes easily, naturally. Even the things he *doesn't* want to do, he does well. And as much as he's hurt my feelings tonight, I wish I were the one out there dancing with him.

"They make a pretty couple, don't they?" asks Marie-Therese, observing them.

I shrug. They do, but I refuse to agree to it. "So who's this Xavier?"

"I told you," she says without interest. "Just someone who went to school with Henri."

"He was cute," I say, waiting for a reaction from her. "Is he nice?"

She nods, barely paying attention to the question. "Very."

"He didn't ask you out?"

She takes a sip of her drink. "He did. I told him I couldn't while we still had company here."

I laugh. "Oh my God. You stick me with a broken ankle and then use me as your excuse? It's one date. Why not go out with him?" *And move on from the priest, since you refuse to act on it. Move on with your life so Henri can move on with his.*

"This town is not so big that you can just go on a single date without repercussions. He's someone I'll have to run into for the rest of my life. And speaking of people we keep running into, André is coming this way."

I sigh. André is perfectly nice, but I'm not interested in him in the least and I'm feeling slightly too tired and disgruntled to be pleasant right now.

He holds his hand out to me. "May I have the next dance?"

I shake my head. "I can't get out there. Not in a cast."

His eyes twinkle. "But you could if they played a *slow* song, couldn't you?" As if on cue, the music changes, and a ballad begins. "Don't tell me I bribed him for no reason," says André with a grin.

He leads me to the dance floor and we pass Henri and Claudette, who are just on the way off. Henri's eyes darken as we pass. "Your cousin doesn't seem to like me too much," says André.

"Don't take it personally," I reply. "He doesn't like me too much either."

He places one hand politely on my waist and clasps the other and we begin to dance the way they mandated in high school, one body width apart. I find myself thinking about last night with Henri and the chocolate bar, the way we were pressed together, that desperation in his eyes when I was on top of him. How was that only yesterday, when today I'm apparently the only unattractive female in the whole town? My God, what a wasted effort this all was.

André asks if I'm having a nice time and I smile at him. "This is my first dance of the evening, so at least I can say it's improving."

The floor crowds quickly and he pulls me closer. "Here," he says, after a moment, "come with me. People are getting too close to your cast."

He pulls me into the hallway and off to a balcony on the other side, and we are suddenly alone. "Oh," I say. "I thought you were taking me to another part of the dance floor."

He pulls me toward him, holding me closer than necessary. "We can still dance," he says, his breath gusting against my ear before he pulls me closer still, throwing me off balance just enough that I land against his chest. "It's better when it's private like this, I think."

I pull back but he doesn't release me. "I think this will look a little inappropriate if anyone comes out here," I say, trying to wriggle from his grasp.

"Who cares?" he asks. "Are you really so worried about what your cousin will say?"

His head lowers as if he plans to kiss me, although I think I've made it amply clear that I'm trying to push him off. I'm saved by Marie-Therese, who throws open the curtains and stands there looking at us with wide eyes.

"Henri is looking for you," she says, nervously. "We're leaving now."

"What a shock," says André drily, slowly releasing me. I stumble in my haste to get away and hobble back toward the ballroom while Marie *thanks* him for watching me and then runs to my side.

"Are you okay?" she asks, steering us down the side hall instead of the main ballroom.

"I'm fine," I say between my teeth. "Although I don't understand why the hell you just *thanked* him for watching me. You treat that family like royalty."

She looks at me uncertainly. "Henri and I have no family at all. No grandparents, no parents, no aunts or uncles. If something happens, we may need to rely on the people of the town to help us, and because of that, alienating anyone is a bad idea, and alienating the Beauvoirs is an especially bad idea, because they are wealthy and employ a lot of people here, and much of the town will take their cues from them."

I sigh. I was about to insist I wasn't going to read to Madame Perot again but I see Marie's point. She can't afford to piss people off, and I only have a few more weeks here, so I'm certainly not going to piss anyone off on their behalf. It's not as if André actually did anything. He just acted like my opinion didn't matter the first moment he had the option to ignore it. What is it Henri said? *Don't judge a man until you've seen him without an audience.* I suppose now I understand what he meant.

"Where are we going, anyway?" I ask.

"To the front," she says, worrying her lip. "Henri has your crutches."

"So he sent you after me like I was a child on the loose," I reply. "I guess that gave him some extra time with Claudette."

Her lips twitch. "Actually I was the one who demanded he wait, because I was worried he would wind up killing André if he went out there and saw the wrong thing."

I groan. "Jesus, Marie! What did you think we were doing out there?"

She lifts a shoulder. "There's only one reason to go on a balcony with a man alone."

Henri is pacing in front like a caged tiger, and he rounds on me the second we emerge, "Had fun out there, did you?"

"Fuck you, Henri," I hiss. "I didn't even know we were going onto a balcony. He said he was worried about my cast and we were going somewhere with more room."

His eyes remain narrowed. "Are women really so naïve in your time that you didn't understand what that meant?"

I move toward the exit. "Maybe men in my time just aren't so underhanded about their motives."

His hand wraps around my bicep to stop me. "Did he try something?"

I glance at Marie, who's looking extremely worried. Her eyes plead with me not to make things worse. "We danced for all of two seconds and he asked me why you don't like him," I snap. "Satisfied? You were so determined all night to make sure I didn't have any fun, and rest assured, I didn't."

We don't say another word to each other the entire way home. He drives, his jaw locked tight, while I sit beside him, my hands clenched in my lap. Only Marie-Therese speaks, chattering on in back about the band and the clothes and the drinks, as if it was the most spectacular night ever, when I know for a fact she didn't enjoy it as much as she wants to pretend.

"And wasn't Amelie lovely tonight, Henri?" she asks as we pull up to the house. "Not a man in the room could take his eyes off her."

I wait. I wait for one kind word and I know he's not going to give it to me.

"Perhaps if her dress was less bright," he replies, "it wouldn't have been an issue."

It hurts. All I wanted from the night was for him to notice me. I've got no business wanting that, but I did want it, badly, and he never gave an inch. Instead, he acted like I was a burden, and it reminds me very much of my childhood. Of feeling desperate for a single word of approval or praise or love and only getting a list of what I'd done wrong instead.

Marie climbs from the car without waiting for him, calling him several choice words in French as she slams her door, and I try to follow, pushing my door open and climbing out less steadily.

"Just wait," he grumbles, turning off the car.

I ignore him, hobbling slowly toward the house over uneven ground.

"Amelie," he shouts, "just wait. You're not supposed to be walking out here without your crutches, especially in the dark."

I round on him. "Don't worry. My dress is so *bright* and *garish* and *attention-grabbing* I'm sure it'll provide sufficient light."

He walks toward me, contrition replacing some of the anger that's been on his face since we left the dance. "I'm sorry," he says. "Your dress wasn't too bright. I shouldn't have said it."

I begin to walk away again. "Come on," he calls. "I said I was sorry. What's the matter?"

I take a deep breath. I refuse to cry over this. I've suffered far worse and I don't need his approval. I'm never even going to see him again in a few weeks anyway.

"When Marie asked you, not once but twice, if you thought I looked nice, all you had to say was yes," I hiss. "Don't worry. I'd never in a million years believe you *meant* it. But you couldn't even do that much. And it wouldn't hurt if you were an asshole to everyone, or maybe it wouldn't hurt as much...but I saw you tonight and you're not. You were only an asshole to me."

He looks uncertain for the first time all night. "Of course you look nice," he offers.

I slowly raise my eyes to his. Every hope I had for the evening is gone, and it leaves me feeling hollowed out inside, emptied. Even replying to him takes energy I no longer to seem to have. "It would already have been meaningless if you'd said it the first two times Marie asked. For you to say it now because you think I'm upset means even less. I don't give a shit what you think anyway. It's just time for me to go home."

I take the crutches from him and walk inside the house, certain I'll hear something about my unladylike mouth before I reach my door, but it doesn't come. Instead he walks up behind me in the kitchen, where not a single light flickers, and places a hand on my shoulder.

"You're exquisite," he says quietly. "You're exquisite when you're outside feeding the chickens and when you're in here scrubbing laundry, sweaty and annoyed with me. You took my breath away when I walked in the room tonight...something I assumed you must realize since no one at the dance could look away from you."

I swallow and turn toward him. His dismissal tonight hurt more than I could even admit to myself until now, and my eyes threaten to well over. He places one hand on my waist and I feel like I can scarcely breathe.

"Then why didn't you say so?" I whisper, my voice rough. "You acted like you didn't even want me there."

He glances between us, at his hand on my waist, at the hint of cleavage rising above the bodice of the dress, and takes a deep breath. "I didn't want you there tonight because I knew exactly what would happen."

"What did you think would happen?"

His lips press to the top of my head. "That everyone would discover a secret I wanted to keep to myself," he says quietly, and then he turns and walks away.

Nothing has changed, and everything has changed.

I was awake for a long time after he left me at the door to my room, facing some facts I probably should have faced far sooner—about how much more I feel for Henri than I should, and how much my feelings for Mark seem to pale in comparison. I don't know what this will mean when I go home, but what it means while I'm here is that I can't look at Henri the way I did before. It's more than a crush or infatuation, and maybe it'll all die away when I leave—it would certainly be for the best if it did—but I know now that a part of me wants it to never end.

I'm sitting with Marie at the kitchen table shelling peas when Henri walks in.

"Good morning," he says.

"Good morning," I reply. I am blushing.

"No jokes about murder today, then?" Marie asks, regarding the two of us with amusement in her eyes.

He glances at me and I flush again. Something has shifted between us. It feels dangerous but also beguiling, like a beautifully wrapped gift I know I shouldn't open. I'm drawn toward this thing knowing full well I should head in the opposite direction.

THERE'S a good breeze and the sun is strong, so when Marie leaves for town I grab the laundry basket full of wet sheets and head outside to hang them on the line, accustomed enough to the cast that I can manage small distances without crutches.

The sheets billow as I hang them and the air is heavy with their fragrance. My dress whips around my legs in the breeze, a stray lock of hair flying across my face. I wonder what it's like here in the fall, in the spring. I picture the winter hard and cold, yet even that has a certain appeal. *I could make Henri cocoa again*, I find myself thinking. A smile crosses my face at the thought when I see Henri climbing the hill, his eyes fixed on nothing but me. I meet his gaze and he doesn't look away. He keeps walking towards me until we stand only feet apart.

His eyes dip to my mouth. "You shouldn't be doing that," he says. "You could fall." His voice seems to come from far away, but his eyes are right here, *on me*, in a way I swear I can feel.

"I'm okay," I reply. "I've gotten used to the cast."

He considers me for a moment. I see the tiniest hint of vulnerability in his eyes. "It's supposed to storm later in the week," he says. "If you'd like to go riding, we might want to go today."

I feel faint. I'm so consumed with whatever this new thing is between us that it's hard to even understand what he's saying.

"I have to read to Madame Perot this afternoon."

"Afterward, then," he says, pulling one end of the sheet from me and draping it over the line.

I smile. "Okay."

His mouth lifts, just a hint of pleasure. "Okay."

HENRI DRIVES me to Madame Beauvoir's a few hours later, the two of us saying little.

"You don't have to do this," he says, "if you don't want to."

I swallow. I desperately *don't* want to do this, and yet I think of Marie last night with her pleading eyes, silently begging me not to cause problems. "She's expecting me. And who will she have to yell at if I'm not there?"

"Isn't that what they have servants for?" he asks with a small smile.

I struggle to return it. I'm probably being paranoid, but I don't want to be anywhere in that house alone with André. Henri, no matter what words come out of his mouth, sees me as an equal. André treated me like property out on the balcony. And something about that strikes me as a dangerous, especially in a time when women have so few rights.

Henri walks me to the door. Today, it's Andre who answers. He and Henri exchange a look before André gives him a broad smile, one that is too amiable to be believed. Did I actually think he was attractive the first time we met? Because the sight of him is making my skin crawl now. His lips press to my hand for longer than they should and I hear a low noise, a growl, coming from behind me.

"Your cousin is in good hands," André says to Henri as I walk in. He starts to shut the door and Henri puts one large foot over the threshold. "I will be back in precisely ninety minutes," he says to me, and then he leaves with one lingering, particularly hostile glance at André.

"If you're not in the mood to read to my grandmother today," says Andre, "perhaps we could go have lunch somewhere? It's a bit warm out but fortunately we live in town so things are close."

I smile. "That's kind of you, but I love reading to your grandmother," I lie. "She was so helpful last time, correcting my accent."

"Come to lunch with me. Your accent is already quite good, as is your French," he says. He smiles conspiratorially at my look of surprise. "I heard you with my grandmother the last time—

there's no way you could have read as well as you did without knowing the language. Don't worry. I won't tell your cousins."

I tighten my grip on the crutches. I am not interested in sharing secrets with André, and if he thinks this gives him some leverage over me, he's very mistaken. "I made a promise to your grandmother," I say, passing him to reach the stairs. "You don't need to show me the way. I remember the room."

He bows his head. "Your dedication is admirable. I'll come up to check on you in a while."

I scurry up the stairs as fast as a woman on crutches can scurry and tap on the door, which is not fully shut and swings open with little pressure. The old woman gives me another narrowed-eye glance and tells me to get on with it.

"It's so lovely to see you today, Madame Perot," I reply in English.

Stop speaking to me in your gibberish and start reading, she replies.

I open the book where we left off and begin, but within seconds she is yelling at me. *Your American accent is like oil in my ears*, she yells. *It's not guh, it's gah. My God they must teach you nothing over there.*

Fortunately, when I ignore her she dozes off. I continue to read, because Henri won't be back for another hour and I'd rather spend time up here than with André downstairs. I begin to read more slowly, though, finally capable of saying the words and translating them as I go.

Madame Perot wakes, her eyes beady, all pupil, and accuses me of talking to the Gypsies outside.

I decide there's no sense in pretending I don't know what she's said. *I didn't see any Gypsies outside*, I reply, *but they've never caused me any problems.*

They're a dirty people, she says, still glaring at me as if I'm lying. *They stole my husband's car once, at the end of the war. A very, very dirty people.*

I'll keep that in mind, Madame, I reply, hiding my smile.

I begin to read again and she soon falls back asleep, which is my preference, as it means I'm being neither hit nor yelled at. Unfortunately, it also means she is snoring loudly when André pokes his head in the door.

"Come have tea with me," he says. "My grandmother won't wake again for hours."

I return the book to her nightstand and reluctantly leave the room. "I don't have time for tea, I'm afraid. Henri will be here to get me soon."

"Then come," he says, "we can sit outside until he arrives."

I follow him to the garden on the side of the yard, which is flourishing in the warm July air. "It must be so dull for you, out on the farm," he says.

My dislike for André intensifies. "Not at all. Henri and Marie-Therese are very pleasant company."

"You're very good to them," he says diplomatically, walking closer than seems reasonable, given that I'm on crutches. His hand extends toward the garden. "So here it is. We've created a little bridge over this pond. A sort of mini Giverny if you will. You've seen Monet's paintings, yes?"

I give him a tight smile. His garden is not Giverny by any stretch of the imagination. "Yes. I study art history, remember?"

"Ah, yes, of course," says André, stepping an inch closer. "We should go visit Giverny together. I know the current owners and it's just a few hours by car. Next Saturday perhaps? We will make a day of it."

I blink. I do not want to be alone with this man even here, a mile from the farm. I certainly don't want to be alone with him in a car, hours away. "I'm not sure my cousins would approve."

He raises a brow. "Henri seems rather proprietary of you, don't you think? It's a bit unseemly."

I move forward quickly, toward a small stone bench. "I'm sure you are mistaken," I say firmly.

He stills, as if he will argue, but then nods slowly. "Either way, I have no right to interfere. I just worry about you. So what do you think of our little garden?"

I'm loath to compliment anything about this man. "It's beautiful," I say, forcing out the words.

His palm slides over mine. "Your beauty makes all else fade by contrast."

I pull away with another tight smile when suddenly his hand lands on my thigh, his fingers sinking into my flesh through the thin fabric of the dress. I begin to slide away but his free hand has already snaked out to hold my jaw, and just as suddenly his doughy mouth is on mine, thick tongue pushing between my lips, his hand sliding beneath my dress to the juncture of my thighs.

"What the hell are you doing?" I demand. I shove him and he barely moves, just presses harder, doing his level best to get his fingers inside my panties.

"I'm giving you a better option than having it on with your own cousin," he says. "Everyone knows you're fucking Henri."

I jump to my feet, grabbing the crutches. "What the hell are you talking about?"

"Anyone with eyes can put together what's happening."

He stands, reaching for me again and I try to step backward but stumble, thrown off balance by the cast, landing on my ass. He leans down and I don't wait for his next move. I grab one of the crutches, which has fallen with me, and swing it straight at his face. I hear the impact, a *thwack*, and his jaw blossoms into an ugly bright red patch that will undoubtedly be a deep purple within the hour.

He holds a hand to it, dazed and astonished. "*Putain*," he gasps. "You think you can do better than me?"

"It would be hard to do *worse* than you," I hiss.

"Fine," he says. "Continue to fuck your cousin instead, American whore." He walks off and leaves me there, lying in the yard with a dirty dress and bleeding hands.

When he's out of sight, the sob that was locked in my throat releases. I'm not even sure why I'm so upset. I wasn't raped. He called me names every woman hears at some point in her life. It's the adrenaline and my absolute helplessness, I think. I'm not in my own time, I'm not in my own country, and I can't even trust my legs to keep me upright when they're supposed to.

All I want in this moment, oddly enough, is Henri. Henri with his smirk and those eyes that are angry as often as they are kind. Henri who does nothing but ridicule my clumsiness and ask how soon I'm leaving. He is all I want in the world right now, and as bizarre as my life has been and continues to be, that's the most puzzling fact of all.

I dry my face on the inside of my dress and brush myself off, limping to the front of the house, feeling a little more shaky and off-kilter than I normally do—and given how off-kilter I've been since breaking my ankle, that's saying something. Henri is waiting beside the car.

I try to smile, but it feels as if my whole body trembles with the effort.

"What's wrong?" he asks immediately.

"Nothing."

He looks me over, head to foot, and I see rage settling over him like a cloak as he takes in the dirty dress, the cut hands. He takes three large strides until he's directly in front of me. "What happened?"

I could lie and tell him I fell, but it's not going to add up, especially once I insist I will never again set foot in this house. "André tried to kiss me," I tell him. "It turns out the crutches make a fine weapon. He won't try it again." I give him a tremulous smile, one he doesn't return.

"Tell me exactly what happened," he says. His voice is quiet, and lethal. "Everything he did and every word he said."

I limp past him. "It doesn't matter. I dealt with it."

His hand lands on my shoulder to stop me. It's a firm grip, just as André's was, but different somehow. Perhaps simply because I trust Henri. "It does matter. Tell me."

I turn to him. "Fino," I say roughly. I sound angry but it's only so I won't dissolve into tears. "He insisted on sitting in the garden with me to wait for you. Then he kissed me and put his hand up my dress and when I yelled at him he called me an American whore..." There's more, of course, but it seems like I've probably told him enough.

His face is blank for a moment and then morphs into a rage so fierce and absolute it scares me. I wait for the outburst to come but there is nothing. After a moment of stillness, he takes the crutches from me and gently helps me into the car. I'm relieved by his lack of response but surprised by it too.

The ride home is silent, his hands gripping the steering wheel so tightly his knuckles pale with the pressure. I stare out the window, arguing with myself about what I *didn't* tell him. Yes, it will be awkward to admit there are rumors about us, but maybe he should know, since he's the one who'll be left to combat them when I'm gone. He hesitates for a moment after we arrive, as if he wants to say something, but then climbs from the car instead, opening my door and offering me a hand, more careful than normal, and also more restrained.

"There's something else," I say, staring at the ground rather than him. "André said everyone in town thinks we're...*together*. Sleeping together, I mean."

"Merde," he hisses under his breath, an expression of disgust on his face. It's the disgust that surprises me. I'd have thought after everything he said last night...I flinch now, wondering if I somehow misunderstood him. Based on the way he looks right now, it certainly seems that way.

He turns on his heel and marches into the house, leaving me to follow. Marie is in the kitchen, but he's heading upstairs without a word. She looks at me. "Are you two fighting again?"

"No," I reply. I can't go through the whole story and it would just worry her if I did. "I don't know what's wrong with him."

We can't go riding since Marie has decided to stay home, but I'm not sure we'd go anyway. He emerges from his room and tells Marie he's not staying for dinner because he's going out *to clear some things up.* Then he leaves the house without even glancing at me once.

She frowns at the door as he walks through it. "You're sure you didn't fight?"

"Yes."

Is he out tonight because of what André said? Will he clear up any illusions about our relationship by sleeping with some slut from town? Or maybe he was just reminded of what he's been missing out on. Either way I find that I am absolutely livid.

"How was reading to Madame Perot today?" Marie asks.

The urge to blame her is strong. She's the one who agreed to have me read there. She's the reason my ankle is still broken. And if none of this had happened, maybe Henri wouldn't be off with someone tonight the way he is.

"I won't go back to that house," I reply, rising from the table. "I don't care what you have to tell them."

IT'S LATE when I hear him pull up outside. Marie has been asleep for hours and I should have been too, but I'm too busy stewing, wondering if he was going to stay out all night and stumble home in the morning with some sheepish grin on his face. I wrap the borrowed robe around me and walk into the kitchen just as he enters, bleary-eyed and unhappy.

"Did I wake you?" he asks. He isn't drunk but he's not quite sober either, and he can't seem to mask his discomfort in my presence, that he wishes he was alone right now.

My lips press tight. "You made enough noise to raise the

dead," I reply, though it's not true. "I assume by your level of sobriety that you went out?"

"Can't get anything by you," he says with a smirk I'd like to wipe off his face. Now that I've hit someone with a crutch the desire to do it again is positively calling to me.

"I'd like a night out myself before I leave," I reply, feeling something mean and spiteful rise up inside me. I want to strike out like a cobra and I have no means to, but something keeps my mouth running. "I imagine there must be someone in the town nicer than you and André."

His smirk is gone, replaced by glittering eyes and a mean set to his mouth. "I'm sure there are. But just so you're clear, in *my* time, decent women don't give themselves away to the first rich man who makes them an offer."

"So I guess you were with one of the indecent ones tonight," I hiss. "That shouldn't surprise me."

His mouth turns up at one end. Another of his arrogant smiles. He runs a thumb over his lower lip. "Ah. So you're jealous. Is that what this is?"

I force myself to laugh. "In my world, you're a 72-year old man, remember? And I'm practically engaged."

He crosses the room until he's a foot away, towering over me. He braces himself against the wall behind me, caging me in. "Except you're not in your world. You're in mine."

His gaze falls to my face, to my lips, and my heart feels as if it's dropped into my stomach. I'm shaking but it's not fear. It's as if my entire body is so primed, so reckless and raw, that it refuses to allow me to remain still.

His head dips. Just an inch. There's no longer a hint of a smile on his face. I know exactly what's going to happen and I want it. I don't care about our respective ages. I don't care that I'm nearly engaged. I just *want*, as if there's no room in my head for any other emotion. The pad of his thumb runs over my lower lip.

And then a door opens upstairs and we jump, separating from

each other. Within seconds Marie-Therese stands at the top of the stairs. "Surely the two of you can contain your fighting to daylight hours?" she demands.

I swallow, guilty as a teenager caught in the back of a car with a boy. I can no longer meet Henri's gaze. "Sorry," I mumble, fleeing to my room.

I'm nearly to my door when I hear him. "Amelie?" he asks quietly. I stop and turn toward him. His eyes flicker over my face. "I wasn't with anyone tonight," he says. "I haven't been with anyone since the day you arrived."

He turns to walk up the stairs, leaving me standing there, relieved and with a bizarre desire to cry for the second time in one day.

THE MYSTERY of Henri's disappearance is solved fairly quickly. When Marie returns from the market she drops the bags inside the door and stares at us both.

"Someone put a cloth over André Beauvoir's head last night and beat him within an inch of his life," she says, her lips pressed tight. "I don't suppose the two of you know anything about that?"

I turn to Henri in shock. *That's* where he was?

He avoids my gaze, lifting his eyes to his sister instead, looking bored. "He insulted our family," Henri replies. "I couldn't let him get away with it."

"*He insulted our family?*" she repeats incredulously. "Are we back in the Middle Ages? What could he possibly have said?"

His jaw grinds. "He implied there were some rumors about Amelie that...I won't have anyone thinking of her that way." I misinterpreted his disgust yesterday, and I've never been so relieved to be wrong.

Marie throws out her hands. "So he said a few things about us. We've lived through worse."

Henri's gaze flickers to me. He is being honorable. The story of what happened is mine and he's not going to share it.

"André did more than insult me, Marie," I admit. "I was able to stop him, but it involved hitting him with my crutch."

She blinks twice and presses a hand to her chest. For the first time since this whole ankle debacle began, she looks guilty. "Oh." She glances at my cast and I see the thoughts as they cross her face. I suppose they cycled through mine as well—that I wouldn't even be here if it weren't for her refusal to fix my ankle.

"Yes, Marie," says Henri with acid in his voice, "you've put her in danger with your stupidity about fate."

She swallows. "I'm sorry," she says to me. "Please...forgive me. I know it doesn't make sense."

Henri's arms go wide. He's as angry as he was when it first happened. "She could have been raped!" he shouts. "Don't apologize—fix it!"

He walks out of the house, slamming the door so hard that the windows rattle and the pans hanging from the copper rack clank against each other.

Marie hangs her head. "I can't fix it," she says, near tears. "But I *am* deeply sorry."

I sigh. I don't know why I care that Marie feels guilty, but I do. Aside from this one odd anomaly, she's been unbelievably kind and gracious throughout my stay. "It doesn't matter. My cast comes off in a week. Though I can't imagine what you believe is going to change between now and then."

Her head still hangs as she walks away. "I don't know either. Not what I hoped."

22

During my final week in the cast Henri spends every afternoon with me, regardless of Marie-Therese's plans. On the last afternoon before we see the doctor, he comes in and tells me the horses are saddled, ignoring his sister entirely. She doesn't seem at all surprised but instead settles into a chair and shrugs.

"Good," she says, "I'll have a quiet afternoon to myself."

He's gentler with me when he lifts me onto the horse, and also when he removes me. I'm not sure if his hands linger at my waist or if I'm just so much more aware of them today. They're so big I think they could span my entire rib cage if he tried.

We are quieter as we sit out on the blanket. He is sitting slightly closer than he usually does. I barely notice the magnificence of the setting sun, the glory of the wildflowers. I'm only aware of the heat of him next to me, the thud of my heart, overloud in my chest.

Is this love? It feels nothing like what I have with Mark. My love for Mark feels like the hours before a big dance, when you are a little giddy with the excitement of it all, when the possibilities for the evening seem fun at the very least and almost infinite.

This feeling for Henri is different. It hurts. It leaves me feeling desperate and reckless and it clouds my brain in a way that makes rational thought difficult. I'm not sure if it's real or just some version of Stockholm Syndrome. I've been with almost no one but him for months. He's the most gorgeous man I've ever seen and we've found ourselves in increasingly heated positions. Maybe any woman in my shoes would feel this way.

I squeeze my eyes shut. *It doesn't matter anyway*, I say to myself. *You can't stay for good. And he's never once implied that he'd like you to.*

"A VERY EXCITING DAY FOR YOU," says Doctor Nadeau when I arrive at his office.

I struggle to smile as I agree. In truth, the experience is bittersweet. I'm eager to regain my mobility, but regaining it also means I must leave. And it's definitely *time* for me to go—there's a chance if I remain too much longer I won't have enough of a spark to even make it back home at all. But I will miss my life here more than I want to admit.

Henri looks a little unnerved as the doctor prepares to saw open my cast. He hovers nearby as it begins, his hands in his pockets, his jaw clenched tight.

When the cast is split the doctor cracks it open into two even halves, revealing my ankle—pale and atrophied, but otherwise normal.

"You'll be weak and stiff for a few days," the doctor warns. "So use caution."

Henri helps me climb off the table. His protectiveness is ridiculous but also sweet. At last I understand the appeal of being treated like something delicate and precious, just as I'm about to leave it behind for good.

He links his elbow through mine and guides me carefully out

to the car. When we reach the door, he stops. "You heard what Doctor Nadeau said. I hope you don't plan to leave until you've got your mobility back completely."

I turn toward him. We are probably standing a little too close for supposed family members, but I don't care. I rest my hands against his chest. I will miss this chest. I will miss the way he looms over me when we stand close. I will miss the way he treats me when his guard is down, as if I am worth more to him than the rest of the world combined.

"No, I think I'll need to stay a bit longer. A week maybe."

His palms fold over my hands for one long moment. "Good," he says. "That's good."

We've entered a new season of Henri, I realize. The one in which he's willing to admit he likes having me here, that he possibly cares. It's probably for the best that he's arrived at this position so late because, with enough time, I might just be persuaded to stay.

WHEN I RETURN HOME, Marie is waiting. She winces at the sight of my weak, pale ankle. "I hope you won't try to leave just yet," she says quietly. "And you might want to test landing on it, just to make sure you'll be okay?" I've rarely seen her look as depressed as she does right now.

I'm sure she'll miss me, just as I'll miss her, but her sadness right now is more than that.

I nod. "I'm sorry. I know you wanted me to come with you to 1918." I suspect she hoped for other things too, but I can't even bring myself to suggest it or I might be the one to cry instead.

She looks at me blankly for a moment. "1918?" And then she laughs, a mournful, resigned sound. "I never thought I'd persuade you to go anywhere," she says as she walks away. "It was rather the opposite."

I SPEND the remainder of the day walking around the farm and helping with chores, waiting for my ankle to lose its stiffness. When it does I'm both relieved and disappointed. A part of me thought I might be stuck here a little longer, but by the time I go to bed my ankle is already feeling close to normal, bringing home the fact that it's really ending, all of it. The horseback rides, the picnics, the afternoons with Henri reading on the porch, sipping on that Beaujolais I didn't care for when I first arrived.

I long for time with Henri alone, but it doesn't come. Marie-Therese, sensing that my departure is imminent, suddenly decides to stick around the house. I spend the day helping her make preserves with my eyes on the window the entire time, hungering for the sight of her brother.

On the third day, though, comes a reprieve. When I walk inside from watering the pumpkins early in the afternoon, Marie is just hanging up the phone and bouncing with excitement over the fact that her friend Jeannette is in labor. She begins hastily packing a basket.

"Her husband is at the Maginot Line so I'll need to stay and mind her daughter until her mother can get here from Paris. Tomorrow morning at the earliest." She looks up at me with the brightest smile on her face. "A baby! Can you imagine?"

I smile back. Ankle ordeal aside, Marie-Therese would make such a good mother, if she would just move on from her crush on Father Edouard. She could settle down with Xavier. Even Luc, as abrasive as he was, could probably give her the things she needs: children, a home of her own, an easier life.

"I think you should go out with Xavier," I tell her. "Just once."

Her brow furrows. "How has the conversation gone from the miracle of life to a boy who went to a school with my brother?"

I shrug. "Because a boy who went to school with your brother could lead to the miracle of life."

She pauses. "Yes, I suppose he could." But her joy is slightly diminished, and it makes me wish I hadn't said anything.

She leaves for Jeanette's with Henri, and when he returns he comes inside rather than heading straight to the fields.

"It might be a nice day for a ride," he says. He throws it out like a challenge, but his eyes are uncertain. All this time our rides have had an element of charity to them, as if they were a debt he was paying for his role in my immobility. Now I don't need them, and he no longer needs to offer them.

There's no denying the slight relief on his face when I agree.

WE RIDE SIDE BY SIDE.

The farm has changed a great deal since I arrived at the end of May. All the colors are more saturated, and everything is full and lush now, the grapes nearly ripe.

"What's it like here, in the fall?" I ask.

He glances over at me for a moment too long. "Beautiful. The sky is a deeper blue. All these trees will look like balls of flame and the air will be crisp. We bring in help for the harvest, but our days are very long. You'd like it, though, I think."

I wish I could stay. I wish for it so much that I have to swallow down the urge to say it aloud.

I've only just realized we aren't heading to the meadow when the lake comes into view. I draw Fleur to a halt. "Why would you bring me here, after what I told you?"

He stops alongside me. "Because I think it's time you faced this fear of yours. Replaced your unhappy memory with a pleasant one. Wouldn't you like to go through your life without shuddering at the sight of every lake? It's no way to live."

I've thought this before myself. Once I have children, the way I've kept myself in a bubble won't be possible. They'll want to swim, and God knows I'll never let them go alone.

What could possibly go wrong if we sit by the lake? Nothing. I'm like Kit as a small child, certain there's a witch in the closet no matter what common sense tells me.

"Fine." I take a quick breath.

He climbs down and then lifts me off my horse, setting me gently on the ground. We walk down the hill, him hovering close in case my ankle gives way. And when we reach the bottom, he untucks his shirt and reaches for the top button.

"What on earth are you doing?" I demand.

His mouth lifts on one side. "Did you think we'd swim fully dressed?"

My jaw drops. A swim is not what I agreed to, by any stretch of the imagination. "I'm not *swimming*! I thought you meant we'd just sit here."

"Come, Amelie. Face your fears. What's the worst that could happen?"

My arms fold across my chest. "Do I really need to detail that for you? My sister *drowned*."

He continues unbuttoning his shirt. "And you think I will drown? I've been swimming in this lake since I was small. I'm not going to let anything happen to you. And nothing will happen to me."

"Absolutely not."

He gives me that shrug of his, so effortlessly Gallic, and pulls his shirt over his head.

For a moment I gape. I've seen him without a shirt from afar, but never like this, standing three feet away. His chest is smooth and perfectly formed, an anatomy lesson of the best possible kind. Every muscle a man can have, he has in spades. He grins, as if he's caught me at something, which he has, and I flush.

"In my time, undressing in front of a woman without her permission is known as exposure and it's a crime," I say primly.

He laughs. "No one is telling you to watch." He reaches for his belt. There's something so sexual about it, so indecent. It's how he would undress for me in some other circumstance. Eager, unapologetic...

"God," I say, facing away from him. I wait until I've heard him splash before I turn, just catching sight of his perfect, broad back and the most gorgeous male ass I've ever seen in my life before he dives under. I hold my breath, waiting for him to reemerge, and don't release it until he's back above the surface.

"Please don't stay under like that," I ask quietly, my voice desperate. It's probably the first time in our acquaintance I've begged him for something.

His face softens and he wades through the water until he stands only a few feet away. "I'm a grown man," he says gently. "Nothing is going to happen to me. This water is perhaps six feet at its deepest point."

I know he's right. Swimming in this lake is far less risky than half the things he does, but knowing that doesn't lessen my fear. "You might hit your head on something. You can drown in an inch of water."

He grins, pushing his wet hair off his face. "Who will protect me from every inch of water once you're not here?"

The question causes a pain in my heart, because I really do want an answer: who will watch over him and keep him safe once I'm gone? Not that I've ever actually kept him safe. I suppose I just like the illusion that I *could* keep him safe if the situation presented itself.

He reaches out his hand. "Please come in. I won't allow anything to happen to either of us. I swear it on my life. You are no longer a child. You can control your gifts. You were brave to come here, and you are brave to attempt the journey home. Be brave one more time. For me."

My heart pounds in terror, but I know that if this is ever going to happen it has to be now. At least Henri understands that I'm scared, and feels some sympathy for it. Mark won't. How could he, when he has no idea why I'm scared in the first place?

"Turn around," I say quietly. When he does, I slip out of the clothes and take a first tentative step on the slippery, moss-covered rocks that lead into the water.

My breathing is shallow, and every bone in my body wants to retreat to the safety of the shore. I keep my eyes glued to his broad back, as if it's the finish line. He has the sort of build featured in magazines at home: pure muscle, tapering to a narrow waist. Mark still has the lanky build of a boy, though he and Henri are the same age.

"Can I turn around yet?" he asks.

"No!" I cry. "I'm only up to my calves."

He laughs. "For a woman who has no problem discussing brassieres in mixed company, you are suddenly quite modest."

"There's a big difference between talking about something and brandishing it about."

"You're forgetting I've already seen you naked."

The water swirls around the middle of my thighs, and then my waist. I feel like I'm not quite taking in full breaths. "You said you didn't see anything!"

"I didn't see *much*," he amends. "At the time I was panicked but..."

"But what?" I take one more step and am in up to my collarbone. "You can turn around."

"But I remembered it later." He turns toward me with a small grin. We are far closer than two naked people should be when one of them is practically engaged to someone else. "And I remembered it often."

I laugh, a hint of nerves underlying the sound.

His eyes search mine. "How are you?" he asks.

I swallow. The truth is that talking to him on the way in distracted me a little. I'm surprised by how okay this is, but my heart is still thudding in my chest.

"I'm...alright."

He begins to back away and my pulse quickens. "Can you

stay?" I ask, the question whistling out on a single breath. "Right where you are?"

Instead, he moves closer and reaches out his hand. I grab it. "Do you want to go under?" he asks.

"God, no."

He smiles. "Just checking."

The two of us stay like that, standing feet apart, our hands clasped. The world is dreamy and quiet, as the sun begins to lower. A breeze, balmy and apple-scented, rustles the reeds that line the far shore.

I'm happy, I realize. I never thought I'd set foot in a lake again, but I'm actually happy right now. I've been happier over the past month than I've ever been in my life. And all the best moments happened with him.

Happened *because* of him.

When the breeze picks up and the sun begins to set, I climb from the lake, struggling to pull clothes on over my damp skin. Once I'm done, I turn around and he climbs out to do the same. The breeze now whips through the meadow so hard that the trees shake.

He lifts me onto Fleur, though I no longer need the help, his hands large and warm and gentle—and then he urges me along while he climbs on Napoleon.

"It's going to storm," he says. As soon as he speaks, I hear the low growl of distant thunder. "Head straight for the house. I'll get the horses put away on my own."

"What am I supposed to do while you're risking your life out in the storm?" I ask.

He grins. "Get dry and open a bottle of wine? That's what I'd do anyway."

≈

I'VE CHANGED clothes and am sitting on the stone porch with a lamp and an open bottle of wine when he gets to the house. He takes the chair across from mine, accepting the glass I've poured for him and breathing in deeply.

I've come to love the smell of wine as well. It's no longer merely a drink—it's an experience. The scent. That first burst of it against my tongue. I sigh happily.

"It's perfect."

He bites his lip. "You've come around then to wine, at last."

"It's one of those things you learn to love," I explain. "I'm not even sure if it's the taste I love or just the things it brings to mind."

Lightning splashes across the sky, causing the lamplight to flicker over his face as he watches me. "So what does it bring to mind?"

I close my eyes and take another sip, letting the answer come to me as I relish it on my tongue. "Being here, with you. Reading. Playing chess. The smell of the rain."

"You'll replace all those memories when you go home," he says quietly.

I shake my head, trying to picture the experiences that could attempt to replace these. My best memories, aside from my time here, are from the one full summer Mark and I spent together. It seemed like a miracle at the time, but now I wonder if it was just different, and anything different seemed good. I picture it all now: drinking with Mark's family at the country club, receptions at art galleries, late nights out with his college buddies. That future I chose for myself—the one that seemed so ideal, so glamorous— suddenly seems loud, and empty, and sad. It could never replace these memories.

"I don't think I will," I reply. "Will you?"

"There will never be a time that I don't step on this porch and think of you," he says quietly.

My heart squeezes. It's easy enough to say, but eventually there will be some other female here in my place, warmed by his presence—taking in his beautiful mouth and his bright eyes and the way he rests back in his chair—and she will be thinking of nothing more than when he will kiss her. I'm so jealous of her I feel dizzy.

He glances at me and bites his lip, leaning back in his seat, the glass floating lazily against his palm. He looks sad, though he says nothing.

I picture myself leaning over, brushing my mouth over those full lips of his. Would he be shocked? Would he respond? I think he might. I think he might lean into the kiss, pull the hint of wine from my lower lip. And my hand would go to his cheek, rasping against the beard that's grown in over the course of the day. I'd breathe him in then, trying to capture him inside me somehow. His smell, his taste, his warmth.

"We should eat," I say quickly. "The wine is going to my head."

He leans back in his chair, watching me in that way of his, like he understands what's going on inside me better than I do. "And what do you suggest we eat?" he asks.

We could do bread and cheese and ham, as always. But for some reason I'm thinking of the night I ran away, when we came back here and divided Marie's latest creation between us with two forks.

"I think we should make a pie."

"*We?*" he asks.

Pie is not something I'd suggest under normal circumstances, particularly as I've only been a part of the pie-making process once in my life. If I'm going to attempt it, I'm not doing it alone.

"You don't expect me to make it all by myself?"

He grins. "Yes, obviously it would be unthinkable, making something all by yourself." He's teasing but he rises, pushing his sleeves above the elbow. "Put me to work, *ma reine*." My queen.

"Is that another word for thief?" I ask.

"Yes," he replies. "But worse."

He follows me to the kitchen and I wrap my braid on top of

my head while he pours us both more wine. "That isn't going to improve my baking skills," I warn as I take the glass.

"No," he says, "but it will help dull our senses before we are forced to taste the fruit of your labors."

"*Our* labors."

I push the apples and cutting board toward him, while I take the seat on the other side and try to remember what Marie did that morning. I watch her measure the flour—exactly two and a half cups, watch as she mixes it with baking powder and then takes the butter and chops it into the flour, with small knives and rapid hands.

"You're doing it again," he says softly. "The shimmering."

My eyes open and I settle into my body, with a need to argue that is almost instinctive. Henri's now claimed to have seen it twice and what does it mean if he's correct? It means this is something I might do in front of Mark. *Will* do, if we live together eventually. And how the hell will I explain *that*?

"I wasn't time traveling," I insist, grabbing the flour and the butter. "Maybe I just lose my place a little when I'm focusing on something."

"There wouldn't be anything wrong with it if you *were* time traveling, you know," he suggests casually, winding the knife with clever hands around the apple's surface.

I measure the flour just as Marie did, and begin to cut the butter into it. "Did I actually shimmer? Tell me the truth."

"You did," he says. "You looked like a candle in a storm."

"God," I say, cutting the butter into the flour with hands moving even faster than Marie's did, but mostly out of distress. "I sometimes do it during tests. Do you think anyone's seen me?"

He raises a brow. "I don't know, but if you want to convince people you don't time travel, you might want to cut that out first."

I sigh as I grab the rolling pin. "Hard to accomplish when I don't even know I'm doing it."

"Then may I suggest that you don't wind up with someone

who has no idea who you are?" he asks.

I flip him off. He doesn't seem to mind. He begins mixing the apples, cinnamon and sugar, but he's watching me more than he is his bowl. He runs a thumb over his lip, a gesture that makes me feel slightly weak-kneed. I've definitely had too much wine. Too much of something, anyway. I carry my bowl to the counter, needing some distance from him.

"Are you really going to sleep with him when you get home?" he asks abruptly.

I glance up. His eyes are on fire now, angry and...something else...as he waits for my response.

The idea of sleeping with Mark merely made me nervous last spring, but now it twists my stomach in knots—and not the good kind. I shouldn't have spent the entire summer away from him. We haven't even seen each other since March, and five months apart would have anyone nervous. If I feel like this when I get home, I won't be able to go through with it, but maybe I'll feel different by then. Maybe things will go back to normal.

"I'm not sure about anything anymore."

My body feels overheated and liquid. He holds my eyes, and I picture sliding over the table to kiss him. I picture him lifting me on the counter, pressed between my legs the way he was the day we fought over the chocolate.

My chest rises and falls too quickly and his eyes flicker there, and back to my mouth. He is looking at me like something he intends to devour, and I can't catch my breath.

I grab the rolling pin and begin to roll out the dough, trying to get my thoughts in order. I don't know who I am right now—it must be the wine creating these pictures in my head, making me sweat though the room isn't warm.

"You're doing it wrong," he says.

I wipe flour off my forehead with my shoulder. "How typical of you to sit there from your relaxed perch and criticize."

He rises, slowly, and moves around to my side of the counter.

I'm about to slide out of his way when suddenly he is behind me, his hands covering mine on the handles of the rolling pin, his mouth near my ear

"You need to put your body into it," he says, pushing me forward, coming with me. Our weight presses into the dough and it smooths out neatly across the butcher block. "Then back," he says. His voice is low and rough against my ear. I move backward with him, with our hands, and need sharpens in my stomach.

"And again," he says softly. He exhales and every tiny hair along the shell of my ear rises in response. I look at our hands. His are large, tan, dwarfing my small, paler ones beneath. Our forearms are pressed together, the same contrast: large and hard next to small and soft. His chest leans against my back, pressing firm and hot to the thin fabric of my dress, which sticks to me now. My breathing is shallow, small gasps and quick exhales, my heart beating hard with the desire to just close my eyes and follow him wherever he takes this.

I don't know why I want to arch against him when he presses into my back, why I want to move my head toward the pulse of his breath against my ear. Why, when his hands grip mine hard enough to hurt, I only want him to hold them tighter.

Lightning cracks outside and the room is plunged into darkness.

I can feel his heart hammering against my back, the rasp of his unshaved jaw so close that it catches on my skin. His hands tighten around mine and for a single moment I'm not sure what either of us will do next.

I want him. I want to give him everything I've refused to give Mark, haven't *wanted* to give Mark. Except a week from now, Henri will be an old man. And I might be getting engaged.

"I don't think we can make the pie now," I whisper. I'm breathless and sound terrified, though I'm not sure that's what I am. Even as I say the words, I'm relishing the feel of his skin on mine, and wanting more of it.

"It might keep for morning," he says, his voice gravelly, warm against my ear for only a moment before he backs away. "Let me get a candle."

I hear the sound of a match striking, and then there is a hint of light in the room. Our eyes meet in the semi-darkness, his burning in a way that's quickly becoming familiar to me. I gather up the dough, avoiding his face, and he covers the apples.

What would have happened if the lights hadn't gone out? My heart thuds with the desire to find out.

"I think I've had too much to drink," I stammer, though I know that's not the issue. My eyes fall to his full mouth, to the broad shoulders that enveloped mine just a minute earlier. I want to feel all of it, to feel his weight over me, consuming me. I am weak-kneed, swollen with desire for it. But giving in right now could ruin everything I've planned for myself. "I should go to bed."

He nods, his jaw locked tight with restraint. When I get to the door of my room I turn. If he were to come over here now and kiss me, I would let him. And then I'd pull him into the room with me and strip him free of those clothes.

He's leaning over the counter, gripping it. Almost as if he's fighting himself not to follow me.

I go through the door before he changes his mind, before he gives into what exists between us.

Because I know in my heart I gave into it a while ago.

MARIE RETURNS at the crack of dawn the next day. I know this because I hear her gasp when she walks in. I throw my dress on and rush out of the room.

I understand why she's gasping. Henri and I managed to destroy the kitchen...there is flour on every surface. "Sorry," I say, rushing in to clean. "Henri and I tried to make a pie and the lights went out."

A slow smile dawns on her face. "You and Henri tried to make a pie? *Together*?"

"Well, we had to eat."

"Interesting."

I want to roll my eyes at her but already I'm remembering the feel of him behind me, so much larger than I am. His hands enclosing mine. His breath against my ear.

It must have been the wine. It must have been temporary insanity.

Henri walks into the room then, looking more tired than usual. "Why are you home so early?" he asks Marie. "It's barely even light out."

She colors. "Jeanette's mother arrived, so I got a ride home."

"A ride?" he asks "Who was available to give you a ride at five in the morning?"

"Father Edouard," she says, blushing fiercely. "Madame LeGrand was worried about the baby and had him come to baptize her just in case, but all was well. And how was it here? If the two of you were making pie together, I assume that means you managed not to be at each other's throats, briefly?"

He was at my throat, I think. Or very near it. I could feel his breath on my skin there. Mark and I have not had sex, but we've done a great many other things. I've been beneath him, practically naked, and not felt a hint of anything. Henri stands behind me and the mere feel of his hands and his breath on me, both of us fully dressed, had me arching like a cat in heat. I just don't understand. I don't want to understand.

"It was fine," I tell her faintly.

Except it wasn't fine. It was dangerous. Every minute I'm around him seems slightly less controlled than the last. I'm not sure what will happen if I stay another week or two as planned. A smarter girl would probably leave before she found out.

23

Two days later I decide to test my ankle. There's always the possibility that I will break it, which could very well keep me here so long that I can't jump home anymore, that 1938 becomes my new present. A part of me isn't as horrified by that idea as I once was.

I wait until Henri leaves to drive Marie-Therese to a farm on the other side of town, since it means I won't inadvertently flash anyone when I return.

I decide I'll only go forward a month or two, and though I have a good reason for using my ability, I'm eager to see what the farm will look like. By early fall the apples will be in and the grapes will be nearly ready for harvest. I want to see it all, and why shouldn't I? I usually feel some guilt about using my gift, but I don't right now. I guess watching Marie jump so shamelessly has had an effect.

I cross the yard and go out to the barn, where I close my eyes, memorizing the feel of this exact moment, preserving it like a page turned down in a book so I can find my place easily when I return. And then I picture a time not too far from now, imagining a crispness to the air, the way the summer colors will be on the cusp of shifting from green to gold. I feel the first hints of it beginning—the breeze, the darkness but am suddenly yanked forward, as if my own time is demanding my return.

I panic and drop out of it, hitting the ground and sliding in the hay before I rise, relieved that my ankle seems to have held up just fine. I glance around me with a happy sigh. I meant to go farther, but it's far enough: there's a soft breeze—not cold, but far more pleasant than the air was a few seconds earlier. Early fall, I assume.

I grab the blanket still hanging in the barn and wrap it around myself before I peek outside. From here I can see the vegetable patch, where my tiny little shoots have blossomed into long, thick vines, with more pumpkins than the two of them could possibly need. Do I dare walk down to the orchard? It's ill advised, yes, but the odds of running into anyone are slim. I begin walking down the lane, surrounded on both sides by grape vines rustling in the same fall breeze that blows my hair around my face and whips the blanket around my legs.

And suddenly Henri is there, twenty feet away, eyes wide at the sight of me. The tool falls from his hand. I suppose I need to explain, and a part of me wonders what kind of reception I'm in for. He's never once indicated he would like me to stay beyond the summer, but if I were to return one day would he be pleased? I guess I'm about to find out.

He moves toward me, stopping only when we are inches apart, eyes on my face in a way I've seen only a few times before. He looks stunned, as if my presence here is some kind of miracle. Before I can ask him what's going on, his hands curve around my jaw, and he kisses me.

It's too much sensation to even process—the feel of his mouth, the firmness of his body against mine, his smell, his desire. I'm still holding the blanket around me but my body sways against his until there's not a whisper of space between us and his arms slide down to my back, gripping me harder, kissing me harder. Kissing me as if he would like to drown in me, as if I'm the only thing he's hungered for in a hundred years. And I am kissing him back. I want to kiss him hard enough to become a part of him, to sear my memory into his skin, sear his into mine.

My arms climb around his neck and the blanket falls to the ground. His hands are on my bare back and I want everything from him, so much I can hardly stand to wait.

Except...

"Oh my God," I whisper, stumbling as I back away from him.

This isn't now. This is fall, when I'm no longer here, and this shouldn't be happening. Even if I didn't have a boyfriend it shouldn't be happening. I don't know what I've just done, but I know I need to escape from it, especially given that I'm now standing in front of him naked. I vanish before I can give myself even a moment to change my mind, returning to the moment I bookmarked so fast that I barely manage to stop as I feel it approaching.

I land and see my clothes resting in a pile, so I scramble back into them just as Henri pulls up. He's climbing out of the truck when I emerge, and the sight of him there makes my breath come short. That kiss was like nothing I'd ever imagined. And I still don't know what happened. He's been restrained with me even at times when *I* would not have shown restraint. What the hell happens in the next week to change that?

We make a mistake.

If I stay another week or two as promised, he and I will make a mistake. We will sleep together or come close to it, changing things for us both. Why else would he kiss me the way he did?

"You're staring at me like you've seen a ghost," he says, his smile fading. "Is something wrong?"

Yes.

"No," I reply, looking away. "I just think it's time for me to head home."

My last full day with Henri and Marie is a sober one. Henri spends most of it outside and Marie spends it baking, worrying her lower lip with her teeth until it is raw.

"What if you're not well enough to get home?" she asks. "Don't you think you should stay a few more days, just to be safe?"

I watch Henri walk to the pump, his t-shirt clinging to him, drinking water he's cupped in his hands. "No," I reply, my voice a little faint. "I think it's best that I get back right away."

Marie stays home that afternoon, so there is no evening picnic, no ride to the meadow to watch the setting sun. Somehow I didn't think it would be over so quickly. I thought I'd have a chance to say goodbye to each of the places I loved with him, but I won't.

Dinner is painfully quiet, and before it's even done, Marie tears up and excuses herself for the night. Henri and I clear the table, and every time his arm or hip brush against mine I'm thinking about that kiss in the orchard, and wanting it all over again.

"Come on," he says when we're done, placing his hand at the small of my back.

I let him push me toward the door. "Where are we going?"

He laughs. "Where else?"

We walk to the hay bale, the site of so many picnics and the infamous chocolate incident. I squeeze my eyes shut for a moment, wishing I could relive each of them.

He spreads a blanket and we sit side by side, leaning our heads backward to glance at the sliver of moon visible through the clouds. "Tomorrow, that and the sun are going to be the only things we share."

My throat swells to the point of pain. I don't want to live in a world where he is not. "It's not enough."

"No," he says softly. "It's not. So are you glad you wound up staying here?"

I laugh, brushing tears from my face. "Of course. Are you glad I wound up staying here?"

He smiles, but his eyes are sad. "Of course. Although I'm going to be spending the rest of my life fielding questions about my beautiful cousin."

I shrug. "Beautiful? As I recall, you told Madame Beauvoir when I got here that you didn't find me attractive but *not all men could afford to be picky.*"

"That's what you deserved for pretending you didn't understand us. My God," he says, his laughter a low rumble in his chest, "your face when I said that. I was certain you'd crack."

"You knew?! All this time?" I exclaim. "Why didn't you say anything?"

"Why tell you? It was so much more fun to say awful things about you in front of your face and watch you try not to explode."

We both laugh and then it fades to silence again.

"I'm sorry about the dance," he finally says.

"Which part?"

"All of it. That I hurt your feelings. That I probably ruined it for you with my jealousy."

I let my head rest on his shoulder for just a moment. "You made up for in the end. I'm just sorry the only person I got to dance with the whole time I was here was André."

He climbs to his feet and holds out his hand to me. "We should fix that then."

My heart flutters, skips several beats. "Oh...okay."

He places a hand on my waist, another holds mine aloft and begins to hum a tune I don't know.

"If anyone comes out here, they'll see you dancing with your cousin."

He gives me a small smile. "I'm sure you realize at this point they all think we're doing a lot more than that."

My breath catches a little at the suggestion of it, but instead of holding myself back, I step closer and let my head rest on his chest, breathing in the smell of him, memorizing the rough feel of his shirt against my skin, his neck against my forehead. His arms tighten.

Tomorrow I will return home to a world in which Henri and Marie may no longer exist. But even if they do, I couldn't bear to see them old and alone. I want them to stay just as they are. And I wish I could stay with them. I wish I could stay with *him* exactly the way we are now. Leaving is going to hurt more than anything has since I lost Kit.

His hands splay across my back, as if trying to cover as much of my skin as possible, and for a moment I feel his fingertips press, pulling me closer.

"I want your name," he says quietly. "Your real name. I want to be the one person in all of the past who knows who you really are."

I smile, blinking back tears. It's been so long I'd nearly forgotten I ever had a name that wasn't Amelie Durand. "Sarah," I whisper. "Sarah Stewart."

"Sarah," he says, resting a palm against my face. "My little thief."

His breath ghosts over my head, and when I glance up at him again, his eyes are fastened on my mouth as if he is hungry, as if he would devour me if he could. And I want him to so badly that I'm strung tight with it.

His head descends, his mouth gently pressing to each cheek, to my forehead and my eyes, and I'm not sure I'm even breathing as I wait for him to find my mouth. I stopped him when he kissed me the last time, but I don't have it in me to stop him again.

But it doesn't come. Instead he releases me as if he's been

burned, flinching. "Go," he says, more to himself than to me. "It will have to be enough."

He walks off into the darkness without ever looking back and I watch him go, feeling sick with the loss. I know it makes sense— why start something with a girl who's leaving forever?

I always thought I'd be relieved to get home. Now I think it might break my heart instead.

24

I lie in bed that night exhausted and unable to sleep. I will miss the crickets. I will miss the silence behind them. I will miss open windows and the smell of heat-pressed grass blowing in to wake me.

I will miss Marie-Therese, who feels like a sister.

And most of all I will miss Henri, who is everything to me. I can only hope it won't still feel like this once I get home, because I'm not sure I can bear it.

I wake feeling exhausted yet jittery, like I've had ten espressos after a night without sleep. My reflection shows that I am pale today beneath the tan I've gained in the summer sun, with blue circles under my eyes. It's not how I want to look when I say goodbye to him.

I don't want to say goodbye to him at all.

If he'd asked me to stay...

I close my eyes. It doesn't matter. I can't stay, and he doesn't care enough to ask anyway.

I begin sweating at the idea of leaving him. My hands shake, and the white dress I've put on for the last time sticks to my skin. I should be conserving every ounce of energy for the trip home but I can't seem to help it. What should I say to Henri? How will I tell him goodbye? Should I warn him that I will appear in a few months? I guess it's not necessary—if I leave now, then whatever would lead him to kiss me the way he did won't happen. I just hope I don't lose the memory. It's one I'd like to keep forever.

I strip the bed and carefully collect all of the items I've acquired or borrowed during my time here—a brush, some books, bobby pins, the hose and gloves—and place them neatly on the small bureau. I will never be in this house again, in this room again, and even *that* makes me sad, because this place has been more of a home than any I've ever known.

When I get into the kitchen, Marie pushes me to the table where bread and cheese and fruit wait. "You need to eat, for strength," she says.

I nod but I've got little appetite. I should be eager to return home—to television, to comfortable clothes and air conditioning and every food imaginable. I should be eager to return to a life where there are no chores, where nothing is expected of me and life seems to function entirely on its own without any labor on my end. But I'm not. There is nothing inside me that wants to go back.

Marie paces while I pick at a piece of bread. "You've only made a trip of that length once and you're going back weaker than you were," she frets. "What will you do if you don't make it?"

"I'll come find you," I say, forcing a smile, "and you will stuff me full of bread once more and send me on my way."

Her own attempt at a smile falters a little. "Do you think we'll be here then?" she asks quietly. "You think we'll survive this war you say is coming?"

My eyes sting. The truth is I have no idea. Marie might survive, but how will Henri? Whether he remains on this farm or not, I know he'll be fighting. If I were to visit again, even sometime in the next two years, he might already be gone.

"I can't imagine you not surviving just about anything," I tell her. "But I wish you'd consider going to the south of France. The farm will still be here when the war is over, I'm sure."

She smiles sadly. "I need to stay for my mother, and also Henri."

I nod, feeling choked up. "I guess you can always break the Germans' ankles and refuse to go back in time to fix them if they arrive at the farm."

"I owe you an apology for that," she says. "My logic won't make much sense, I suppose, but my mother...she thought you were in love with Henri. She said it was the reason she told you what she did when you visited. So when your ankle broke..."

"You thought it would give us more time together," I conclude. I'd suspected as much already, but I can only admit to myself now that I was grateful for it.

"I see how ridiculous it was now," she says. "Even if things had worked out, you'd have to give up far too much to stay back here with us."

I swallow. If Henri had ever tried to convince me to stay, he might have changed my mind. I suppose it's for the best that I'm leaving now, before it can happen.

I stare at my lap. "Maybe not as ridiculous as you think. But love requires two people in your time, just like it does in mine. Is he even coming to see me off?"

She swallows and stares at her feet. "He was gone when I woke and there's been no sign of him. Just know that his absence is not due to a lack of feeling."

My heart cracks. He's not coming to say goodbye to me, which means I will never see him again. I don't plan to seek either of them out when I get home. Maybe years from now, when it's all more distant and my life has moved on enough, I'll be able to stand to learn what became of them both. But it won't be anytime soon.

"I guess there's no reason to put it off then."

I rise, taking a look around the small house that feels like mine. I wonder if I will ever have this experience again. Even if things work out with Mark, any home we have won't be this: a place where every real piece of me is allowed to reside.

Since I landed in the barn, I decide I should leave from there too. Marie says she'll come with me, and takes my hand as if I'm a child to walk me there.

"You are the only sister I've ever known. I know things are so much better where you are. But please know if you ever decide you want to come back, whether to visit or to stay for good, no one would be happier than I." She smiles through her tears. "No, that's not true. I suppose Henri might be happier."

I squeeze her hand. "Thank you for everything you've done. Please tell Henri—" my head drops and I clench my jaw to ward off tears. What do I want to say to Henri? Too many things, so I settle for none. I shake my head. "Just tell him I said goodbye."

She nods and releases my hand, taking a step away. I close my eyes and begin to focus on home. The year, the place. But at the last minute I turn to take one last glance at the hillside where Henri and I spent so many nights. I look out over the field and try not to long for the sight of him. I let thoughts of home fill me instead, and at last I can feel myself growing light, the air around me dimming as if suddenly night is falling.

And in the very last seconds, when the air begins to whip around me and my body feels the overwhelming tug of home, I see Henri running up the hill. And I'm not sure if it's because I'm scared of what he will say, or if it's just too late for me to stop, but the world goes dark and my body heads for home. The sight of his anguished face is the last thing I see before I go.

25

1 987

I land in a strange place, striking a brick wall hard. It's daylight, but beyond that I can't think. I don't recognize anything. And I'm too tired to figure it out.

I know I need to fight the exhaustion, at least hide away somewhere. But all my thoughts and impulses are caving in along with my vision. I'm sucked into a spiral, and the truth is I don't really care. It feels like I left something vital with Henri, or maybe the vital thing I left was him.

I RECOGNIZE the astringent smell of a hospital before I realize I'm in one. I have no idea how long I was asleep, but a doctor is speaking to someone rapidly, and it occurs to me through my half-functioning brain that my French improved dramatically while I was gone. Despite his speed, I understand him. There is no longer that heavy pause while I pick through the words to make sense of them.

We still don't know what she's taken, he says to the nurse. *Have the police come up with anything?*

They think I'm on drugs. I suppose it makes sense, given how they must have found me.

I try to speak but my throat is so dry it's a struggle to form the words. "I haven't taken anything," I reply, turning my head toward him. "*Je n'ai rien pris.*" He ignores me.

I try to push my hair out of my face as I sit up and discover that I can do neither. I'm tied to the bed, long white bands securing my torso, my forearms, my ankles.

A new fear arises. What if I have not made it back to my own time? What if I'm held captive in some strange middle era between 1938 and 1987 until my ability to leave is gone completely? I'm too weak to jump anywhere at the moment. This I know for certain.

"Let me go!" I demand. My wrists shake against the restraints and go nowhere. My breath comes too fast. I know I should be calm and reasonable right now, but the onset of panic is making it impossible. "*Laissez-moi partir!*"

"Mademoiselle, you need to calm yourself," he says, completely unmoved. He looks bored.

Rage and adrenaline—they entwine together and I gasp with the effort of reining them in. I'm not strong enough to jump so they can do whatever they want to me, but it's his ambivalence that upsets me most—a reminder of what I really lose by refusing to time travel anymore. It just takes one person—an angry cop, a pissed-off ex-boyfriend, a suspicious doctor without a shred of empathy—to strip you of your freedom entirely.

"Why am I restrained?" I demand.

"It's standard protocol for patients who come in high," he replies crisply.

"I'm not high!" I scream, losing any semblance of calm. "Get me out of these things!" My heart begins to thud loudly in my chest.

The doctor asks the nurse to hand him a syringe. They're going to sedate me, and then I won't have a chance of escape. I won't even be able to talk my way out of this. "No," I beg. "Please Don't."

"You need to calm down," he repeats. The needle presses into my bicep and I start to scream, closing my eyes to jump out of this bed, out of this skin.

The cool liquid is seeping into my blood when a man comes to the room. He's black, so large he seems to take up most of the door.

"*S'arretez-vous!*" he orders. He grabs the doctor but it's too late. I can already feel my eyes growing heavy. *She is the granddaughter of Cecelia Boudon,* he announces, *and if you've hurt a hair on her head, you will be very sorry.*

I'm relieved to have someone, *anyone*, intervening. But I have no idea who Cecelia Boudon is. And I'm definitely not her granddaughter.

～

WHEN I WAKE, I'm in a sunlit room, one that does not smell or look like a hospital. *General Hospital* is playing on the TV across from me, overdubbed in French. The windowsill and nightstand hold a wealth of flowers.

A nurse stands beside me. *It's just a blood pressure check*, she says testily. At first I assume she's talking to me, but then there's a low grunt from the corner of the room: *D'accord*, someone says.

It's the man from earlier. His jacket has fallen open just enough to reveal the holstered gun at his side. No wonder she sounds so defensive.

Just once I'd like to land in a version of France where I'm not greeted with guns.

"Who are you?" I ask. My voice is hoarse.

He startles a bit at the sound of my voice. "I'm surprised you're awake. They gave you enough sedative to fell a horse for a week," he says. "My name is Philippe. I'm one of your grandmother's bodyguards."

I glance at him warily. I know for a fact that both of my grandmothers are dead, and that neither of them were French, or had bodyguards. Sooner or later, he's going to realize I'm not who he thinks I am. I'm still not strong enough to jump, so my only chance to escape is now, before this *Cecelia Boudon*, whoever she really is, arrives to rat me out.

"When...when is my grandmother coming?" I ask. The nurse is leaving and I'm no longer restrained. Surely there will be a moment when this large man has to step out of the room.

"I'm calling her now," he replies, picking up the phone.

I sit, pulling the blood pressure cuff from my arm, swinging my legs over the edge of the bed and he rises. "I'm just going to—" I begin.

He cuts me off with a low laugh and a wide smile that makes him seem slightly less dangerous. "Slow down, Mademoiselle Besson."

I gasp. "What did you call me?" That's when it occurs to me to lift my wrist.

Amelie Besson, the hospital bracelet says. DOB: 5-8-1966.

My made-up French name. My actual date of birth.

He hangs up the phone. "Madame Boudon has asked me to reassure you she is a friend of the Durand family."

A friend. Does that mean Henri and Marie-Therese asked her to look out for me? But how could they, when they had no idea where and when I'd be arriving? Does it mean they're alive?

Maybe she is Henri's daughter, or his wife.

My throat tightens at the thought.

Please God, don't let it be either of those. I wanted Henri to be happy after I left, and I do hope he had a family. I'm just not ready to witness it firsthand.

WITHIN THIRTY MINUTES there's a bustle at the door, and a woman strides in with a retinue behind her. She is in her early forties, perhaps, wearing a Chanel suit and subtle but clearly expensive jewelry. There's a diamond on her finger that could easily pay for my last year at Penn. To my relief, she does not look at all like Henri. She's blonde like me, and blue-eyed as well—but they are not the eyes of a time traveler, which is also a relief.

She dismisses Philippe and the men who followed her in with a mere nod of the head, and perches elegantly on the edge of my mattress.

"Hello, Amelie. I'm Cecelia," she says with a fond smile. "You're probably a little confused right now."

I meet her gaze warily. "How...how do you know who I am?"

Her smile grows slightly wistful, sad, and my stomach drops. I pray she's not thinking of Henri and Marie-Therese when she smiles like that.

"You're so young. I hadn't realized how young you were," she says, a hand smoothing over my hair. "But I think it might be best if we exchange very little information. It was brought to my attention that your arrival here would go...poorly. And perhaps I should not have intervened..." her brow furrows. "I hope I've made the right choice. I didn't want you to suffer the way you would have."

She knows I'm a time traveler. I feel a small skittering panic and try to rein it in, running my tongue over my dry, chapped lips.

"So you're friends with Marie-Therese and Henri?" I ask.

Her expression gives nothing away. "Naughty girl. Don't try to trick me into giving you information. Now I've rescued you, but I have a condition. It will probably sound a bit extreme, but I need to know that my rescue will not change what's going to happen from here."

"What *is* going to happen?"

She laughs to herself and shakes her head. "I'm not telling you that, because telling you would change it. So here is my condition: the next three weeks need to go as they would have, had I not intervened. So you must remain in Paris for that period of time, and you can't see anyone until it's through."

I open my mouth to object and she holds up her palm, very clearly a woman used to getting her way. "Are you glad now that Marie-Therese wouldn't fix your ankle?" she asks abruptly.

My mouth falls open. How she knows what happened is a mystery, but I can't argue with what she's saying, even if a part of me wants to. Denying that I'm happy I stayed also means denying all those afternoons with Henri. It means wishing away our hours on the porch spent reading, the days we went riding, or watching the sun descend. It means there'd be no dancing, there'd be no kiss.

"Yes," I admit. "I'm glad."

"I know for a fact that you want the future you will have if you remain for the next three weeks and do as I say. And I don't know that you'll still have that future if you leave before then."

I want to trust her, but she must have a motive of some kind. "Maybe I'll have a future I like just as much."

She gives me a look—exasperated and amused, as if she already knows what I will decide but is humoring me by continuing to debate this. "You will gamble so many times in the coming years. Please don't gamble with this."

"How do I know you're actually trying to help me? How do I know you're not just trying to keep me here so I *don't* do something I'm supposed to do?"

She smiles. "You don't. I suppose this is the first of your many gambles."

I look at her. She seems nice enough. She did rescue me, and if she wanted to stop me from leaving, she probably has the power to keep me drugged for the next three weeks.

"Okay. So what am I supposed to do here?"

"Recover," she says. "It's what you'd have done anyway, just in much more difficult conditions. I've arranged a hotel room for you, and everything will be taken care of. You won't see me again, but Louis or Philippe will be nearby at all times and can get you whatever you need."

"I don't think I need..."

"A guard? I'm sure you do not," she says with a soft smile. "But I cannot risk any harm coming to you here, and I'm changing the past a bit, simply by interfering, so let me reassure myself you'll come to no harm."

A bodyguard *is* better than being locked up for the next three weeks. I nod, reluctantly, and she rises. "Be well, my friend. We will see each other again."

She leaves, and I find myself alone and awake for the first time since I got back. There's a TV on the wall across from me. A menu on the nightstand that probably offers all the foods I missed. I ignore both, closing my eyes, trying to picture what Henri and Marie are doing now. *No, not now*, I correct. In *1938*, what are they doing? It's nearly lunch. Marie is probably teaching English or German and Henri is in the fields. In a month or two he will see me again during my attempt to try out my ankle—and what will happen then?

My last memory is of him running up the hillside, perhaps to change my mind, and his last memory of me is yet to come—it'll take place two months ahead, and I pray it isn't a memory of me stumbling away from him after he's kissed me.

God, I wish I'd done things differently. I thought I'd be grateful, *overjoyed*, to get home. Instead I'm so weighed down by regret I don't even want to open my eyes.

∿

I SPEND most of the next three days sleeping in the yellow room, which I'm informed is a private hospital on the outskirts of Paris. I'm too exhausted, for the most part, to give it much thought, but during the time I'm awake I wonder why this is happening. Who Cecelia could be and why she cares enough to rescue me in the first place.

I'm fed at regular intervals, though it turns out that hospital food is still hospital food, even in France and even for the wealthy. I occasionally catch glimpses of Phillipe or a similarly intimidating man in a suit, but they remain outside the room and silent.

As I recover I find I'm missing 1938 more rather than less. I spend my lucid time watching TV, trying to keep my mind off a past that does not belong to me, but it doesn't work.

On the fourth day, when I'm finally recovered enough to get restless, Louis—the other guard—tells me we are going to the hotel, and hands me a small bag from Gucci. Inside I find black heels and a black sheath, very *Breakfast at Tiffany's*. Things I could never afford and would have few places to wear.

I glance at it, and back at Louis. "I'm supposed to put this *on*?"

"Unless you'd prefer to wear a hospital gown."

Where the hell are we going that I'd need to wear this stuff? I have sudden visions of some party for the extremely wealthy, where I'm trotted out like a circus freak for viewing and questioning. I set the bag on the bed and fold my arms across my chest.

"I thought we were going to a hotel," I say. "Why is all this so fancy?"

There's a glimmer of amusement in his eyes, but his face betrays nothing. "We *are* going to the hotel, and I believe Madame Boudon would not consider these things fancy. She's merely chosen for you what she herself might wear."

I guess it makes sense, as much as any of this makes sense, except the stuff in this bag is easily worth a thousand dollars, and

I'm struggling to understand why Madame Boudon would spend a thousand dollars on a broke girl she doesn't know.

THE LIMOUSINE that picks me up from the hospital reaches the highway quickly, and just as soon is weaving through the streets of Paris. The city itself doesn't look so different than it did when I was here with Henri. The traffic is heavier, and moves faster, but the biggest difference is the people. Their clothes, the speed with which they walk down the street. They don't seem to look at each other quite as much as they did.

We turn just off the Champs Elysees and come to a stop. "We are here," announces Louis.

Here is the Ritz Carlton.

And, as I discover five short minutes later, *here* is also a suite. Two bathrooms, a living area and a bedroom. It's got more square feet than my shared apartment in Philly, along with a plush couch, huge mahogany bed, and a fruit tray on the four-person table. I forget everything else and go straight to it, like a child set free in a chocolate factory, popping a massive piece of pineapple in my mouth. It dissolves on my tongue in an explosion of sweetness. Okay, *pineapple* I have definitely missed.

"Mademoiselle Durand," says Louis quietly, nodding at the bellman who's watching, stupefied, as I shove another piece in my mouth.

"Oh," I say, attempting to swallow. "Um, *c'est tout*?" Louis' mouth curves upward. He tips the bellman and then laughs when the door closes behind him. "It is customary to *tell* the bellman that is all, rather than to *ask* him."

I smile, a bit sheepish. "I haven't spent a lot of time dealing with bellmen."

He grins. "Yes, I gathered as much."

I bite my lip. The fact that Louis is capable of smiling encourages me. Mostly it encourages me to pry a little, because I'm dying to know exactly who Cecelia is, and why she's helping me.

"You know Madame Boudon well?" I ask. "You've worked for her a while?"

His smile fades and he folds his arms across his chest. "Yes. And that is the last question about her I will answer. Phillipe or I will be outside at all times. You have appointments tomorrow also, so please be ready to leave by 10."

My head shoots up. They somehow acquired my passport and credit card from the woods in Saint Antoine, but I'd still rather not spend money I don't have. And the money in my savings account is for tuition, nothing more.

"Appointments?" I ask. "I don't need..."

"It is taken care of," he replies.

I squirm. I can just picture my mother's reaction if she knew I was blithely accepting such largesse from an absolute stranger, especially one I've come to meet because I time traveled. "I don't feel comfortable—"

"Madame Boudon is the wealthiest woman in France, and among the wealthiest in the world. Do not insult her by refusing her generosity," he says, and with that he walks out, shutting the door behind him.

I spend the rest of the day in the room, shaking off the last of my fatigue. The suite has three TVs. I turn each of them on and back off, wondering if it's possible ease and happiness don't have as much overlap as I once believed.

It's been a week since I left 1938. Henri and Marie are probably used to it now, life without my casted ankle knocking about and my ineptly made bread, but I can't get used to being gone. I order a burger and look out the window. Paris waits outside for me, but I don't have the heart for it just yet. Will I hold every future trip to this city against the day spent here with Henri? I will, and I'm pretty sure they'll all fall short.

THE NEXT MORNING Philippe taps on the door just as I'm finishing my omelet. I'm wearing the black dress and heels because I have nothing else and I feel sort of ridiculous.

"Where are we going, anyway?" I ask.

"First, to get clothes."

I frown. "I need an *appointment* to get clothes?"

"At the stores Madame Boudon frequents you do."

The limousine drives me only three blocks, which seems silly, although I wouldn't have wanted to walk them in these heels anyway. It stops in front of Chanel.

My head swivels to Philippe. "I can't shop here. Even a t-shirt probably costs a thousand dollars. Can't we just go to, like, The Gap? Or whatever the French version of that is?"

"Madame insists," he says.

Cecelia appears to know something about my future—does all this mean I turn into the kind of woman who will only wear couture? Mark's mother is, but that has never been the kind of luxury I was after. I just want to be able to pay for my kids' braces and replace the washing machine when it breaks. I want the luxury of not *needing* to time travel, not needing to risk lives, in order to meet my family's needs.

I follow him inside. The women working there fawn over me as if I'm someone famous, or wealthy, which just makes me feel worse. I've been given the distinct impression from Philippe that I'm not leaving until I pick out something, so eventually I relent and buy one dress and one pair of shoes I might wear at home if I was attending something especially nice.

He relents once we get outside and gives me enough cash to get a pair of sneakers, a pair of jeans and a few t-shirts at a cheap place nearby, all for less than the cost of a scarf at Chanel.

That afternoon I'm taken downstairs to the spa where I undergo the kind of transformation I've only seen in movies.

Pedicure, manicure, facial. My brows are plucked, my skin is waxed, my hair trimmed. It's as if Cecelia is trying to get me ready for Mark's proposal. Maybe this is part of the future she promised I'd want, but all I feel when I imagine it is dread.

I SPEND the next days wandering the streets of Paris. I go to Montmartre, to Trocadero and Les Invalides, the Louvre and yes—the Eiffel Tower, despite how much Henri maligned it. I take day trips to St. Malo and Mont St. Michelle and Omaha Beach. The driver takes me to the Normandy American Cemetery, and I chicken out at the last minute. There are French graves there too. I'm terrified I might see Henri's name.

I go to Giverny, which is now open to the public. I go to Versailles but spend most of my trip there sitting beside a rectangular pool outside its perimeter. I'm not scared of the water so much anymore, and I guess I have Henri to thank for it. That's probably why I spend the entire time thinking only of him.

Eventually I end up back in Saint-Germain-des-Pres. Les Deux Magots and Cafe Flore are still there, but they are now packed with photo-taking tourists. The restaurant where he and I dined is gone. But I continue to wander the streets anyway, trying to find what is missing.

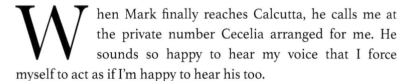

26

When Mark finally reaches Calcutta, he calls me at the private number Cecelia arranged for me. He sounds so happy to hear my voice that I force myself to act as if I'm happy to hear his too.

"My flight gets into Paris on the 16th," he says. "I can't wait to see you."

I bite my lip. I don't want him to come here to have the *I need some space* conversation, and I don't want to have it by phone. And perhaps it won't even be necessary, because I'll see him and things will finally feel right. But I'd rather not take any chances.

"If you want to fly straight home to New York you can," I suggest. "You've got to be sick of traveling. I can just meet you there instead. My flight gets in on the 22nd."

I want him to agree. I want it desperately. "Are you crazy?" he asks. "It's Paris. And you're there. Of course there's nowhere else I want to be. Where should I pick you up?"

I hesitate. He knows I can't afford the Ritz Carlton. "I'm pretty far outside of the city," I tell him. "Why don't I just meet you somewhere?"

And naturally he suggests the one place I don't want to share with him: Saint-Germain-des-Pres.

ON THE EVENING of the 16th, at the appointed hour, I wear the Gucci dress with the Chanel heels and I insist that Phillipe, my guard for the evening, sit this one out.

"I'm probably not coming back tonight," I tell him. I wait for him to protest, and when he doesn't, I grow more aware of a sick, swirling feeling in my stomach, one that's been here every time I've considered what tonight entails.

I know what Mark's expecting, but I can't go through with it. When he touches me, I will crave calloused hands on my skin that are not his, Henri's weight and size and smell pressing against me. I'm missing those things more and more with every hour that passes.

I take a cab to the corner of Quai Voltaire and Rue Bonaparte. Mark is already waiting, a wide smile on his face when I emerge from the car.

He looks good, tan and a little thinner from the weeks in Nepal. I smile back, still nervous but also relieved. This isn't some stranger. It's Mark, who I've adored for two full years. And if my adoration is a bit more tempered than it was, perhaps that's for the best. There's always been a piece of me that felt like he could do better, but that piece of me is gone. He's a good man, but if I was enough for Henri, I'm enough for anyone.

I cross the street and his arms band tight around me, his mouth landing on mine. It's the way he's always kissed me, but it feels as if I'm experiencing it all from a distance, like an alien noting all the aspects of some strange human custom, perhaps wondering what possible purpose this joining of the mouths could have: the texture of his tongue against mine. Moisture on my lips. It's not like kissing Henri. It doesn't make my limbs melt, it doesn't make me forget where we are.

I don't want this, I hear a voice in my head saying, and it makes me panic, because *this* is what I have, and it's what I've planned for. I want to become the version of me who thought Mark hung the moon, who truly believed this was the best path I could take, because I'm not sure where we stand if I'm no longer her.

I pull away and he smiles down at me, pushing my hair back, leaving his palms on the sides of my face. "I'd forgotten how beautiful you are," he says softly. "I'll try to behave for the next hour or two but it's not going to be easy."

For the next hour or two. My chest tightens. I'll deal with it when the time comes.

We get a table at Café Flore. A drink or two will calm my nerves, I promise myself. It will put me back, mentally, in the year I belong.

Mark flags down a waiter and orders himself bourbon. He starts to order me a margarita and I stop him and ask for a glass of Beaujolais instead.

"Look at my little sophisticate after a summer in France," he says. "I thought you'd never come around to drinking wine." There's a shade of condescension in the words. I guess there has been before, but it's never bothered me until now.

For the next hour we talk. I tell him the little I can about my time in France, which isn't much, but mostly he talks about Nepal. The conversation is interesting, but it lacks something. We don't banter, and the only time he laughs is when he's recalling something funny that happened on his trip. No matter what we are discussing—whether it's art or music or movies or the future —it all feels a little empty, like a conversation you have to pass the time while stuck in line.

My roommate that summer in New York called us Ivy League Barbie and Ken, and I'm sure that's exactly what we look like right now, a perfectly matched set of blondes in expensive clothes. But I'm not enjoying this, and I don't know how to fix it. Mark is a lovely man, but Henri is like the cornerstone of a building and Mark is merely a decorative element on its exterior, pretty but ultimately meaningless.

He squeezes my hand. "You seem different tonight. Is everything okay?"

"I'm fine," I lie, smiling at him across the table. "I think I'm still a little under the weather is all."

He leans forward to take my other hand. "Maybe it's time we went back to the room?"

My pulse rises. "No," I reply too quickly. "I'm not tired at all."

He laughs. "I know you're nervous about tonight. Don't be, okay? It's going to be good. I'll take care of everything."

I slowly release a breath. I'd be nervous under the best of circumstances. I'd be nervous if there were no Henri, if I'd never gone back to 1938. But this is different. It's not nerves. It's an absolute unwillingness.

"Mark," I whisper, "I'm sorry. But it's not happening tonight. I'm just not ready."

Just then a waiter bumps our table and Mark gives him a dirty look. "Watch it," he snaps.

It's a tiny show of irritation, but it reminds me a bit of André, the way his kindness came easily to him when things were going well and abandoned him completely when it didn't. I've never seen Mark when things aren't going well for him, I realize. It's probably the kind of thing I should become familiar with before this moves forward.

He forces a smile. "It's fine. Let's just go to the room. Nothing has to happen."

WE WALK along the Seine to his hotel.

I'm in Paris, wearing couture and walking along one of the most famous rivers in the world under a full moon with a man who thinks he wants to marry me. It's my most ridiculous high school fantasy on steroids. And yet I'm longing for a different man and a different place entirely.

"What a perfect night, huh?" he asks, grabbing my hand. "Look at that moon."

I do, and all I think when I see it is that it's the same moon Henri is looking at in another time. I can't bring myself to think of him in the past tense. The moon is as close to infinite as anything can be, neither past nor present, and I choose to believe somewhere Henri exists under its glow still. Will he think of me when he sees it?

"Have you given any more thought to transferring?" Mark asks.

I stumble a little, jolted from my thoughts and surprised by the question. "Mark, I've only got one year left. I want to graduate with my friends. And besides, I can't transfer from Penn this late in the game. It'd take a year just to get in anywhere."

"So take a year off," he says, as if it's the simplest thing in the world. "You don't even have to work, or if you wanted to, I'm sure there's a gallery somewhere that would be all over a super-hot receptionist who majored in art history."

The spark of irritation I felt flares into something else, something far greater than I remember ever feeling with him. "So you're suggesting that instead of graduating from an Ivy League college in one year, *less* than a year actually, I should give it up to become a receptionist somewhere?"

He exhales heavily, pushing a hand through his hair. "I already said you don't *have* to work. You can stay at my place, hang out, and start at Columbia when your transfer comes through. It'll give you a whole year to plan a wedding. Women love that shit."

I pull my hand away and turn to face him. "You could have

gotten a job anywhere. If it's so important that we're in the same place, get a job in Philadelphia."

He rolls his eyes. "Get real, Sarah," he says. "I just got hired by JP Morgan. I'm not moving to *Philadelphia*."

I stare at him, thinking *Henri would never ask this of me*. What did he say when I told him Mark had asked me to move? *If what was best for the woman I loved was for her to stay where she was, the one thing I'd never do is ask her to give it up.*

I picture Henri's face on the last night we were together. The longing I saw there, and his refusal to act on it. And again when he kissed me in the field that day...looking at me as if my presence was a miracle, as if I was all he'd ever wanted.

I picture it, and am suddenly struck hard by a thought. What if the reason he kept silent wasn't because he didn't care enough, but because he cared so much that he wanted what was best for me, rather than what was best for him? What if he didn't kiss me because things were going to change between us, but because he thought I'd chosen, on my own, to return to him? That I was there to give him the things he refused to ask for—my heart and a life that could be spent much more safely and comfortably in my own time.

The thought makes my breath stop. God, I want it to be true. And the more I let the possibility crash through my brain, the more likely it seems.

Mark sighs and steps close to me, placing his hands on my waist. "I'm sorry I said it like that. I just love you so much that I don't want to be away from you, okay? But tonight is special. We don't have to figure it all out now."

Exactly, says the old version of me. *Just find a way to make this work.* But there's a new voice now, a louder one, that insists otherwise. I remove his hands and take a step backward.

"I disagree. I think this is definitely a conversation we need to have right now."

I see irritation flicker across his face again. "Jesus, Sarah," he says, pushing a hand through his hair. "Since when are you so argumentative? I want you in New York because I love you and I don't want to be away from you. Why is that suddenly a crime?"

"Pushing me to give up what I want isn't love."

His mouth falls open. "I thought what you wanted was *me*."

I look at him, at his handsome, *incredulous* face. He's right. He's right to think that what I wanted was him, because for our entire relationship, he *did* matter more than anything else. Or maybe not him, but the life I saw with him—one where I could be a different person, a person I didn't hate quite so much.

Except, I realize suddenly: I'm already that person.

I'm not sure when it changed. Maybe it was all those weeks watching Marie use her gifts to help her neighbors, to make all of our lives slightly better ones. Maybe it was finally admitting my role in Kit's death, and seeing for the first time that my guilt is normal, and human, and a burden my mother should have shared.

But mostly I think it was Henri. It was being seen by him as I am, and being loved for it.

Mark doesn't see me as I am, and whatever it is he thinks he cares for...it isn't me.

"I'm sorry," I tell him. "I changed this summer. And I think I might be in love with someone else."

MARK ARGUES. He gets mad, and then upset, and after a minute or two of this the limousine pulls up and the driver steps out.

"Madame Boudon thought you might be ready to leave."

Mark stares at him and then glares at me. "Who the fuck is Madame Boudon?"

"Possibly my only living friend in this country," I reply. I throw my arms around him, whispering one last apology in his ear, and then I climb into the back of the car and begin to weep.

How stupid I was. How impossibly stupid I was.

I'm in love with Henri in a way you never find twice.

I don't merely lust for his pretty face and his full mouth and the broad shoulders I used to watch from afar. I adore him, and even if it means I'll do nothing more than sit on the periphery of his life and exist near him, I'd agree. I will gladly milk cows and cook and hang the laundry and all of the other tasks I complained about so vehemently, just for the gift of his sudden smile, his surprised laugh.

I'm still not certain Henri wants me there for good. I could return to 1938 to discover I misinterpreted everything he ever did and said. And even if he does want me, returning will be terrible in more ways than I can name. I won't finish my degree. There will be rationing and hunger. I might die in the process, and he might too. And the next time I come to 1987, I'll be an old woman, if I reach it at all.

But in the end it comes down to a simple truth, one that matters more than all of the other truths: I don't want to exist in a world where he is not.

27

My mother is stiff when I call, and formal. She tells me how my brother is doing—Steven has long been the only subject we have in common. His wife just miscarried again, she says, adding that it's sometimes for the best. There's no doubt in my mind she's thinking of me when she says it.

"How was your trip to Paris?" she finally asks without interest.

I glance around my suite, thinking how disgusted she would be if she could see me now. My mother thinks time travel is something I should be deeply ashamed of, and the ways I benefit from it sicken her. She'd see this suite as one of those ways.

"I'm still here, actually. Mark and I broke up, so I'm planning to stay a while."

"I can't say I'm surprised," she replies. "No offense, but I never understood why he was with you, aside from your looks, and pretty women are a dime a dozen."

It's amazing to me that a few months ago I'd have *agreed* with her, and I'd have thought Mark dodged a bullet in getting clear of me.

"I was the one who ended it. And it might surprise you to

learn that some men don't object to women with magical gifts," I reply, "particularly ones that can fix mistakes and guarantee unlimited wealth."

She doesn't like that. In my mother's silence I hear the sound of a snake as it retracts, preparing to lash out. "So you've found someone new then," she replies. "Try telling him you killed your own sister and see if he's still so enamored of your gift then."

I've heard these words, or some version of them, many times before. Normally they can silence me like nothing else, but today they don't.

"I think you mean *we*," I reply. "*We* killed Kit, the two of us. Me, an innocent 11-year old who had no idea I was going to time travel and you, Kit's mother, who knew I might start time jumping any day but still entrusted her care to me instead of watching her yourself. So *we*, and I'm being generous with that."

"How dare you blame that on me?" she asks. "You were jealous and you allowed it to happen." Her voice wobbles, rasps. I've never heard her cry once since Kit died. Never heard even a second of vulnerability. For a moment I feel guilty: why make her share the burden of Kit's death? If blaming it on me is what allows her to continue living, I should let her have it.

I open my mouth to apologize, to take back what I said. "I'm —" I begin, but she cuts me off.

"If you'd died when you got meningitis, I'd still have my daughter." She's weeping.

I'd be lying if I said it didn't hurt, if I said there wasn't a part of me that didn't still wish I had a mother who approved, or at least didn't despise me. But it doesn't hurt the way it once would have.

"Actually, you'd have two," I reply just before I hang up the phone. "And now you have none."

TWO DAYS LATER, three weeks on the dot since I returned to my own time, I'm ready to leave it again. This time, I hope, for good.

Cecelia made yet another spa appointment for me after I broke up with Mark, which made me realize she was never trying to get me ready for a life with him in the first place. She somehow knew, or at least hoped, that my life would end up back with Henri.

I hope she's right.

"I'm not sure what to do with all this stuff," I tell Louis on my last day. When I failed to buy myself a new wardrobe at Chanel, clothes began to arrive. More clothes than I could wear in a year, along with shoes and purses and toiletries.

"It is yours," he tells me. "Madame Boudon says she will keep them until you return to visit us again."

"I'm...I'm not planning to come back."

He bows his head. "We'll keep them just in case you change your mind."

I take one last look around my suite. It's been like a dream, but I have another dream, one that is so much more compelling. Saying goodbye to my own time is far easier than I ever thought it might be.

28

This time when I jump from the woods near 11 Rue Ste Genevieve, I know exactly what I hope to find on the other side. I picture eyes the color of the forest at dusk and the slow curve of a smile meant only for me. And as everything begins to blacken around me, there is no panic. There is only relief.

I could try to land the day I left, but I choose not to. I have no right to steal days from them that they lived without me, although I suppose this is what I'll be doing from now on. But who knows what might have happened while I was gone? Marie could have won over her priest or discovered the prophecy is about her. She might have decided to move to the south of France like I asked.

Even if what's changed hurts me—if Henri is now with Claudette, for instance—it would be wrong for me to erase those weeks from their existence, rewrite it all with me present for them, just because I wish it was so. So I proceed carefully, skipping through decades and then years and then months and finally counting days until I'm fairly confident I'm exactly where I want to be—August 22, 1938, three weeks after I left.

I land in the hay again, of course, and land badly, but the heaviness of the journey is already settling on me and there's no time to waste. I bolt from the stall, grabbing the blanket that hangs on a peg to the left. I wrap it around me, and though sleep has begun its siren's call, I keep pushing forward. I knew I missed Henri, but I had no idea how much until this moment, until he's so very close and I have a few conscious minutes at most to lay eyes on him.

I rush into the yard just as he is climbing out of the truck. He sees me and for a moment only stares, as if I'm a ghost. That same longing is there, but uncertainty also. I have no time for his uncertainty, however, so I run, or try to anyway, stumbling over the long blanket at my feet, hair flying.

I throw my arms around his neck and feel his heart thudding beneath my ear. My eyes flutter and the fatigue settles over me like a weight I can no longer push away. I tip my head up toward him. "I'm back," I whisper, as I sink into oblivion. "I made it back."

29

I wake in the room next to Marie's, which is flooded with morning sun. A chair sits next to the bed, with a blanket tossed over the arm and a dog-eared book on the table beside it.

My limbs are as heavy as ever when I rise, and the simple act of climbing out of bed feels like it requires more strength than I might have, but the breeze coming through the window is refreshing, not sweltering, and I'm motivated to get downstairs in a way I wasn't the first time I arrived. In spite of the journey and the days I've probably spent sleeping, a quick glance in the cracked mirror on the wall confirms I still haven't lost the sheen of my spa day. I'm ready to begin my life here...as long as Henri wants that too.

I hear the sound of feet racing up the stairs just as I've pulled the white dress over my head, and suddenly Marie comes running in. "I thought I heard you moving around!" she cries, throwing her arms around me. "At last! I want to hear everything, but first things first. You'll eat while I draw you a bath, and then—"

I glance out the window. I've craved the sight of Henri's face like a drowning man craves oxygen, and for far too long. "I just…I think I need to talk to Henri first."

She waves my words away. "There's time for that later. You've been asleep for days and you need your energy. Just take a quick bath while I go get him."

She heads toward the door but turns back just as it opens. "I'm so, so happy you're here," she says. "I hope you plan to stay."

That's in your brother's hands, not mine. I think of how uncertain his face looked when I ran to him and the doubt in my stomach begins to spread through my blood. "I hope it all works out."

I take the world's quickest bath and dress again before I hobble downstairs. I'm holding my breath, bracing for Henri, but when I reach the kitchen I find only Marie bustling around, having already placed an obscene amount of food on the table.

"Where's Henri?" I ask.

"I'm leaving to get him in a second, but first you must eat." She bites her lip. "And I thought perhaps we should talk."

My stomach falls to the floor. I take a chair at the table, not sure I can continue to stand. It's only been a few weeks. I thought he might be dating someone but he couldn't already be serious with her, could he?

"Talk? About what?"

Her eyes are worried. "I think there are some things you need to understand. When you—"

The door opens, and her words stop short.

Henri stands at the threshold. Our eyes meet, and I start to rise but Marie's hand presses to my shoulder. "You will stay where you are, and you will eat. And you," she says, turning to Henri, "will sit politely at the table, and wait until she's done."

He looks more worried than pleased to see me here. Did I misunderstand the things he said? "Marie," he says, his eyes never leaving mine, "get out."

"Do you not *care* how well she recovers?" Marie asks. "Stop being selfish and take a seat."

Henri sighs and slides his large frame onto the bench across from me. I watch, wondering how there ever could have been a time when I didn't know I loved him. When I didn't want that full, pouting mouth of his on mine, when I didn't want his calloused hands—currently clasped tight above the table—on my skin. There is so much we need to say to each other, so much I need to know, and the fact that it can't be said with Marie here makes me feel even more choked, even more desperate, than I already did.

"Tell us what happened," Marie says breathlessly. "What brought you back?"

"What made her change her mind is none of your concern, Marie," snaps Henri. "Don't you have errands to run or children to teach?"

"All in good time. She deserves a chance to tell her side of the story," she says, shooting Henri a look I can't quite interpret. She turns to me. "Start at the beginning."

I'm not sure what she means by *my side* of the story, as if there was a fight. Henri can't be mad that I left—he never once asked me to stay. With one last glance at him, I begin to tell the story between bites of bread and cheese and sausage: how I woke, tied to a gurney, under the command of a doctor who was certain I was an addict. And the mysterious Cecelia and how she rescued me from all of it but would never tell me why. The whole time I'm talking, however, all I want to do is drink in the sight of him. I can barely look his way, however, without forgetting what I've just said.

"And you still have no idea who she was?" Marie asks.

"None. She said she was a friend of yours," I reply, "but she isn't even born yet, so that seems unlikely. And she told the hospital my name was Amelie Besson."

Marie looks slightly alarmed. "Could she have been...one of our children? Mine, or Henri's?"

I shake my head. "I think she would have said so. And she had a different last name and looked nothing like either of you. But anyway, she agreed to take care of me until I recovered. She seemed to know my arrival there would have gone really badly if she didn't intervene."

"But what happened when you landed that made things go so wrong?" she asks. "I hope you were at least able to get to your clothes before you fell asleep."

I bite my lip. I hate not knowing what could have happened to me during those missing hours between my arrival in 1987 and waking in the hospital. "I'm not sure. I remember landing, but I wasn't at the farm. I was in an alley somewhere. It was like I fell into the wall and that was it. The next thing I know I was in the hospital."

Henri buries his head in his hands, looking even less happy than he did a moment before. "*Dieu. Anything* could have happened to you."

"But it didn't," says Marie, grabbing my hand. "And look at her. She's never looked healthier."

Henri doesn't look reassured. I came here for him, willing to give up everything, and he seems to wish I hadn't.

"And Mark?" he asks, his shoulders rigid. "Did you see him?"

I'm not sure what's happening between us, but the air is thick —with tension and desperation and unanswered questions—and there's just too much there. Like colliding weather in the heat of summer, there will need to be a storm before we can have clear air.

"Yes, I saw him. He came into Paris before I left."

Henri's eyes darken until they're nearly the color of night. "Meeting in Paris. I assume that means you called him."

"Yes," I snap. "That's generally how people get in touch with each other."

Marie's glance darts between the two of us. "So back to

Cecelia," she says, her voice overly cheerful and loud. "She took care of you?"

I nod, still watching Henri. "She put me up in a suite in the Ritz Carlton."

Marie sighs dreamily. "So you lived like a queen for three weeks. What did you eat? How did you get clothes?"

I swallow and look away from Henri. "I felt like *The Little Princess*. Anything I could possibly have wanted, I had. She even took me to Chanel and when I didn't want to buy anything, she began sending designer clothes to the hotel, more clothes than I could have worn in a decade."

Henri's eyes have narrowed to slits. "It sounds as if you should have stayed."

If he'd reached into my chest and ripped my heart in two, it couldn't hurt more than his words do now. "I'm beginning to wish I had," I reply, rising with my plate in hand, torn between weeping or throwing something at his head.

He pushes away from the table, grabbing what I left behind and following me to the counter. "Marie," he hisses as he slams the butter and bread down beside me. "It's time for you to leave."

"Please," she begs, "you both need to—"

"Go," he growls. "*Now*."

The door shuts and neither of us blink an eye. He's wounded me, but only rage feels safe right now. "Do you have any idea what I gave up to come back here?" I ask. "And what I risked making the trip?"

"Do you have any idea what it was like to be stuck here knowing you were with someone else?" he demands. "For all I knew you'd already *married* him."

"Well I'm here now!" I cry. "And it's like you don't even care!"

He tugs at his hair with an angry laugh. "Don't *care*? I've spent the past three nights watching you sleep. That's how much I *don't care*. And given how horrified you looked when I kissed you last week, and the way you vanished when it happened, I can't imagine why you'd choose to return."

"Last week?" I ask. "But..."

The day I jumped ahead. I thought it was fall, but could it have been an unusually pleasant August day instead? Yes, it absolutely could have been. No wonder he's been so uncertain since I arrived. "That wasn't last week for me," I whisper. "It happened back when I was still staying here with you."

"And you couldn't have explained that? You left me feeling like I was another André!"

I throw out my hands. "I thought I could prevent it happening if I left early!"

The light in his eyes dies and I realize the error I've made immediately. "I'm not saying I wanted to prevent it. I just didn't know..."

His mouth becomes a flat line. "Didn't know what?"

I take a deep breath. "I didn't know I was in love with you. And I didn't know if you'd want me to stay—"

I don't finish the sentence. That's how fast he closes the distance between us, pushing my back to the refrigerator as his mouth crashes on mine. A hard, possessing kiss with his hands tight on my hips. What I've longed for all these months.

"All I have ever wanted was for you to stay," he says, his mouth moving to my jaw.

"You never said that. Not once."

He huffs a pained laugh against my skin and pulls back, framing my face with his hands. "How could you not have known? Marie knew. The *whole town* knew. I haven't been capable of wanting anything else since you arrived."

His mouth moves over mine again, and I melt, arching against him, heedless of anything but this desperate want inside me. Unbound at last after a whole summer of deprivation and restraint, with his arm wrapping around my waist and rib cage, pulling me tighter and tighter, his lips moving over my jaw, my neck. His fingers slide from collarbone to the top of my dress and my breath comes in tiny pants, frantic to feel that first button pop free. But instead, he eases away, his breathing heavy, his forehead pressed to mine.

"I..." he swallows, wincing as if in pain. "I want so much from you right now, but you just arrived. I should...let you rest."

I grab him by his shirt and pull him back to me. "I want a lot of things right now too. And none of them are rest."

I see the war raging inside him, the heaviness of need, tempered by doubt.

"Henri," I whisper against his lips. "I'm not fragile. Remember the guy who pinned me to the dirt over a chocolate bar? That's the version of you I want right now."

With a low growl, he lifts me then, wrapping my legs around his waist as he carries me to his room, kicking the door shut behind us. And then I'm in his soft bed and he's beside me, rolling me to my back. He finds my mouth, his tongue stroking mine, creating a sharp, desperate pulse between my legs, an emptiness that demands a cure. His hands slide down to my ass, sinking in to pull me hard against him.

I wasn't raised in a convent, but this is all new to me—the way his erection pressed to the juncture of my legs is enough to make my knees spread wide. The way the rasp of his breath and small groan of desire against my skin make my heart rate soar. I spent so many years proud of my self-restraint, proud I hadn't given in when everyone I knew had, but if Mark had made me feel anything close to the way I do now, I'd have given in within minutes. Seconds. The way I have every intention of giving in to Henri right now.

His hand goes to the top button of my dress and then he stops, with an expression of pure tortured lust on his face. He swallows. "Is this okay?"

When I nod, he unbuttons it to the waist with frenzied hands and pushes it off my shoulders, revealing the lace bra I bought that day in Paris months ago. "*Dieu*," he says, running his finger over my tight nipple, visible through the sheer lace. "You have no idea how the thought of doing this tortured me." He lowers his mouth and his warm breath washes over the tight peak of one breast before his mouth lands on it, through the lace, softly clinging with his teeth as he pulls away. I arch, stifling a cry.

"I want to hear you," he groans. "I want every single one of your sounds because I've been imagining them for months. *Tell me* what you want."

"I have no idea," I gasp. "Just more."

His mouth descends to the other breast, repeating the action, while his hand is gliding along the soft skin of my inner thigh, lightly pressing against the outside of my panties. My breath hitches and then stops entirely as his fingers slide beneath the hem, gliding along my core.

"*Merde*," he groans, his eyes fluttering shut. "Ask me to stop. I've wanted this too much, and for too long. Ask me to stop or I won't."

I reach for his belt, tugging it free. "I don't want you to stop," I whisper, while I fumble with his buttons. "I don't care about waiting. I don't care about marriage. I just want this."

His eyes blaze, but his mouth tips into an almost-smile as it descends. "*I* care about marriage," he says beside my ear, his fingers still moving. "Just maybe not for the next hour."

My hand slips into his pants. I can barely wrap my fingers around him, but when I attempt it his whole body stiffens.

"God," he says hoarsely. "Yes."

"Are you ready?" I ask.

"My readiness was never in question," he says with a gasp as my hand glides over him. "But yours is. The first time can be..."

"I know and I don't care," I breathe, arching into his hand. "I'll never be more ready than I am now."

He kneels above me, between my spread knees, still almost completely dressed: shirt in place, pants hanging halfway down his hips, and pushes my skirt around my waist before tugging my panties down. It bears no resemblance to all my fantasies about what a first time would entail—a room lit by candlelight, me in a negligee, nestled in a sea of pillows—but that's because I never realized before what it meant to truly want something. I don't need a perfect setting or a pretty story—I can't imagine being able to notice anything but him.

His eyes have gone hazy, feverish. "If you had any idea what you look like right now," he says, the words trailing away as he takes in my spread legs, the way I'm bared to him with my dress half off. He flinches. "You're sure?"

"Yes," I reply, arching toward him. "Now."

He pulls his cock free and leans over me, letting the wet tip glide, press to my entrance and then, slowly, he begins to move, entering me in tiny pulses, forcing me to stretch wide enough to accommodate him.

"You're alright?" he asks, his eyes unfocused. The heavy thickness of him feels like too much, like something that could break me. But I can see the effort it takes for him to restrain himself, teeth sinking into his lower lip, breath coming fast.

"Don't go slowly," I tell him. "Just do it."

He hesitates for only a second and then gives into it, the urge to thrust, to fill, to push until he can't go any farther. He falls forward with a small cry, bracing himself above me, and by the time he's opened his eyes to check on me that initial shock of pain is leaving and in its wake is another feeling—full, stretched. It still hurts, but there's pleasure there too, some deeper craving that now thrums inside me, wanting.

"More," I demand, and then his mouth is on my neck, on my breasts, as he withdraws and pushes back in, once, twice, three times. And suddenly all the pleasure, all the craving—it seems to center itself, a circle of flame he hits with every thrust.

Ohhhh. It's so much more than I realized it could be.

"I don't ever want this to stop," I gasp.

His eyes are squeezed shut as if he's in pain. "I'm afraid that's not possible," he says between gritted teeth. He stops moving, but his fingers go to my clitoris and begin to circle there. With him fully inside me, nothing has felt better in my entire life. I tighten around him. "Please," I beg. "Move."

He thrusts once, hard, and the sweet sharpness of it has me gasping, digging my fingers into his back. His face is desperate, tight with restraint, groaning low in his chest as I clamp down on him.

"Again," I demand, my legs wrapping around his back for leverage, meeting his thrusts, demanding they come harder and swifter until that ache inside me tightens, tightens and finally explodes.

I cry out, arching off the bed pulling him against me, greedy and desperate, and his movements grow frenzied—swift, stabbing thrusts that prolong my orgasm, making me feel like I'm suspended in mid-air for seconds, a full minute, before he gives a single hoarse cry and pulls out, gripping himself, spilling across my stomach and chest.

He falls against me, his mouth pressed to my neck. "I've wanted that for so long," he groans against my skin. "From that first day in the barn."

I laugh, pulling him closer. "When you were holding me at gunpoint?"

"Yes, even then. And nothing from my fervent imagination could match the reality of it." He presses small, sweet kisses to my brows, my cheekbones, and finally my lips. "You're...okay? It didn't hurt too much?"

I pull his lips back to mine. "It was a lot better than okay. They probably heard me clear to the other end of town. Although we shouldn't make a habit of doing it without protection," I say. "It doesn't matter today because my cycle just ended, but it will matter a lot going forward."

"Protection?" He looks at me blankly for a moment. And then

he sighs, realizing what I'm saying. "Contraceptives are illegal— selling them here means six months in jail, so even on the black market they're hard to come by. Our version of protection is what I just did. That and watching the calendar."

My God. If a man back home were to suggest pulling out and the calendar method as ongoing forms of contraception, any female would laugh in his face. "Maybe we shouldn't—" I begin, just as his lips press to my neck, and I forget my point.

His fingers slide over one breast, which tightens in response. "I love that," he says with a soft groan, rolling over me to place his mouth at the tip. "This about killed me that day in the field when we fought over the chocolate."

"If I recall correctly, you walked away like it was no big deal."

He laughs. "I walked away like it was no big deal so I could... take care of an issue you created."

A small moan escapes my lips at the thought of him *taking care of an issue.* "I want to watch you do that." He leans down, fully hard again, sliding his hands behind my neck as he begins to kiss me.

My legs spread and he pushes inside me once more. "It might be a while," he says, biting his lip, "before I'm willing to do anything but this."

When I wake, Henri is entering the room with a tray. He's shirt- less, wearing only the pants from before, which are half buttoned and hang from his hips.

"You're not wearing a shirt," I say, eyeing him as if this is something I haven't seen before. To be fair, it's something I've mostly seen from a distance, back when sliding my palms over all those hard muscles and smooth skin was something I wouldn't allow myself to do.

He gives me a half smile. "And you're wearing nothing at all, beneath that sheet," he says, placing the tray on the bed. "Which is something I'm going to try not to think about until you've been fed."

It's only now that I notice the haziness of the light outside. "It's dusk? I slept all afternoon."

He laughs. "You exerted a great deal of energy this morning. You needed your rest." He takes a spoonful of stew and holds it to my lips. "Eat."

I obey him and then look over his shoulder at the door. "What's Marie going to think?" I ask. "I should go out there."

"Marie is gone for the evening," he says with a small smile. "She left a note saying she was staying with her friend Anna and would return in the morning."

My cheeks grow hot and I cover my face with my hands. "I never heard her come in. Does that mean...do you think she heard us?"

He pulls my hands away, grinning. "I think most of the town probably heard us, that last time."

I groan, picking up the tray and setting it off to the side. "We'll need to be more careful once she gets home."

"I plan to remain every bit as *careful* as I was earlier."

Earlier. I think of it, and I want him again—the thick press of him entering me, that dazed, desperate look on his face before he came, the frenzied way he thrusted as he did. My stomach tightens with want, in a way I'm barely familiar with, and my fingers go to his thigh.

"I'm sure earlier was an aberration. It won't be like that with us most of the time."

There's a dangerous light in his eyes, which now linger on my mouth. "An *aberration*, you say?"

I struggle not to smile. "An aberration. I'm sure it will be calm...*subdued*, even, from now on."

In a heartbeat he's pulled me down beneath him, and his mouth is on mine. He pins my wrists with his hands and sits up just enough that he can see my face. "How calm do I seem to you now, little thief?"

I arch against him. Even through his pants I can feel how hard he is, wedged against my stomach. "Very calm. Nearly asleep."

He goes to his knees, pulling the sheet back as he tugs down his pants. "Then," he says softly, "I think it's time I woke up."

IT'S EARLY in the morning when I broach the topic of Marie again. "She'll be here in a few hours," I sigh. "We probably need some... ground rules."

He runs a lazy hand over my breast. "We won't have sex when she's in the same room. That's all I'm willing to agree to."

I laugh, but it fades quickly. "Henri...she's religious. I can't imagine she'll approve of this."

"What occurs between a man and the woman he's marrying is not her concern and she knows it," he says. "She's probably just relieved we're both in one piece."

I swallow. "Marrying?"

He raises a brow. "I said the conversation could wait an hour, not forever."

"It just seems a little sudden," I reply, "given that you were telling me I should have stayed in my own time a few hours ago. I must be ridiculously good in bed."

He laughs. "You are definitely that. And it's not really sudden for me—I've been picturing it for months."

I lean back against the headboard. "You pictured being *married*? To *me*?"

"I'm trying hard not to be insulted by how astonishing you seem to find that."

My smile fades a little. "I guess I was so certain it wasn't possible that I never let my head go in that direction."

His eyes darken. "Because of Mark."

I keep forgetting that for him, Mark is still an issue, still *competition*. He doesn't understand how completely I've left the idea behind. "No," I say with a vehement shake of the head. "Just that it would mean giving up home, and my own time, which seemed impossible. Plus...the coming years are bad. It's nothing I ever dreamed I'd enter into voluntarily."

His lips press together. He focuses on the tray, his thoughts unhappy. "I should have the strength to tell you to leave, but I don't, not yet. But if this war comes like you claim, I want you to go back."

"Are you insane? You think I'd leave you here during that? It's going to be years and years."

"If something happened to you, I'd never be able to live with myself. And you could come back to find me when it's done...you wouldn't even need to wait. You could just jump ahead to the war's end."

"And I'd never be able to live with myself if something happened to you because I wasn't here to help. Do you know how many people die during the war? You might not even be alive when I get back."

He hangs his head. "All the better reason for you to stay safe in your own time."

"I'm not going anywhere," I reply, my jaw set hard.

His nostrils flare. "What about children? You'd want to raise children during a war? When there might be rationing or worse?"

"Children?" I ask, startled. "You're getting way ahead of yourself."

"Believe me," he says grimly, "if you remain here, a child or two is almost a certainty. No matter how careful we are, there are going to be many, many times when we are not. And there's something else I need to tell you before this goes any further."

I place a hand over my stomach, waiting once more for pain.

"You've been dating that girl from the church," I say quietly. "Claudette?"

His brow furrows. "*Claudette*?" He gives a short, abrupt laugh. "No. I wish that's all it was. I have a feeling it's very different where you're from, but here, in this time, people are less tolerant of differences. You probably wondered why the Beauvoirs didn't even consider Marie for André?"

I nod. I wondered it many times, actually.

He sighs. "It's because of our mother."

My jaw drops. "They knew she was a *time traveler*?"

"No," he says, his tongue darting out to wet his lips. "They knew she was Jewish."

My jaw remains open. Stunned. How, in all the time I was here, could they not have mentioned it? "Not a particularly devout one obviously, as she married a Catholic and raised us as such," he continues. "But the town has a long memory."

My eyes close. Will that matter during the war? Will it be enough to get them sent to a concentration camp? If I'd known, I'd have pushed them so much harder than I did to leave.

"I'm sorry," Henri says formally, rising from the bed. "I didn't realize it would matter to you."

I quickly grab his hand and pull him back to me. "Of course it doesn't. But...it may matter once the war starts, to all of us. I just don't know what the Germans consider Jewish by law."

He rests back against the bed frame and I lay my head on his chest. "Unfortunately I do know the answer to that," he says. "They've already decided it. Something called the Mischling test. If you've got even one Jewish grandparent you're removed from civil service in Germany. If that changes your mind about this, I understand."

I shake my head. "No, of course it doesn't." But it changes other things. It makes the odds that he and Marie-Therese will survive the war that much worse. It means any child we have could end up in a concentration camp too. When I was warning them about the war, I was so focused on their personal safety I didn't even mention the extermination of the Jews, when it turns out to be the most important piece of information I could give them.

God, this whole thing just got so much worse.

"I need to tell you more about what's coming," I say quietly. "And then we are going to make a plan."

30

When Marie gets home around lunch, Henri looks nearly as sheepish as I do. I'm fairly certain if there's some kind of record for the number of times two people can have sex in twenty-four hours, we just demolished it.

She looks from one of us to the other. "I assume it's safe to enter?"

Henri's hand slides through mine. "Relatively, yes."

"And I take it you're staying?" she asks with a broad smile.

I exchange a look with Henri. "More or less," I reply with a sigh. "Henri thought I should go home during the war, and I disagreed. So we've decided to compromise."

She looks between the two of us uncertainly. "Compromise?"

Henri runs a hand through his hair. "I want to know that, if nothing else, Amelie has the ability to escape if she needs to. So she'll stay here, but return to her own time as often as necessary, just so she doesn't lose the ability to jump at all."

"And once the war is over," I add, "I will remain here for good."

Henri's hand brushes against mine. We've intentionally left out an important part of our agreement—the most important part: sometime over the next year, the three of us will relocate to the United States. I didn't want to spring this on her upon my arrival, but soon we'll have to tell her. Their safety, with a Jewish mother, depends on it.

But only if they've already made it through the war, a voice whispers in my head.

Henri's fingers twine through mine and I squeeze them hard. I won't lose him. I won't lose either of them. Somehow.

With Marie-Therese back in the house, Henri and I reluctantly acknowledge that it's time we return to something akin to normal life. He leaves the house to do the chores he's neglected for days, his gaze lingering on my face before he walks out the door. The moment it shuts, Marie pounces on me.

"So...?" she asks, eyes bright with excitement. "How was it?"

I laugh uncertainly. "You want me to tell you what it was like to have sex with your brother? Because I have a brother myself, and honestly I'd be scarred for life if someone provided me that information."

She flushes and smacks her head. "Ugh. *Dieu*. No. I meant the reunion. I'm going to forget you even said the rest."

I bite my lip, trying to recall the parts of our reunion that *weren't* sex. "It was great," I say vaguely. I think of him pushing me against the refrigerator and want to chase him into the fields for another round. "We argued a bit. He was worried I wouldn't stay and I was worried he didn't want me to stay and then it all worked out."

"Yes, I figured all this," she says, waving her hand. "But what are your *plans*? Have you set a wedding date?"

I glance at her. I don't understand how we went from no talk of marriage whatsoever to *setting a date*. "Um...not yet. I just got here. I'm not even thinking about marriage yet."

She raises a brow. "Well, that makes one of you, then. I'm certain my brother would not say the same."

I throw out my hands. "We haven't even *dated* yet."

"*Dated*?" she asks with an incredulous laugh. "What did you think occurred here all summer? Did you think Henri always takes picnics and goes riding and watches the sunset each night on his own? The two of you courted more than any married couple in this entire province. Possibly more than any couple in this country, if you look at in terms of hours." Her smile fades. "Amelie, I love you and I want nothing more than for you to be with my brother, but if you're not serious about him, you can't do this."

"I just gave up living in my own time!" I cry. "Of course I'm serious about him. What I did is far more serious than any stupid piece of paper."

"Except that *stupid piece of paper* is all Henri will have to know you're bound to him," she replies. "And you were perfectly ready to agree to that *stupid piece of paper* with a man you *don't* love just a few weeks ago, so why not with Henri? If you're still unsure, I think you need to tell him that."

I know I'm not unsure about him, but she has a point. Why am I so reluctant to go down that path? If Henri and I were living in *my* time and he asked me to marry him, I'd agree with ease. I suppose because I know that world. I know who I am in it. But I don't have a place in this one yet.

"In spite of my months here, I don't really know how to function in your time," I explain. "It's just...a lot."

"But I'll help you," she says eagerly. "I'll teach you to cook and show you how everything is done. And when you have children, we'll figure it out together, I suppose."

I exhale. When I came back here, I wasn't picturing much of anything beyond moments with Henri. It seemed so easy to give up my own time because I wanted him. And I still do, enough to suffer in all the ways I will to stay. But I'm not sure that life on the farm is what I want forever. I can learn to cook and clean and do the laundry and rear children in a rural village, but the part of me that wanted to finish college and have a career is still there. And she doesn't want to spend long afternoons over a copper tub scrubbing laundry or making cassoulet. That future I laid out in Paris, when Henri asked what I'd do if I had to stay—was it a ridiculous fantasy for him? Because it wasn't for me.

"It's not that I don't think I am *capable* of doing these things," I finally reply. "It's just that where I'm from, women at least theoretically have the same opportunities that men do. There are fathers who stay home while their wives work, and there are couples who share all that stuff. So I'm willing to live in 1938, but Henri will need to be willing to make our lives a little more modern than he may want. It's not that I'm worried I'll change my mind. It's that I'm worried he'll change his."

She glances at me uncertainly. "I know my brother will agree to any condition you lay out, but there's not much here for a woman to do. You could teach, or work in a shop, I suppose. And you've seen how much time the farm takes for Henri. You can't expect him to come home after that and start making the bread?"

I swallow. "No, of course not."

I leave the conversation there, because Marie does not understand that Henri isn't exactly wed to this life either. He's doing this for her, but once she's made her choices, once she's no longer his to hide and protect, he'll be free to do anything. And I hope that he will.

I remain inside through the afternoon with Marie, helping her complete all the mind-numbing domestic tasks that are a part of her day. Despite what I told her, she is determined to teach me how to do these things on my own. It's impossible for her to understand how much easier life will be very soon— that machines will replace so much of her labor.

And all afternoon as I make the bread and scrub the floor and help with dinner, I'm looking out the window, longing just for the sight of him.

"Thirty-six," Marie says out of nowhere.

"Excuse me?"

She smiles. "You've looked out the window thirty-six times in the past two hours."

I shrug, trying to pretend I'm not embarrassed to be called out. "I did just travel back five decades to see him, you know."

"You looked out the window back then too," she says. And then she laughs. "Ah. Poor Amelie. So stricken any time he went to the pump for water."

I raise a brow. "I can't believe I'm taking shit from a girl infatuated with a *priest*."

Her mouth purses. "I have no idea what you're talking about. But if you want to tell Henri that dinner is nearly ready, go ahead."

I glance at the stove, where the water isn't even boiling yet. "Dinner's nowhere close to being ready."

She bites her lip, barely hiding her grin. "Yes, but I thought it might take you an hour or more to get the job done."

He is walking up from the field as I approach, with a smile so sweet I can feel it in my blood. He draws me against him, his hands on my face, his mouth seeking mine. He smells like him— soap and skin and freshly cut grass. God, I've missed that smell and I'm so grateful it's now mine to keep.

"How were things in there?" he asks, nodding at the house.

I tip my head. "You say that as if you expected them to be bad."

He grabs my hand and starts leading me toward the orchard. "If I know my sister at all, she's already rung Father Edouard about dates for our wedding and has begun suggesting names for our children."

I sigh. "Both topics were raised, yes." When we reach the orchard, he sits and begins pulling me to the grass, but I hesitate. "We don't need to worry about snakes?"

He laughs. "Snakes? There are no snakes here. I was just trying to get you on my blanket."

Ah, to have known these things at the time. "But you didn't even like me then. Why would you try to get me on your blanket?"

His back rests against the tree as he regards me, a small smile on his mouth. "I liked you then too, believe me." His hand slides out, and he twines a lock of my hair around his finger. "You looked troubled just now, when I asked about Marie. Did something happen?"

He wraps an arm around me and I rest my head on his shoulder. "Do you remember when we were in Paris and you asked me what I would do if I had to stay in your time?"

A laugh comes from low in his chest. "If I recall correctly, you were going to live in Paris with a legion of staff and find struggling artists to support." That laugh of his does not bode well. He makes it sound like I'd planned to breed unicorns. When I'm quiet he pulls away so he can see my face. "What is it?"

I sigh. "It wasn't a joke for me," I say quietly. "I mean, no, I didn't think at the time it was a serious possibility, but—"

"But you don't think you want to be the wife of a poor farmer," he concludes.

I glance up at him. He's saying what I couldn't bring myself to say, but hearing the words from his mouth, I'm no longer sure they're true. "If I have to choose between being with you and the future I'd planned for myself, I choose you," I tell him. "But in an ideal world, I wouldn't have to choose."

He searches my eyes. "What will it take to keep you, Sarah? Name it, and if it's in my power it's yours."

He is willing to give me anything. Give up anything. For the first time in my life, I realize, I am not alone. He will follow me no matter how far I fall, no matter what I need to do or become. That small part of me that was holding back, scared and uncertain, flutters away. I wrap my arms around his neck and kiss him, breathing in and out.

"I love you," I whisper, kissing the corners of his mouth, his jaw. "I love you so much."

His breathing sharpens as my mouth moves to his neck. "If you keep doing that, this conversation might need to take place at another time."

I'm not sure who he's turned me into, but the mere suggestion of sex with him has my entire body primed and ready. My nerve endings seem to rest on the very surface of my skin, a thousand tiny points of need. I climb into his lap, my knees on either side of his hips. My teeth go to the lobe of his ear.

"Oh?" I ask. "Why's that?"

He inhales. "Because in about thirty seconds you will have me promising to buy Versailles for you."

I pull my dress out of the way, let my weight rest on his. He's already swelling against me and I feel stupid, blind with want for it. "It *would* be fun to live in a palace," I tell him. My hand goes to his belt.

"It's yours." His voice is rough and low, wanting. "We'll leave tonight."

His hand slips inside my dress, cupping a breast, flicking at it with his thumb in a way that makes me gasp. I reach into his boxers. He is thick and heavy in my hand, my thumb spreading over the tip until he is slick there.

"*Dieu*," he groans. "You're not sore?" His eyes are closed and he sounds breathless, desperate.

"I'm fine," I say, rubbing against him. In truth, I'm sore. But it doesn't stop the want in any way, shape or form. If anything, it makes it worse.

He reaches between us and pushes my panties aside, lining his cock up with my entrance—swollen with need, and raw. I sink into him, head thrown back. It is pleasure and pain at once, exquisite in a way I can't begin to explain to him. It hurts like hunger, like something that won't go away until it's been sated.

I ride him slowly, drawing it out though I've felt close since the moment I grabbed his belt. His mouth is on my neck, fingers flicking open the buttons of my dress to go lower. My nipple draws tight in his mouth while he seems to grow inside me, stretching me further than I imagined possible.

His lids are heavy, eyes dazed beneath them. "You're going to get tired of me," he says. His hands go to my waist and he pulls me down on him hard, jerking upward to meet me. "I will want this every day. Every hour. You'll get tired of it."

I can no longer keep my eyes open. I wrap my arms around his neck and bury my face in his shoulder, moving faster. "I'm not ever going to be tired of you," I say, gasping as he thrusts upward again. "Oh God, I'm close."

He increases the intensity of the thrusts. His fingers dig into my back. "It's so hard not to let go," he hisses. His index finger trails down my ass, brushing lightly against the puckered ring there, and I gasp.

"Did you like that?" he asks.

I ride him harder, blind now, desperate to finish. "I don't know."

He laughs. Allows his finger to brush again. Once, twice—as he meets me with another thrust—and I am done for. I clench him tight as I go over the edge, dissolve into nothing beyond the feeling of us joined there. He flips me on my back and drives into me with four sharp jabs and then he's cursing, pulling out, coming on my chest, my neck.

When his eyes open he looks a little shocked. "Well that escalated quickly," he says with an uneven laugh.

I glance down at my ruined dress. "When we move to Versailles, I think I'd like some more clothes. And a washing machine."

"Anything, *ma reine*," he says, collapsing beside me.

MARIE'S BROWS go to her hairline when I return an hour later, my dress grass-stained, hair a disaster. "Well then. I guess having a baby in this house will liven things up."

"I'm taking a bath. And you bite your tongue," I reply. "No children. Not until after the war."

"If you say so," she murmurs behind me, sounding as if she is holding in a laugh.

I fill the tub and sink inside it for the second time today, smiling as I lean my head backward against the edge. We did end up talking just a bit in the orchard. I think he would be happy enough to stay on the farm if that's what I wanted, but I saw that spark in his eye when I talked about moving someday. Living in a city where we can both finish our degrees, where he no longer has to work so hard to make people *not* take notice of his family. Much of that depends on Marie, of course, but by the time the war is over, she will probably have chosen a path for herself. Perhaps found a spouse who isn't a priest.

Except maybe it's Edouard she's *meant* to end up with. While a priest seems like the least likely candidate to help produce some kind of supernatural being, if the "circle of light" is a child, there's a lovely sort of symmetry to it: my strict, religious family saw time travel as evil, and from my few interactions with her, it seemed my grandmother viewed organized religion in the same way, but this would be a union of those things. Marie already exists in both worlds, and if there was ever a priest capable of rising above his beliefs and his training to accept something new, it would be Father Edouard. He would do it for Marie, I'm certain.

I put on a fresh dress and emerge from the bath to begin helping Marie with dinner.

"So did you and Henri talk?" she asks mildly, shoving vegetables toward me over the butcher's block. "Among other things."

I stifle a laugh. "You're not going to shame me, you know. Where I'm from women talk about sex all the time."

She looks at me warily. "I obviously don't want...specifics, given that it's my brother we're discussing. But, is it not painful? It seems like it would be extremely so."

"I doubt I'd have sought it out if it were," I reply. "No, it's the opposite. It's like a miracle. Or a drug. You'll see some day, if you ever agree to go on a date."

Her smile falters. "Xavier asked me out again last week. I put him off, but perhaps...perhaps I should."

I've never seen a woman look more grief-stricken or reluctant to go on a date with a handsome man.

"When you're in love with someone," I say softly, "no one else appeals to you. You can convince yourself they do, the way I did with Mark, but it won't work. It can't."

She swallows. Her hand clenches around the knife's handle and her head goes down, as if suddenly she's in so much pain she can't unclench herself. "Then what am I supposed to do?" she asks, her voice rough. "How do I make it stop?"

My heart hurts for her. I know better than anyone what it's like to want something so badly and be certain you can't have it. "Before you abandon the idea of Father Edouard entirely, ask yourself what you'd risk by trying. I've seen the way he looks at you. There's not a doubt in my head he'd give up everything with a little encouragement."

Tears drip down her face onto the butcher's block. "What if he finds out what I am, though? Even if I chose to hide it, there are times when it might happen. Or we could have a child...like your parents did. And then what? How do I explain what I hid from him? How do I allow a child to be raised the way you were, as if there's something poisonous inside her? I couldn't."

I shake my head. "Do you think Edouard would be that man? If you do, then perhaps you don't love him like I thought. Or *shouldn't* love him in any case. The person you're describing does not deserve your affection."

She looks up at me, and swallows again. "You really think he'd accept it?"

It shocks me that she could possibly think otherwise. I suppose even people with loving parents doubt themselves occasionally. "I think he'd accept you, exactly as you are. And I think you will never move forward if you don't try."

She bites her lip. "You could perhaps jump ahead," she whispers. "You know I can't. But *you* could go forward a few years and see where things are. If it would all work out the way you say."

My stomach swims at the idea. I'm not sure I want to see the next few years. We will suffer at least a little, and possibly a great deal, and I don't want to know. It would seem like the wrong decision anyway.

"I love you, but I won't do that. Anything the two of you become will happen because you opened yourself up to the uncertainty. He would need to risk a great deal. I'm not sure you'd become everything you should be together if you didn't risk as well."

She laughs through her tears. "You're punishing me for the ankle, aren't you?"

I smile. "No, I've got a different punishment planned for that."

"Oh?"

"A hideous maid of honor dress. Absolutely putrid. Lime green and covered in bows from head to foot."

She smiles at me. "I will gladly wear the putrid lime green dress. There's nothing I want more than the two of you together."

"Perhaps there's *one* thing you'd like more?" I tease

She flushes. A quiet happiness has come over her face. "Yes. Perhaps."

31

The next weeks are blissful. A promise of things to come. Marie is once again absent a great deal, finding ways to spend her afternoons and often her evenings in town. If she's spending them with Father Edouard, she doesn't mention it.

The weather grows crisp. When the grapes are ready we all work together, along with the hired help. Marie and I both wear shirts and trousers since there's so much time in the dirt, and at night when I go to bathe my arms ache so much I can barely remove my clothes—it's something Henri would, no doubt, be willing to help with, but he is gone. Out in the fields before I rise, returning long after I've gone to sleep.

With the hired hands on the farm, our interaction is constrained to lingering glances and a brush of hands as we pass, and on Sunday we don't even get that much: Henri remains in the vineyard while Marie-Therese at last succeeds in dragging me to mass, insisting that no work should be done on Sunday. I'm once more the object of stares, and this time I have to suffer them alone while Marie sits with the choir, watching Father Edouard with lovesick eyes.

The moment mass concludes I am approached by Madame Beauvoir. I assume she still has no idea that Henri is the one who beat André up or she wouldn't be speaking to me.

"I thought you'd gone back to America," she says. I have no idea what people were told so I'm not sure how to respond, but to my vast relief Marie-Therese appears just in time.

"Madame Beauvoir was just saying she thought I'd gone to America," I tell her with a pleading look.

Her eyes go wide, and then she nods. "Yes. How fortunate for us that storms kept her ship in Le Havre long enough that she changed her mind."

Madame Beauvoir is looking me over once more like a prize calf. "I will come call today, then," she says. "I'd like to hear more about your plans."

I wait for Marie-Therese to make an excuse but she merely gives a small, pained smile. "That sounds lovely," she says.

"WHAT IS WRONG WITH YOU?" I demand once we're walking home. "Why in God's name would you tell that woman it would be *lovely* if she came to see us?"

Marie shrugs. "We live in a small town. We can't afford to alienate our neighbors."

"You saw the way she was looking at me," I reply. "She's only coming so she can find a way to foist her son on me again."

"Well this time you'll be there," says Marie with a hapless smile, "so I won't be able to agree to anything on your behalf."

I shake my head. "I definitely will not be there," I retort. "This is on you. And let me assure you, if you agree to anything on my behalf this time I will clear it up myself and I won't be nice about it."

We get to the house and I continue walking, searching the fields for Henri. I'm tired and irritated and it just feels like I've had enough of being away from him, of sharing nothing more than a lingering glance or the vague memory of his arrival in bed well into the night.

I find him at the far end of the vineyard, alone, since the farm hands don't work on Sunday either.

When our eyes meet, he drops his shears, taking five large strides to wrap his arms around me and press his mouth to my neck. "God I've missed you," he says with a sigh. "You seem...upset?"

I groan. "Madame Beauvoir is coming here to try to set me up with André again. Marie didn't even try to discourage her."

His breath ghosts along the shell of my ear and goose bumps rise on the back of my arms in response. "A ring on your finger might cure that," he suggests.

I laugh. "And how do you propose we explain that I married my own cousin?"

His hands drift upward, cupping my breasts. "No one who's laid eyes on you would blame me if it were true."

My head falls to his chest and for a single moment I allow his exploration, sighing as I force myself to stay his hands. "The calendar suggests you'd better stop doing that," I tell him. "Unless you've found black market condoms, that is." The few he found last month are long gone by now.

But he doesn't stop. Instead his hand slides inside my bra, teasing me until I rest on that fine line of pleasure and pain. "You're sure?"

My breath rasps. "We need to be responsible, Henri. At least right now we do." But he persists, growing hard, his breathing tight as he shifts against me. "You're torturing both of us for no reason."

He kisses me with the kind of intensity he does during sex sometimes, when he is on the cusp of losing his last ounce of restraint, and nods at the grass. "Sit down," he says, his voice rough, his eyes impossibly dark.

The grass will stain my dress and I know that we can't continue whatever it is he is planning, but I can't bring myself to stop. I do as he says and he drops to his knees in front of me. His hands slide the dress up slowly, reverently, to mid-thigh, his mouth hanging open a bit as he takes me in.

We've done so much more than this. But for some reason his eyes on me, on my pale thighs in daylight, is almost unbearably intimate. His hands splay over the skin there and he takes a deep, steadying breath. He loosens the garters and carefully peels my stockings off, first the right and then the left. His hands slide up the inside of my thighs until his fingers land at my core and slip beneath my underwear. His eyes flicker to mine, obsidian now.

"Lay back."

I do as he says, feeling a small tug on my underwear just before it slips down my legs. He pushes my knees farther apart, his fingers teasing me again, circling, and then...his tongue flickers over me. I gasp in shock at the sensation—hot and cold at the same time, almost too exquisite to bear. I've stopped him when he's tried this before, because it doesn't seem like there's much in it for him, but today, just for a moment, I allow it. A second and third time, but it still feels as if I should stop him.

"Henri—"

"Let me," he growls, and there's something so desperate and determined in his voice that I wouldn't say no if I wanted to, and obviously I don't.

He resumes the movement, and when he slides his finger back inside me it becomes something else entirely. Sharp, a fire I crave. "I want to do this to you," I plead.

He groans. "You will," he says. "Very soon." I arch against his mouth, wanting more, and with a groan he gives it to me, his fingers pushing harder inside me, that flickering tongue never resting until I gasp, my hands in his hair.

"It's good, Sarah. Let go," he begs. It's the desperation in his voice that undoes me more than anything else. I cry out, arching free of the ground, and the moment I settle, he is over me with his cock in his hand. I reach for him, swirl my tongue over the top before it slides down his length.

His eyes are squeezed tight. "I'm so close already," he gasps.

I take him entirely into my mouth, gagging a little as he thrusts, hitting the back of my throat. There's nothing comfortable about it but I'm unbelievably turned on by this, by his desperation, by the way he's lost control of himself. "I'm going to —" he says. I grab his hips, holding him in place so he knows it's okay, and he explodes with a coarse shout, coating my tongue and my throat. He gives three more slow slides along my tongue, wringing out the last of it, before his eyes open.

"I want to do that again," I tell him.

His answering laughter is slightly breathless. "You are going to make the most perfect wife."

32

Once the grapes have been harvested, half are sold to a winemaker and half remain for us to process ourselves.

Henri and I begin to talk about a wedding. I will need papers of some kind, so he goes to Paris for the day to check into it and comes back with the name of someone who can forge a passport and birth certificate for me once I've had my picture taken.

And Marie listens, excited for us and also…uncertain. Quieter than normal, keeping something to herself she doesn't want to share. There is a strain to her smile when we discuss the future.

I ask in roundabout ways but get nothing from her until the afternoon she returns from town telling me Jeanette needs to go to Paris to check on her ailing mother.

Marie relays this information, biting her lip. "She's going to Paris to check on her and is wondering if we can watch the children."

I look up from my terrible attempt at knitting with a surprised laugh. "Are you *asking* me? It's your home."

Marie frowns. "It is yours as well, though, and will soon be more yours than mine."

My chest tightens a little. I think of what Henri predicted that night in the orchard: that his marriage would make Marie feel displaced. I suppose I thought I would be the exception. "It will never, ever be more mine than yours," I reply. "I would not have returned if I thought you'd feel that way."

She gives me a small smile, though I'm not sure she's convinced. "So it's okay?"

I swallow. The last small child I was asked to care for was my sister. But I can't live in that shadow forever. "Of course."

On Thursday afternoon, Marie and Henri drive to Jeannette's to pick up the children, while I wait at home feeling slightly ill. I've already told Marie I don't want to be in charge of the baby, but three-year-old Charlotte is scary enough. I keep picturing her seeing through me the way my mother did, spying some hidden evil inside me. Knowing it's ridiculous doesn't seem to help.

Marie walks in the door a short time later, carrying a swaddled bundle that must be Lucien. And behind them, a little girl with huge hazel eyes and curls past her shoulders, her tiny hand tucked into Henri's.

He has the widest smile on his face, so wide my heart twists a little. Whoever this little girl is, she's got him hooked around her finger already.

He walks her toward me and then squats low, so they are nearly the same height. "Charlotte, this is my fiancé, Amelie."

I've never heard him call me that. I can't help but smile as I squat down beside them. "Hello, Charlotte."

She stares at me with her wide, serious eyes for a moment. Long enough for my stomach to begin the inevitable slide to my feet. And then she reaches into the small bag she carries and pulls out a book, pushing it into my arms.

"Do you want me to read it to you?" I ask.

She nods. I cast a last nervous smile at Henri and then take her by the hand out to the porch. I take one seat, expecting her to take the one beside mine. Instead, she scrambles into my lap, puts her thumb in her mouth, and waits eagerly for me to begin.

I look back into the house, where Henri is watching us. He smiles again and I know he's seeing his future, when this is our child out on the porch in her mother's lap. And I smile back, because I finally see how magnificent that future will be.

ALL AFTERNOON and into the evening, Marie tends to Lucien while Charlotte has us at her beck and call. Her initial shyness evaporated quickly, and we've now heard all about her doll and her tea set, her best friend and her papa, who is very brave and will be home soon. I read to her, and Henri is in charge of games, including a ridiculous one that involves holding each other's chins and slapping the first to laugh, which Charlotte finds unbelievably funny. Dinner is lively, the three adults passing the baby while we take turns eating, all of us marveling aloud at Jeannette, who somehow is handling this all on her own.

At bedtime I take Charlotte to the room upstairs, the one that belonged to me when I first arrived, but minutes after I've tucked her in and said goodnight, she's downstairs again, saying she's scared. I tell her I'll lie down with her for a moment and do so, surprised to discover how much I like having a three-year-old curled up beside me.

It's Henri who wakes me, his hand on my shoulder. "Come to bed," he whispers. I blink and look at Charlotte, her tiny face on the same pillow as mine, her thumb tucked in her mouth.

He smiles softly. "You're spoiling her."

I open my mouth to argue and he stops me. "I like that you spoil her. You're going to be a very good mother." He gently pulls me to my feet. "But right now I'm more interested in seeing how you'll be a very good wife."

"When *will* I be a wife, by the way?" I ask as we walk downstairs. Henri mailed my photo to the forger just a few days ago, but now that it's really underway I'm impatient for it.

"Your papers will be ready next week," he says. "As soon as possible after that."

"Now we just need to plan a honeymoon," I say. "Unless people don't do that in your time?"

He laughs, pulling me close as he shuts the door behind us. "Yes," he says, against my ear, "we definitely honeymoon in my time. Where do you want to go?"

My lips skate over his collarbone and then his neck. "A beach. Somewhere private where we can have sex on every available surface and swim naked."

He groans. "I'm not sure where this magical place you're describing is, but let's definitely find it. We have the money as long as we don't tell anyone where we went."

"The Riviera, maybe?" I suggest as I unbutton his shirt.

His fingers press into my hips. "It's October now and it will be November by the time we're married. We can go but I don't think we'll be doing any swimming."

"Further south then. Italy?" I reach for his belt.

"You'll have to go further," he says with a groan.

I drop to my knees. "Greece?" I ask, wrapping my hand around his girth, already hard and beyond ready.

"Yes," he says with a hiss as I take him in my mouth. "That's perfect."

THE NEXT DAY when it's time to go, Charlotte clings to me, her arms tight around my neck. I feel the pinch of tears. "Perhaps I'll see you tomorrow at mass," I reply, trying to reassure myself as much as her.

She looks from me to Marie, not understanding. "Charlotte is Jewish," Marie says softly. "So she doesn't go to mass."

My stomach drops. All this time I was worried about Henri and Marie.

But there are thousands of little girls like Charlotte in France, many of whom will not survive the war. I can't save them all. I might not be able to save any of them.

They leave and I bury my head in my hands. How am I going to approach the coming years? Because it's clear this is a situation I'll find myself in, again and again. I can make things better for Charlotte and her brother by getting involved, but if they died during the war, nothing I can do will change that. Which means I also might be *risking* their lives by getting involved.

Perhaps it would be better to do nothing, but I already know I'm not capable of it. I can't watch them marched off to a concentration camp while I simply *hope* they survive it.

"You need to make Jeannette leave," I tell Marie when they return. "It's not safe for her and the kids."

Marie shrugs. "If it's safe enough for us to stay, I'm sure it's safe for Jeannette too."

My eyes meet Henri's and he nods slowly, his hand sliding into mine.

"Marie," he says, "we need to talk you about something. We're moving. We have some time, but next spring, next summer at the latest, we need to leave for the United States."

Her eyes go wide. "The United States? But this is your home."

"I meant all three of us," he amends. "*What?*" she gasps. "Why?"

"It's not safe here," I whisper. "Truly, it isn't. Especially for you and Henri. If I'd known about your mother, I'd have been on my hands and knees begging you to leave when I was here before. Hitler doesn't just dislike the Jews. He will do his level best to eradicate them."

"That won't happen *here*, though. And we are practicing Catholics," she insists.

From my perspective her stance seems insane, but I understand it. If someone swore to me back home that all the people in my town or my college were about to be annihilated, I'd have struggled to believe it, regardless of the source.

"I'm not sure it will matter. War brings out the best and the worst in people. And there's always someone who will inform on you just to get a leg up. Always. Do you really think that André Beauvoir won't be the first to tell the Nazis your mother was Jewish if he sees a benefit to it?"

Her jaw sets. "Even if that's true, I can't leave. What if my mother comes back looking for us? She'll have no idea where we went."

Henri's shoulders sag. "Marie...she's not coming back. You know this. She's had two decades to get back to us if she was going to."

"But she might escape!" exclaims Marie. "Perhaps she's been held somewhere and when the war comes she'll escape at last, and return to an empty home."

Henri slumps at the table, running frustrated hands through his hair. "We've gone over this so many times. This obsession with waiting for her to come home...it's just your way of avoiding the truth. If you don't care for your own life, think of mine, and Amelie's, and any children we might have over the next seven years. Are you willing to risk all of us just so you don't have to face facts?"

She lifts her chin. "Then go without me. I'm not asking you to stay behind."

Henri shakes his head. "The one thing that will *not* happen is you remaining here on your own."

Her arms fold. "I've stayed here and led this quiet little life, as you and Maman wanted. I've done everything you've asked. But I'm an adult now, and I won't be pushed into doing something that isn't right for me. So I won't leave, not until I know for certain she's gone."

His eyes meet mine, tight with worry, when even he can't fully realize how bad things might be. Unless I can change Marie's mind, I know one thing for certain: the odds of us surviving the coming years just got dramatically worse.

MARIE BARELY SPEAKS for the rest of the afternoon. She chops vegetables for the bouillabaisse with a ferocity that scares me.

"You got to decide," she says out of nowhere. "You decided to come here, to go home, to come back. You decided you wanted to go to college, and you decided you would leave. All I'm asking is for the right to decide for myself to remain in my home. Nothing more."

I get the feeling her resentment has been brewing for a long time. Not at me, necessarily, but at the lot she's been dealt. Watching me flit around and do as I please probably hasn't helped, and now she's stuck here, lovesick for Father Edouard while Henri and I bask in our relationship. It must seem unbelievably unfair.

"You're right," I tell her. "And I'd feel the same way. But this isn't the only chance you'll have to make a decision for yourself. You have your entire life ahead to decide whatever you want."

She shakes her head vehemently. "My entire life has been *ahead*. All of these things that will be possible later—when exactly do they happen? When does Henri decide we don't need to hide ourselves? When do I get to make my own decisions?"

I don't know what to tell her, because it won't be any time in the near future. "Give me the knife," I say, "before you cut your finger off."

She sets the knife down entirely and pulls off her apron. "I'm going to town. Which appears to be the only decision I'm allowed to make on my own."

I watch in silence as she walks out the door. When I was a child I always thought that in any argument someone was right and someone was wrong. As an adult I realize that often isn't the case, and it certainly isn't here. Marie deserves to make her own choices, but her brother should be allowed to do what's necessary to keep his family safe.

I head out in search of Henri once she leaves. I don't have to wander long—he's on the far side of the barn, chopping wood as if it's life or death. For a moment I just watch: his shirt is off, his bare chest rippling with muscle and flecked with sweat and sawdust.

He swings the ax viciously and the wood goes flying, nearly to my feet. His eyes widen at the sight of me, and he carefully leans the ax against the tree stump and turns to me. "Have you been there long?"

I shake my head. "Just briefly admiring the view."

He gives me a small smile. "I'm filthy. You have strange taste." He glances at the house. "Is Marie still mad?"

I close the distance between us. "It was a lot to throw at her. She went into town to cool off a bit."

His hands go to my shoulders, his thumb grazing my collarbone. "You're so small," he says quietly. "I forget sometimes how fragile you are, how vulnerable."

"I'm not *that* vulnerable," I reply with a grin. "I can disappear when necessary, remember?"

He swallows. "That you can disappear is never far from my mind," he says heavily. "But you're far more vulnerable than me in the one way that matters right now: your future isn't already decided. Mine is, and Marie's as well."

I stiffen. I already know where he is going with this. I knew from the moment Marie refused to move that we'd circle back to the point where we began.

"I want you to marry me," he says. "And then I want you to leave. Just until the war ends."

I lay my head against his chest. Sweat, sawdust...I want all of it. I want all of his highs and lows, as long as we can be together through them. "I already promised I'd go home just enough that I can escape if necessary."

His arms tighten around me. His heart is hammering now, just beneath my ear. "It's not enough. Anything can happen. What if you get pregnant and I'm gone? You'll be stuck here."

"Then I won't get pregnant."

He laughs unhappily. "After the past two months are you still under the impression that it's entirely within your control? And don't expect me to believe you'd vanish if trouble came. You won't leave me, just as I would not leave you."

My hands clasp his face. "I'd rather have a few years with you than an entire life without you." Something calm settles over me as I say the words aloud for the first time. Yes, I still want a future with him, but even if I don't get much more than what I've had, it's...enough. If I had to trade every future autumn in order to keep the one we just spent together, I'd do so without hesitation.

I just hope it's a choice I'm not forced to make.

THE AIR IS thick with tension when Marie gets home that night. I decide I've created enough trouble, and quietly excuse myself, leaving them in the kitchen and going to the room I now share with Henri. As soon as the door shuts, the arguing begins. First, a quiet, hissing sort of anger, followed by shouting on both sides.

"This is ridiculous!" Henri cries. "I don't even know who you are right now."

"How easy for you to say when everything has always gone your way," she snaps. "Our mother left and *your* life didn't change at all, whereas mine completely stopped. If you truly loved her, you'd understand why I'm determined to stay."

"My life went *on*?" he asks with an incredulous laugh. "You have no idea what I've given up. And Amelie has made every one of those sacrifices worthwhile. If I lose her because of your stupidity, I will never forgive you."

"Don't put that on me!" Marie screams. "*I'm* not asking anyone to stay."

She needs to know about the prophecy. In another world, she might have time to choose a course for her life, but this isn't that world. When he goes silent, I'm certain he's thinking the same thing, so I walk into the kitchen and take the seat across from him. He meets my eye—*should I?*—and I nod.

"There's something you should know," he finally says. "You'll be angry that I didn't tell you sooner, but I was doing so at Maman's request."

Her eyes go wide as she looks between the two of us, wondering what's coming.

Henri's shoulders sag. He leans forward, hands clasped above the table. "Maman thought the prophecy was about you. She believed you were the hidden child. And I suspect she was right."

Her face is completely blank for a moment, and then she laughs. "*Me? Why?*"

He exhales. "You meet all the requirements: you were conceived during a great war and born after it. The *day* after it. In France."

"But—" she begins.

"I know," he says, cutting her off. "You can't be the only one to meet that description. But Maman didn't tell you the most important part of the prophecy: the hidden child is a product of one of the first families."

She slowly drops into a chair, looking shell-shocked. "Why didn't she tell me?" she finally asks.

"She thought it might be a burden, that it might change things for you. She wanted you to at least choose a direction for your life free of that responsibility."

Marie nods, staring at the floor. "Is that why she went back to 1918? Because of me?"

Henri's teeth grind, hating the way this conversation has turned. "I think so, yes."

Her eyes well over. "And that's why you're so insistent on staying here with me, in spite of the danger. Because you promised her you would."

Henri looks at her. "I stay because you're my sister and I want you to be safe. I'd stay whether I'd promised her I would or not."

We are all quiet for a moment. My stomach is clenched tight, praying that she'll change her mind about leaving, now that she understands what Henri has given up on her behalf.

"I will go with you to the United States," she says. My head and Henri's jerk at the words, but she holds up the palm of her hand. "Hear me out. I will go, but only once I know what happened to our mother."

Henri groans, sinking low in his chair. "So in other words, nothing has changed. You will wait here, decade after decade—if you manage to survive the war at all—on the off-chance she returns."

"No," she says softly. "I'm going back to 1918 to find her."

My gasp is audible. "Marie," I whisper. "Please...don't. It's not safe. Who knows how many of our kind have gone there and not returned? It's like some kind of Bermuda Triangle for us."

"I have no idea what a Bermuda Triangle is," she replies, "but it doesn't matter. I want to move on with my life as much as you want me to. And I can't, until I've done this one thing."

I look to Henri, hoping he will slam his hand on the table and forbid it and threaten her with any power he has. But he sits, beaten, knowing she has made her mind up. The same stubbornness that led to her to refuse to fix my ankle is guiding her now.

"I can't stop you," he says quietly. "I realize that. But please don't. If I'm off fighting, you and Amelie will need each other. What if we have a child? Even a child who is one of your kind wouldn't have the ability to jump, not for years. Amelie will need help."

It's shocking to consider I *could* have a child like me. I love Marie, and I liked her mom, but I still don't want to bring another of us into the world.

Marie isn't dissuaded in the least. Her face is, instead, vivid with excitement. "I could leave tomorrow and be back in a week," she says. "I just want to know where she went. I'm not planning to run into a burning building."

Henri raises a brow. "If you saw our mother in a burning building you absolutely would go in after her."

Her mouth purses. She doesn't deny it. And I watch the weight on Henri's shoulders grow, because he knows Marie is not capable of being rational where her mother is concerned. She needs someone older and wiser there to make sure she doesn't do anything stupid, and he's not able to be that person.

But I could be.

I hear Kit's words again. See her desperate face, shivering with cold in the coffin she will never leave: *You have to find them.* And suddenly I know, deep in my heart, that it was always supposed to happen this way. That the *them* I was supposed to help was never Henri and Marie, at least not in the way I hoped.

I meet Henri's eyes across the table, a wordless apology for what I'm about to say, before I turn to Marie. "I'll go with you."

"No," he growls. "Absolutely not."

I lean forward, silently pleading with him to understand. "She needs someone there to watch her back, and there's strength in numbers," I tell him. "Like she said, we're not going there to wage war. She just needs to see how the story ends."

He slams his hand on the table. "If you're going to jump anywhere, you should be jumping home! Dammit, Amelie! Every time a dangerous situation presents itself you seem to be right there, insisting on becoming part of it."

Marie, too, is shaking her head. "I don't want you to do that. You just came back to him. I know I've been awful lately, but the two of you deserve some happiness. Especially if things are about to get as bad as you say."

"If it's no big deal, then it should be no big deal for me to come with you," I reply.

She bites her lip. "I can't stop you, and I suppose it would be helpful to have someone who knows how to drive."

Henri's chair scrapes across the floor. He walks out of the house without a word to either of us, slamming the door behind him.

"He's going to be panicked until you're home safe again," Marie says, watching the door.

My heart twists. I never dreamed that returning here would make his life so much harder. "Then we should probably go right away. Do you have a plan in mind?"

She rubs a finger over her lower lip. "I'm not sure how long we'll need to recover once we arrive."

She's being diplomatic, using the term *we*. Jumping back a few decades won't affect her at all. *I'm* the problem. "It'll take me a day, I think. Two at most."

She nods. "So we should aim for November 11th, since she told you to go on the 12th. We'll jump back and stay in the barn," she says. "We can sleep in the loft until you're strong enough. My mother will be in the process of giving birth, so I doubt we'll be seen."

I stare at her across the table. "Marie, I need to come back to him, okay? We both do."

"Of course," she says. "I just want to watch from a distance. I just need to know for certain...that she's gone."

I think of the hour after Kit drowned. How I dove, looking for her, and screamed, and flailed, long after it was too late. I'm not quite sure Marie understands the way desperation will make you do insane things.

"You've got to promise that no matter what you see, you'll only watch. If you decide to intervene, I'll have to as well."

She reaches for my hands. "I want to know what happened to my mother," she says. "But what matters most is that you come home to Henri. I swear I'll put you first."

I don't want her to put me first. I want her to put herself first. But if protecting me is what will keep her safe, so be it.

I FIND Henri out by our hay bale, staring at the moon.

I sit beside him and pull his hand into my lap as I rest my head on his shoulder. "I'm sorry," I tell him. "I hate that I'm making you worry."

His lips brush my hair. "My mother used to tell me when I was younger that I should enjoy my life while I could, because once I fell in love, I'd never know a day that was completely without fear. Now I see what she meant."

Have I made a mistake? Perhaps I should have just left him alone, to marry a normal girl and lead a normal life. "It never occurred to me I'd be making your life harder when I came back here."

"My life was going to be hard whether you were here or not. And if worry is the price to have you, I will gladly pay it."

"It's going to be fine," I promise him. "Marie and I talked it out. We'll watch from a distance. If there's even a hint of trouble, we'll leave. She'll be gone three days at most. It might take me a bit longer, since I have to recover there a day or two, but that's a worst-case scenario."

His hands dig in his hair. "That's hardly the worst-case scenario," he says, his eyes dark as night. "When will you go?"

He isn't going to like my answer, but we definitely need to get it done as soon as possible. Not simply because of the stress this is causing him, but because I suspect that even after Marie knows her mother isn't coming back, she's not going to want to move.

Not when Father Edouard remains here. And we've now got less than a year before the war begins.

"Tomorrow. I just want to get it over with "

He flinches. "You said we'd be married before you jumped again."

I rest my head on his shoulder, wishing he truly understood how I feel about him. "A piece of paper isn't what's going to bring me back to you."

"No, but when you're not here it's all I'll have to prove you were mine."

Were. The word sits uneasily in stomach. "You make it sound like I'm not coming back."

He stares at the ground. "I will never know for certain that you are, any time you leave. And…" he stops himself, shaking his head. "I have a bad feeling about this. Perhaps it's because I just got you back, or because I'm so close to having everything I want in the world. But I wish you'd reconsider."

I can't say his words don't give me pause. But what option do we have? "Marie is going whether I'm there or not. And neither of us will be able to live with ourselves if we let her go alone and she doesn't come back."

He rises and begins to pace. Unable to agree, unable to disagree.

I follow him, resting my head on his back, wrapping my arms around his chest. "I swear I'll return," I whisper. "Go pick up the papers. I'll marry you the minute I'm home."

He remains silent. I slide my hands away, preparing to retreat, and he spins, catching me and pulling me tight against him, finding my mouth. I feel his desperation in the pace of his breath, in the urgency of his hands. In the fingers, making quick work of my buttons, of his belt and his pants. He lifts me to the side of the barn and pushes inside me so fast and so hard that I forget how to breathe. He's acting as if our time is about to run out.

And suddenly I'm no longer certain it isn't.

33

Neither Henri nor I get much sleep. I know he's exhausted, but when I wake with a start in the middle of the night, he's lying there watching me, like it's a deathbed vigil. I pull him on top of me, and it's just as urgent, as desperate, as it was before.

When it's over he presses his mouth to my eyelids and tells me to sleep, but he's still watching me when my eyes open again, just as the first rays of light flicker over the barn. I dress and walk into the kitchen, where Marie sits, flushed with excitement. This is a problem—I want Marie cautiously optimistic at best. *Cautiously* being the key word.

"You look like a kid waiting for Santa to come," I sigh.

She smiles, with an embarrassed shrug. "I'm about to see my mother for the first time in three years. Who wouldn't be excited by that?"

I wouldn't, for one. "Marie..." I begin.

She raises a hand to stop me. "Yes, I know. We're just watching from a distance. I won't go after her. I won't even *speak* to her. Just let me have my happiness, Amelie. There've been too few of these moments since she left."

Henri walks into the room and she bounces up. "Are we ready to go then?"

His jaw grinds. I know he's struggling with his resentment—none of this would be happening if it weren't for her. But none of this would be happening if it weren't for me either.

"You go first," I tell her. There's no point in trying to go together since the jump through time is always a solo enterprise. "I'll be right behind you."

Henri hugs his sister and quietly asks her to be careful. She hugs him back. "Amelie will be perfectly safe. I promise."

And with a quick, hopeful grin at me, she vanishes.

I swallow. I don't dare jump from the house. With my luck I'd land inside it in 1918. I hold out my hand. "Walk me to the barn?"

His fingers slide through mine, all his worry and fear in the pressure he exerts. We walk slowly, unwillingly. When we reach my jumping point, he turns me toward him. "I would give anything in the world for this to not be happening."

I wrap my arms around his neck, press my lips to his. "A week from now we'll be married and it will all be behind us. Our biggest problem will be finding somewhere warm enough to honeymoon."

He clutches me to him. "Swear to me you'll find your way back. No matter what happens, no matter how long it takes, you'll return."

I press my mouth to his. "Of course I will. You just need to promise you'll wait."

His eyes close. "I will wait for you until my dying breath."

THE TRAVEL IS difficult this time. I pop back evenly through the years, but have to proceed at a painfully slow rate once I reach 1919. From there I count back months and then days until I reach November 11th, 1918.

I land. My head is heavy and my body aches. Sleep calls to me, but not as badly as it has with other jumps. I'm able to stagger up to the barn, but just as I reach it, I hear the small, joyous cry of a child. I slide into a dark corner, and watch a little boy chasing chickens through the yard with their feed, shouting "*Poulet, poulet poulet!*"

Henri, at age three, dark-haired and rosy-cheeked.

I feel a burst of love for him, but there's grief in it too. He's so young and innocent and unburdened. He has no idea that his father is dead, that his mother will disappear on him. Or that the girl he will love might leave him and never return.

It's the fatigue, I'm certain, that has me weeping. I slide down the side of the wall, shivering and watching his small legs recede in the distance.

"Amelie," Marie whispers from the top of the loft. "Can you get up here?"

I force my head in the motion of a nod, though even that seems more effort than I'm capable of. I crawl to the ladder and cling to the first rail. There are at least fifteen rungs to go and I'm exhausted already. I get to the second and rest my head.

"Think of my brother right now," Marie urges. "He's worried sick for you, and all you need to do is climb a few more rungs to safety."

I nod and grab the next, and the one after that. I'm so weak. So terrible at this. How did I ever think I could help her at all?

"Don't think," she says. "Just move. Now."

So I do, somehow, and when I get close enough she grabs my hand and drags me the rest of the way. She is already clothed, in a dress that sweeps her ankles.

"Come," she says, "I've got you some clothes."

"Sleep," I reply, and plant face first into the hay.

WHEN I WAKE it is dusk, and I'm somehow dressed and bundled under a pile of blankets with Marie snuggled against me. Between her and the hay and blankets, it's almost warm enough. Certainly warm enough for me to fall soundly back to sleep.

When I rise again, it is fully dark—I'm not sure of the hour but it has that heaviness of the middle of the night, when nothing good happens—and Marie is gone.

"Marie," I hiss.

There is no response. My heart rate begins to pick up, imagining worst-case scenarios, but given that I don't see her clothes lying around I can at least rule out the worst of all: that she time traveled somewhere without me.

I convince myself she's just heeding nature's call and fall back into fitful sleep. It feels like only minutes later that Marie is kneeling by my side, trying to wake me. "It's time to go," she whispers. "Do you think you can make it back down the ladder?"

I nod, pushing my hair off my face. "So what's the plan?" I ask. "You said you knew how we'd get to Paris."

"I do," she says. "But it will involve some theft." For a woman who spends so much time at church, Marie has a very loose relationship with a few of the commandments.

"What *kind* of theft?"

"A car," she says, wrapping food she's stolen in a blanket. "Madame and Monsieur Perot have the only car in town. I've heard people complain about how awful she was during the war. She wouldn't lift a finger to help anyone, so I don't feel especially guilty depriving her of it."

I'm less troubled by the ethics of the situation than I am the legality. Spending a night or two in a French prison because I don't have the strength to jump away is not particularly appealing. "Don't you think someone will notice if the *only* car in town is driving away?"

"Well," she says, "they haven't noticed it yet. I've got it parked on the far side of the barn, but we should try to get close to Paris before it's light, I think."

I groan. "My God, Marie. It's like you searched for ways to make everything riskier."

"The term you seek, I believe, is *resourceful*. And you're welcome. I just saved your barely mobile self from walking to Paris."

I follow her down the ladder and out to the road. "How did you even get it here? You don't know how to drive."

She points at the bashed-in front bumper and broken headlight. "I didn't say I stole it *well*."

THE CAR, for all its luxurious finishes, drives more like a tractor, with rudimentary gears and a steering wheel that takes unbelievable strength to turn. Fortunately, I learn how to drive it on mostly empty roads. Aside from a horse and cart I nearly run right into, we see almost no one.

I laugh quietly to myself. "You realize *you* are the reason André's grandmother will have a lifelong hatred of Gypsies, right?"

Marie shrugs, picking at some bread she stole from the Perots along with the car. "You can't make an omelet without breaking some eggs."

It takes well over an hour to get to the city, driving as slowly as we must, and when we arrive just after dawn, our progress slows dramatically. I hadn't realized that in 1918 there were still so many horses and carts. They don't operate like carriages in New York City, which remain on paths in Central Park or stay off to the side of the street. They march right down the middle of the road as if they own it, and all I can do is roll along behind them, which gives me a chance to look around. There are few women out this early, but they definitely look like the product of another time:

dresses that hit just above the ankle, and a kind of modesty in attire that will disappear entirely over the next decade.

"Isn't it amazing," says Marie-Therese, voicing my thoughts, "how much things will change in just a few years?"

I glance at her. "They change just as much between your time and mine," I reply.

"Is it entirely for the better?" she asks.

I bite my lip. Life is so much better in my time for women, for minorities. But it's grown less personal as well. "Mostly, but not entirely."

We weave through the city toward Sacré-Coeur, as Parc de la Turlure—where Marie's mother would have headed—sits just behind it. Our plan is to wait there, beginning at sunset, for Madame Durand to arrive, and follow her as best we can. Though we are many hours ahead of schedule, it seems wisest to get the lay of the land before we do anything else.

We park the car a few blocks away, and find Parc de la Turlure easily, just a stone's throw from the basilica. To my dismay, the square is not nearly as small or uniform as I'd imagined. There are lots of large trees, with nooks and crannies between them, which means Madame Durand could easily disappear somewhere in here without us ever noticing.

"I don't like this," I say quietly.

Marie smiles, untroubled. "Look what I found," she says, pulling a necklace away from her collarbone. "It was my mother's. I found it in the pocket of my dress. I think it means we'll have good luck today."

I hope she's right. I somehow doubt it, however. "Let's be cautious anyway."

Marie shrugs as if the admonition is obvious, but she's already ahead of me again and walking too quickly for me to keep up with, given how leaden I am from the trip here.

"Marie," I hiss. "Slow down."

She turns back to me with a giddy smile. "I'm sorry," she says, clasping my hand once, quickly. "I'm just so excited. In a few hours from now, I will lay eyes on my mother again."

"Not if we don't get a better vantage point," I reply. "There are too many hidden corners here."

"The rooftops?" she suggests, glancing up to the right.

I smile. "How do you plan to get up there, Spiderman?" Even if we could reach the roof, there are so many trees that no view is perfect.

"*Spiderman*? I don't know this word. But you make a good point." She shrugs. "So when we come back this evening, we will stake out the main entrances. You'll take one and I'll take the other."

Already she is ignoring our agreement to stay together, and I barely have the energy left to argue with her. Why is this so much harder for me than her? She has enough energy for a *village* of time travelers while I can barely keep my eyes open.

"We were supposed to stay together," I reply. "You promised."

Her mouth opens to argue and then closes. "Fine. It will probably be many hours away, anyhow. We'll come back at sunset and remain here. If my mother hasn't shown up by dawn, we'll jump back to a few hours and try another entrance." She cocks her head. "I'm wondering if you'll even be able to stay awake that long, however."

I'm wondering the same, but I'm not sure what option I have. I don't dare sleep in the back of the stolen car. "I'll be fine. Just stop walking so fast."

She pushes me toward a bench. "You sit here while I check out the other entrances. And then I'll steal some money and get us a place to sleep."

I do as she says, yawning. "Since you're continuing your life of crime anyway, can you steal enough money to get food as well?"

She turns to me, her smile thrilled, slightly manic. "Now that's the spirit. I'll be right back."

She darts across the square and I let my eyes close just for a moment. I'm so tired I think I could probably sleep right here, but within seconds movement in the brush behind me has my eyes opening wide. The sound was too loud to be an animal and

Something pierces the skin of my neck. I open my mouth to scream but no sound emerges. I try to turn my head and my body won't move. I flop forward, unable to block my fall as my face flies toward the grass in front of me.

"That's two we've caught," says a voice above me, "and the day's not even begun."

**SARAH AND HENRI'S STORY
CONTINUES...GRAB IT TODAY!**

ACKNOWLEDGMENTS

First, a shout-out to the members of The Parallel Spoiler Room, The Across Time Spoiler Room, and Elizabeth O'Roark Books. Your enthusiasm for the Parallel/Intersect/Across Time world thrills me on a daily basis.

Second, a huge thanks to Tbird London and Stacy Frenes, two editors who saved the day at the last minute, and Janis Ferguson for her amazing copy editing skills. Thanks so much also to Emily Wittig for the gorgeous cover, and Nick Llellenberg for checking my translations.

And last but not least, many thanks to my beta readers: Kimberly Ann, Katie Foster Meyer, Brenna Rattai, Laura Ward Steuart, Jill Sullender and Courtney Danseizen Wetternach. Your feedback and support made such a difference for this book.

Finally, to my wonderful children, who are extremely tired of hearing about WW2.

Made in the USA
Las Vegas, NV
03 December 2023

82018545R00168